Critical Accla

'Few, if any, contemporary writers are as entertaining as the remarkable H. R. F. Keating'
Len Deighton

'Keating reveals, not for the first time, his criminal versatility in *The Rich Detective* . . . a delight'
Marcel Berlins, *The Times*

'Classic crime from a master of the genre'
Nottingham Evening Post

'Masterly as ever'
Times Literary Supplement

'Another first-class mystery from one of the doyens of British crime writing'
Sunday Times

'Superior fare from a master'
Good Book Guide

'Few who pick up the latest offering from a master will be disappointed by the superior fare on offer'
Crime Time

'An engaging and exemplary book'
Sister Wendy Beckett, *Good Book Guide*

The Dreaming Detective

H. R. F. Keating, a Fellow of the Royal Society of Literature, was the crime books reviewer for *The Times* for fifteen years. He has served as Chairman of the Crime Writers' Association and the Society of Authors, and as President of the Detection Club.

He has written numerous novels as well as non-fiction books, but is most famous for the Inspector Ghote series, the first of which, *The Perfect Murder*, was made into a film by Merchant Ivory and won a CWA Gold Dagger award, as did *The Murder of the Maharajah*.

The Dreaming Detective is the fourth Harriet Martens novel, following *The Hard Detective*, *A Detective in Love* and *A Detective Under Fire* (all available in Pan Books). It will publish alongside the hardback edition of the most recent novel in the series *A Detective at Death's Door*.

H. R. F. Keating is married to Sheila Mitchell, the actor, and lives in London. In 1997 he was awarded the CWA Cartier Diamond Dagger.

By the same author

Death and the Visiting Fireman
Zen there was Murder
A Rush on the Ultimate
The Dog it was that Died
Death of a Fat God
The Perfect Murder
Is Skin-Deep, Is Fatal
Inspector Ghote's Good Crusade
Inspector Ghote Caught in Meshes
Inspector Ghote Hunts the Peacock
Inspector Ghote Plays a Joker
Inspector Ghote Breaks an Egg
Inspector Ghote Goes by Train
Inspector Ghote Trusts the Heart
Bats Fly up for Inspector Ghote
A Remarkable Case of Burglary
Filmi, Filmi, Inspector Ghote
Inspector Ghote Draws a Line
The Murder of the Maharajah
Go West, Inspector Ghote
The Sherrif of Bombay
Under a Monsoon Cloud
The Body in the Billiard Room
Dead on Time
Inspector Ghote, His Life and Crimes
The Iciest Sin

Cheating Death
The Rich Detective
Doing Wrong
The Good Detective
The Bad Detective
Asking Questions
The Soft Detective
Bribery, Corruption Also
The Hard Detective
A Detective in Love
Breaking and Entering
A Detective Under Fire
A Detective at Death's Door
The Strong Man
The Underside
A Long Walk to Wimbledon
The Luck Alphonse
Jack, The Lady Killer
In Kensington Gardens Once . . .
Murder Must Appetize
Sherlock Holmes: The Man and his World
Great Crimes
Writing Crime Fiction
Crime and Mystery: the 100 Best Books
The Bedside Companion to Crime

H. R. F. Keating

The Dreaming Detective

PAN BOOKS

First published 2003 by Macmillan

This edition published 2004 by Pan Books
an imprint of Pan Macmillan Ltd
Pan Macmillan, 20 New Wharf Road, London N1 9RR
Basingstoke and Oxford
Associated companies throughout the world
www.panmacmillan.com

ISBN 0 330 41940 4

1 3 5 7 9 8 6 4 2

A CIP catalogue record for this book is available from
the British Library.

Printed and bound in Great Britain by
Mackays of Chatham plc, Chatham, Kent

Chapter One

'Who killed the preacher?'

The chill hostility in the new Chief Constable's voice as he had shot out the question sent an answering buzz of queries through Detective Superintendent Harriet Martens's head.

The preacher? What preacher, she thought, is Mr Newcomen talking about? And why did he shoot out his question the moment I took my seat in front of his desk? And why . . .? Why is he setting out to antagonize me? Look at the way he's sitting there, leaning sharply forward in that tall, black-leather chair. And look at his hands, flat on the desk, fingers stiffly pointing towards me. Like . . . Like, yes, so many plunging kamikaze planes.

Then, abruptly, the answer to the question the new Chief had snapped out came into her head.

The preacher. Of course, he must mean the famous Boy Preacher who was murdered here in Birchester, thirty or more years ago. The sweepingly popular figure who at the height of his nationwide ministry had been killed . . . killed here in the city where his first fame had come to him. Had been murdered, as they say, by a person or persons unknown. Or, if I

1

remember rightly all that I heard about it when I was still at school, by one of only six or seven people.

'Do I take it, sir,' she ventured, aware that this was the first time she had actually met the Chief face to face, 'that you're referring to the notorious unsolved Boy Preacher case here in Birchester back in the sixties?'

'I could hardly be referring to anything else, could I?'

Yes, hostility. No doubt about it.

And now she thought that she could guess the reason for it. The rapidly risen Chief must be over-conscious of being, as the media has repeatedly told the public he was, the youngest chief constable in the country – damn it, I'm actually a year or two older myself – and so he's determined to live up to the reputation the publicity has given him, to establish himself as dynamically efficient. And hasn't he been busy doing that since day one?

And so, yes, he's doubly resenting the media attention I have acquired, like it or not. That dreadful label the 'Hard Detective' stuck on me ever since I ran my 'Stop the Rot' campaign in Birchester's worst streets. Damn it, without us ever having talked, the man's conceived a sort of hatred for me.

Yes, that's it. He wants me out.

What's that husbandly quotation John's always producing for me? Yes, something about fearing *a rival near the throne*. So can it be that Mr Newcomen has called me in at this late hour of a Friday afternoon to give me a task he hopes I'll make an almighty mess of? Even to resigning point? Is he working on a twenty-first-century version of the knights King Henry sent to Thomas à Becket? *Will no one rid me of this turbulent priest?*

And, of course, the task he's foisting on me is Birchester's most famous murder, unresolved thirty years ago and even more impossible to solve now. *Who killed the Preacher?*

The Chief's next words fully confirmed the guess.

'I don't suppose, Superintendent, that you saw in the *Chronicle* this morning a small item about the old Imperial Hotel?'

Harriet had seen it. Birchester's once most prestigious hotel, the paper said, was at last to be demolished. And the Imperial was the scene of the famous crime.

But can I up and point out that I, too, regularly read, as part of my duties, the *Birchester Chronicle*? When, no doubt about it, Mr Newcomen wants to score off me by knowing something that I don't?

No, give him his little victory.

'No, sir, I don't think I saw anything about the Imperial. What's happening about it now?'

'Work on demolishing that dreadful old pile is about to begin, Superintendent.'

All right, time to show some signs of knowing what's what.

'Ah, I see now, sir, why it was you were asking me about the notorious Boy Preacher case. Wasn't it at the Imperial that the murder took place? You think that before the building's knocked down someone should take a last look at the scene?'

'I would hardly have drawn your attention to the

3

place being demolished for any other reason, Superintendent. But I think we can do rather better than *take a look at the scene*. It can't have escaped your attention that with the advances being made in the use of deoxyribonucleic acid we are now in a position to resolve crimes that have taken place even as long ago as the 1960s. There was that extraordinary development in the Boston Strangler case quite recently, for example.'

Right, I'm not going to let the fellow try to blind me with science any longer.

'Yes, sir, I read about that, too. Long after the death of a man who had confessed under pressure to a string of sexual murders DNA evidence cleared him of it. That's what you're referring to, isn't it?'

Bad move.

The look of resentment on the Chief's schoolboyish face, that short-back-and-sides haircut, the fresh rosiness of hard-shaved cheeks, became an undisguised glare. Can the man be actually paranoid?

'I'm glad to find you have some knowledge of forensic advances, Superintendent. I had thought your reputation as a detective had been acquired solely in the newsrooms of our local press. That slogan of yours – what was it? – Stop the lot?'

The rot, the rot. But don't attempt to correct him. Not that, damn it all, preaching that slogan was a bad thing, not by any means. And, yes, it's clear now. He's certainly desperate for publicity.

'But perhaps your knowledge doesn't quite extend to realizing we are now in a position to do rather more than use DNA to achieve results in cases where, although evidence had been preserved, it was never possible to bring about prosecution with any hope of success. But now with the recent refinements in analysis, all that is changed. I don't suppose you realize that as recently as fifteen years ago a whole drop of blood or saliva was needed, whereas now the merest trace is enough.'

Harriet had realized, long ago.

She said nothing. With a sudden bark of mirthless laughter the Chief went on.

'If such testing had been available in Dostoevsky's time, *Crime and Punishment* would have been no longer than a short story.'

Harriet managed some sort of chuckle in response. It brought an abrupt arrival at specifics.

'Yes, Superintendent. Thanks to us having the top garments worn by every one of those who had access to the Boy Preacher murder scene, we won't even have to seek DNA matches on the national data base, as other forces have been doing with success. I am told that the person who leant over that young man and throttled the life out of him cannot have escaped being spattered with the spittle the Boy would have expelled as he fought against asphyxiation. Of course, thirty years ago there was no possibility of detecting his DNA on any garment that spittle had landed on. But now there is no reason why, after thirty long years, Greater Birchester Police should not bring to justice the man, or woman, who committed that murder.'

He gave Harriet renewed intent scrutiny.

'Very well, I am tasking you with the inquiry, Superintendent,' he said. 'Once the science people have given you a DNA result, go to the man or woman who thirty years ago became soiled with the dead boy's saliva and get out of them a full confession. I expect a result within two weeks. At the very most.'

Oh, yes. All very fine, Mr Newcomen, with your unblinking faith in the latest discoveries in forensic science. But what if DNA doesn't come up with an answer. It well may not, in fact. That spit might not have reached whatever garment the murderer was wearing. And all of those garments, in the course of thirty years, may well have been contaminated in some way. Or the chain of evidence may have lost some necessary link.

But what then will be the situation for your supposed rival in the media's affections? My situation? If I come to you, whether in two weeks' time or ten, and say I've not got a result and can't see how one can be arrived at, then are you going to put it about that the Hard Detective is not after all so very hard, so very successful? That all she's fit for is whatever lowly tasks can be found for her? If there's any task at all that she can be entrusted with?

I rather think that's what you secretly hope. And I'm not sure there's going to be any way out of the trap you've set for me.

Chapter Two

As Harriet left the Chief Constable's suite, Mrs Balfour, the Chief's secretary, a police widow, fluffy in both manner and appearance despite her head of rigidly gold-tinted hair, hunted about among the papers piled on her desk to find a book. Mr Newcomen, she babbled out, had told her it was to be given to Detective Superintendent Martens.

'He said it was to be on your— Well, on your way out,' she waffled on.

It's no wonder, Harriet thought, that canteen gossip credits the lady, rightly or wrongly, with seeing the world through permanent hangover muzziness.

'And, yes. Yes, there was something— No, it's this, the Chief said, the book – it's precious – was presented to Greater Birchester Police by the author. But I've forgotten his name. No, I haven't. It's Michael Meadowcraft. There it is on the front.'

Harriet glanced at the lurid cover of, she saw, *Who Killed the Preacher?*

A thank-you-for-nothing gift, she thought. And she found she was even unsure, thanks to Pansy's stream of confused information, whether it was actually a gift or whether it had to be returned, on pain of terrible condemnation, to the Headquarters library.

However, she thanked Pansy. And got in return a new spate of breathy directions.

'Oh, and Mr Newcomen wanted me to tell you that— Now I've forgotten. No, no. I've remembered. I was to tell you you're to have an office here at Headquarters while you're investigating all this. For security reasons. I think he said security reasons. He doesn't want anything in the papers, you know, or not until . . . But, I mean, it was all thirty years ago, and I don't see . . . And, yes. Yes, he's arranging for you to have a detective constable to assist. Yes, assist. I think that was all. The office isn't quite available yet. It's got to be cleared of what's kept— Well, some things have got to . . . But I don't suppose . . . Well, as it's the weekend . . .'

Sitting out in the garden with John an hour later, relishing the last rays of the early summer sun, Harriet confided to him the fears she had about the new Chief's plans for her. And her rage at how he seemed to have put her into a no-win situation.

'A crime going back thirty years. Thirty years, mind. All right, here and there, every so often, some police force somewhere in the world does resolve a case as old as that. What they delight in calling *a cold case*. But, however brilliant the scientists are, they can't use the magic of DNA if there turns out to be no evidence linking a victim from the distant past to a murderer in the present. If it turns out not to be there, it isn't there.'

'Yes, I certainly see that,' John said soothingly.

'But what you don't understand is it's precisely that which Mr Newcomen's counting on. Either I find that there's no result to be had, whatever investigation I carry out on other lines after – Yes, by God – after thirty bloody years. Or DNA does lead me to an arrest, if the murderer of that boy is still alive to be arrested. In the first case Mr Newcomen'll say I'm not worth the rank I hold, and in the second he'll claim it as his personal triumph and say that any junior officer could have done the actual work. I'm on a hiding to nothing. I really am.'

'All right, perhaps he has arranged all that. But, you know, it's likely on the whole that a man who's risen to the top of his profession as rapidly as he has isn't quite such a devious character.'

'Oh, isn't he just? Look, he's only been in his post for a couple of months, and already he's roused a hell of a lot of anger. And not only among the lower ranks, whose overtime he's abruptly restricted and whose dress standards he's been pernickety about to the point of farce. They call him Mr Newbroom, and it's not for nothing. But even among the senior officers there's been plenty of resentment. He preaches, you know. Preaches on any and every occasion, to meetings of CID officers, to traffic officers, to the admin people. He tells officers of my rank, and even above, how they should do their jobs, and implies that before he came along things had been allowed to go totally slack. Which is just not true.'

'Oh, come on. In any organization, not excluding my employers at Majestic Insurance plc, if someone's been at the helm for too long standards do tend to fall.'

'Okay, okay. I know that. And I dare say some of the things Mr Newbroom wanted changed did need improving. But what I hate, and I know most of my colleagues feel the same, is the way the damn man must always be one hundred per cent right. His methods, and only his, are the ones everyone should adopt, regardless of anything else.'

'All right, I can see that sort of thing rankles. But there are people who want to control, if not the whole world, at least as much of it as falls under their eye. We all of us, in fact, want to control as much as we can. Ideally nothing would ever happen that we hadn't personally arranged for in advance, or granted permission for. But we don't live in an ideal world.'

'All right then. So why does Mr Newbroom want to believe that he lives in a world he can control by preaching at it day after day?'

'Well, we all do, to an extent.' He gave her a wryly amused look. 'I mean, Harriet Piddock, that Detective Superintendent Martens has been called in her time, don't forget, *Miss Eyemright.*'

Harriet sat for a moment in silence.

'Okay,' she said at last. 'You win, John Piddock. I suppose I do believe I get things right as much as Mr Newcomen believes he does. Or almost as much. But I don't preach about my every passing belief. Or do I?'

John laughed.

'Not to me, anyhow. And, all right, all right, no, not

10

to anybody as excessively as your Mr Newbroom seems to do. Satisfied?'

'Satisfied. But look at this wretched book he said I was to be given, presumably echoing his view of what happened at the Imperial Hotel thirty years ago. I tell you one thing, I'm damned if I'm going to read it tonight.'

First thing on Saturday morning, however, Harriet did settle down to go through the 150-odd pages of the fatly bulked-out little volume. It might be, she conceded, a way of getting the basic outline of the thirty-plus-year-old murder into her head. John had gone with some work colleagues out to a farmer who occasionally offered them some rough shooting. So she had the garden – it was another wonderfully sunny day – to herself.

But a glance through the book's preliminary pages set up in her a fluttering of distrust. Not only did they contain a long list of the author's previous works – *Deplorable Tendencies* was one catchpenny title that caught her eye – but the publication date, she saw, was 1969, the same year that the murder had taken place. So, even if the book had not come out until a few weeks before Christmas, with the murder taking place in May, it must have been a rush job, doubtless hurried out to cash in on the heavy press coverage. She remembered that even the solidly serious newspapers allowed through the gates of her school had written of a mystery worthy of Agatha Christie. And how eagerly the senior girls – juniors, of course, were not allowed to see any newspapers – had sucked in every detail.

A vivid fragment of that past abruptly presented itself. In the prefects' commonroom they had been sitting round a present someone had been given, something called – the name suddenly came back – a Tennis Court cake. Tennis Court cakes had been all the rage at that time: perfectly ordinary cakes, but topped with a layer of marzipan and then iced, with their whole surface made green by – was it? – chopped pistachio nuts. On them the outlines of a tennis court would be traced in white icing and a little model net would stand up stretched across the whole. But as, with schoolgirl appetites, they had gobbled down generous slices, it was the Boy Preacher murder that was being discussed. What had the other girls said? What did I say? No idea. All vanished. Except for that cake and the memory of everyone's keen interest in the affair.

She found now she was having some difficulty in concentrating on *Who Killed the Preacher?* She had had a bad night. Despite trying to follow John's tactful advice to forget the dilemma she saw Mr Newbroom as having contrived for her, she had not succeeded with her usual getting-to-sleep routine. She had hardly even, thoughts hammering away, managed its first step: lying flat on her back, shutting her eyes and getting her whole body to relax. Usually after five or ten minutes of that her subconscious would begin to flick on to the screen of her mind one or two of those curious, unrelated-to-anything colourful scraps bubbling away inside. But none had come. She had made herself prowl time and again across that blank dark

screen, probing into its deepest corners where sometimes a bright image might lurk. Without result. Wide-
awake thoughts and fears had forced their way to the
front.

At last she had just rolled over and hoped for
oblivion. It must have come at some stage because the
next thing she knew she was waking from a nightmare. She had been crossing some enormously wide
motorway and two lumbering vehicles – absurdly
unlikely, had one been a circus merry-go-round? – had
approached her at speed from opposite directions.

For a moment, to shake it all off, she had sat up,
breathing deeply, conscious of feeling unpleasantly
sweaty. She had managed then to get back to sleep
without disturbing a snoring John. But it had not been
for long. Half an hour later she was awake again, heart
thudding. She had dreamt this time she was wearing
what seemed to be a heavy winter coat and trudging
along at the steeply shelving edge of the sea somewhere, its heaving waters scintillatingly blue. Then a
devil, horns, trident and all, had come suddenly rushing down towards her.

Did I actually dream that, she asked herself now,
blinking in the sunshine. It really seems too much of
a classic reflection of what I talked about with John
last evening. Between the devil and the deep blue
sea, for heaven's sake. Had it been, in fact, only part
nightmare, and part half-awake wandering thoughts?

But the devil and the deep blue sea situation Mr
Newbroom put me in yesterday was not anything I
dreamt. He said what he said. He gave me the orders
he did.

But now she took a deep breath and made herself get down to the little book's fat pages.

What, after all, had been the exact circumstances, back in 1969, that had made this murder a nine-day sensation? Let's see if Michael Meadowcraft makes it clear.

His first paragraph did to an extent, at least as far as the sensational nature of the affair was concerned. The phrases came popping off the page like so many fireworks – *There they are, five men and two women, the only people who were able to go into the magnificent ballroom of Birchester's premium hotel, the Imperial, where in deep meditation sat alone the young preacher so soon to be brutally done to death.*

Then a few lines further on, *This barbaric attack on a youth whose pure preaching of five simple precepts had entranced the whole nation, 'Do not kill your fellow men', 'Do not yield to Mammon', 'Do not bring children into the world without the care of both mother and father', 'Do not give way to drunkenness' and 'Do not let drugs alter your mind'. But one of those seven watchers just outside was to take, with evil throttling hands, the young man's innocent life . . .*

Hardly the prose of the Dostoevsky that Mr New-broom brandished so happily in my face. But facts are beginning to emerge, for all the sequinned slush they're covered in. The Boy Preacher – actual name not yet revealed and I can't quite recall it – killed by manual strangulation, in the ballroom of the Imperial Hotel now on the point of demolition. And apparently only seven people had had the opportunity. So much for the third item of the familiar trinity, *means, motive*

14

and opportunity. And *means*, of course, present no problem. Everybody has hands that can strangle, though there may be something to be learnt from the size and strength of those hands. I'll see about that when I get to read the ancient files. So what about *motive?*

She went back to the pages.

And almost at once word-splattering Michael Meadowcraft gave his answer. *So who was it who emerged from that deluxe ballroom having carried out their vindictive purpose? Because there can be no possible doubt that sheer vindictiveness lies at the heart of this atrocious crime.* All right, Mr Meadowcraft, we'll see about that when you give us a few facts concerning those *five men and two women*. If you ever do.

Pages swiftly turned.

And, yes, here we go. One by one, analyses of each of the seven suspects.

Let us take them in turn and see what it is that may have driven a twisted mind to commit the act that can never be taken back. First, an Indian long domiciled in an England that may yet regret having offered him sanctuary, Harish Nair by name. Nair, who is in his late fifties, is a distant relative of brutally-done-to-death Krishna Kumaramangalam – Ah, that's what the Boy Preacher was called – *and he, too, has been, after a fashion, a preacher, an occasional lay preacher, at one of Birchester's nonconformist chapels, a man claiming all the virtues of humility, dressing always in simple cotton shirts and cotton trousers, earning a bare living as a self-employed tailor. But one wonders what, as he poured forth the words of his sermons to captive congregations, was going on in the depths of his mind. Was he vindictively jealous of the young relative who lodged in his own house, yet whose preaching had far outshone his own? He is a man of notably short stature, and – I make no accusations – it is a well-known fact that small men are often jealous of others taller than themselves.*

Well, no beating about the bush there. Michael Meadowcraft's prime suspect planked down for all to see. But let's have a look at how he treats the remaining six who, he says, had that opportunity.

Mr Lucas Calverte. Ah, a different layer of society now. Harish Nair was given no preliminary *Mr.* And, yes, though there are no details of where and when Lucas Calverte was born, there seems to be a thoroughly obsequious later biography.

Mr Calverte is a distinguished Birchester barrister who recently gained the honour of being made Undersheriff for the county of Birrshire in appreciation of the many services he has given to the community, including having held the chairmanship of the Birchester Council for Immigrant Welfare. It was this post, no doubt, that accounted for his presence among the somewhat odd collection of people one might call the Boy Preacher's Clique, the few who provided him with assistance of different kinds, the few who alone were in a position to enter the empty ballroom of the Imperial Hotel at the time of the murder. Not, one would think at a first glance, a man likely to commit murder, Undersheriff Lucas Calverte. And yet . . . who can probe the depths of the human heart?

Oh, clever Meadowcraft. Writing your book when it had become clear that no immediate arrest was going to be made, you must have had to maintain an Agatha

Christie interest in keeping all the possible suspects in play. All right, you've done that, in your way, with little-likely Lucas Calverte. So who next?

Yes, one of the women. Michael Meadowcraft knows what will best hold his readers' attention.

Miss Priscilla Knott. Right, with that *Miss* we're still in the comparatively higher reaches of Birchester society in the sixties. And, yes, *Miss Knott is a teacher* – Oh, of course, back then teachers were still respected – *now in her early twenties (One must not ask a lady's age too scrupulously!). When I met her to discuss what she had seen on the terrible Sunday evening of the Boy Preacher's last meeting, I at once formed the impression that I was talking to someone who could only be described as 'a good woman'. She holds the strongest views about what is wrong with present-day society and evidently is prepared to do all that she can to see that the evils around us are brought under proper control.*

Well, when I get to see Miss Knott now – unless I find that her vigorous opposition to *the evils around us* brought her to an early grave – I wonder what she'll have to say about our twenty-first-century drug problem and our numerous single-parent children. What was the Boy's precept? *Do not bring children into the world without* . . . whatever his actual words were. I somehow doubt that Michael Meadowcraft reports them correctly.

Okay, let's see if he's managed to keep even this moralistic lady within his circle of suspects. Oh, right, he has. He has. How about this? *But strange are the workings of the human mind. How often have we seen a golden model of good behaviour prove at the final outcome to be quite the opposite.*

Next, please.

Barney Trapnell. Down in the lower depths again now? And, yes, *Barney is one of the Boy Preacher's humbler followers. A watch repairer by trade, he has a small shop in the working-class area to the north of the Birchester–Liverpool Canal. And, poor fellow, he is, too, a cripple, having been afflicted in infancy by poliomyelitis leaving him with a leg fastened between iron callipers. Until I met him, in his turn, I wondered how it had come about that someone of his type had become one of the Boy's Clique. As soon as I saw him I could see what the possible reason was. Though Barney's leg is weak, his brawny arms and hands are, in compensation, markedly strong. If the Boy, who was a frail creature indeed, needed physical help, as I have learnt that he did, here was the person to provide it. To provide it, but with those very strong hands to provide what else? Can a sudden fit of twisted bitterness have led him to one appalling moment of revenge on life?*

Oh, nasty Michael Meadowcraft.

But read on. Time for a second female appearance, I think.

Yes, here it is. *Barbara Willson, known to one and all by the sobriquet, Bubsy. And Bubsy, your author is constrained in the interests of truth to report, is not a very savoury young lady. She has, in fact, appeared more than once in the Magistrates' Court charged with indecent behaviour in a public place. Nor is her personal appearance any more attractive. When I tried to interview her in the course of my researches she refused to meet me. But I was able to see her at a slight distance, and I have to report that her outer garments were, if not wholly dirty, certainly such that no decent mother would approve of them. Nor is her visage any tribute to female beauty. She is solidly round-faced, and on that pasty white surface, the lips slashed with ill-applied scarlet, there sprout half a dozen wirily thick black hairs. By no means a pretty sight.*

Come on, Meadowcraft, leave the poor girl alone.

More, from what I have learnt from reliable witnesses of the scene at the time of the murder, she was no more wholesome on that day. Her excessively colourful blouse was stated to have been stained with recently spilt tea and her manner in tramping up and down the foyer of the Imperial ballroom clearly left a lot to be desired.

Quite enough said about Bubsy Willson to put her squarely into the number two spot if, in the years after *Who Killed the Peacher?* was written, poor Mr Nair should be conclusively proved innocent. As I suppose he has not been in fact.

But two more to come.

Who's this? *Sydney Bigod, street trader. Mr Bigod is another of the doubtful characters the Boy Preacher, in his charity, appears to have allowed to enter his immediate circle, the Clique as I have called it. As far as I have been able to ascertain Bigod appeared in Birchester a year or two before the terrible day that saw the brutal killing of the Boy Preacher. How and when he managed to attach himself to the Boy I have been unable to discover. Mr Bigod, if Bigod is his real name and not one given to him because of his foul mouth, is not a man to vouchsafe details of his past. Nor have I been able to discover very much about his present activities. Sydney Bigod left Birchester, in a hurry, immediately after he had been interviewed by Detective Chief Inspector Kenworthy, in charge of the inquiry into the murder.*

Another useful fall-back candidate, if the money Michael Meadowcraft puts on poor Harish Nair proves not to be a good bet.

Now for the last of the seven.

Marcus Fairchild is a figure of mystery.

Oh ho.

His stay in Birchester was remarkably short, though during it he contrived to become a member of the Boy's Clique, by what means I can only guess. As far as I have been able to ascertain he arrived just two or three days before the Boy met his appalling end, and, like Sydney Bigod, as soon as he had given his details to DCI Kenworthy he left the city.

Ah, but here's a footnote.

* Marcus Fairchild was reported killed in a London traffic accident shortly before the publication of this book. He must therefore be eliminated as a suspect.

So one possible murderer put beyond the reach of Mr Newbroom's predatory hands, if on somewhat illogical grounds.

Right, that's that. Seen all I want to see, and learnt enough to be going on with.

Something else I can do, though, to get a better picture of it all. I can visit the scene. The Imperial Hotel, dilapidated though it may be, is still intact, and its ballroom where that poor boy was, in Michael Meadowcraft's thunderous words, *brutally done to death* should equally be there for me to see.

Chapter Three

Harriet stood in the shelter of the grimly shut-up Imperial Hotel's pillared portico contemplating, beside its firmly closed doors, an eight-inch rust-rimmed hole where once there must have been a bell. Had there been a round plate of gleaming brass enclosing it? Wrenched away, if so. Or had there been the words *Night Bell* in sturdy black letters on a fat white enamel disc? In fragments now perhaps. Or had a solid brass knob asked to be given a commanding tug? Now, somewhere down inside, only a frayed end of sturdy wire remaining.

Whatever . . . But no way of getting access to the other side of the blank, time-dried, once noble wooden panels facing me. Tramp round to the back quarters of the block? But it occupies the whole section of the street. If there's nothing else for it, I will. However—

She raised her fist and brought it down once, twice, a third time on the crack-lined panel nearest her. Not without a painful jar at each blow.

She waited then.

And at last there seemed to be a slight juddering of the door's surface. Bolts being withdrawn? Yes, there was definitely a regular mechanical squeaking coming from the far side.

But it was taking a long time to produce any result. Harriet imagined a foot-long bolt, almost solidly rusted into place, being swivelled with difficulty to and fro. Squeak, pause, squeak, pause, squeak.

Would whoever was wrestling with it ever manage to get it free? And, if they did, would there be another bolt down nearer the floor inside that would have to be—

No.

One leaf of the tall door began slowly to be drawn back, its bottom edge emitting a low grinding noise.

Now, into the foot-wide aperture that had been contrived there swam a face. The face of a man some four or five inches shorter than herself. Protuberant blue eyes behind rimless glasses were perched on a little podgy nose. The round red dome of the head above had a few lines of grey hair scraped across it. There was a faint grey-white bristle over cheeks and chin. Below the neck, only just visible in the gloom inside, a brown shopman's coat covered a neatly rounded pot belly.

'Yes?'

'I am Detective Superintendent Martens, Greater Birchester Police.' She flashed her warrant card. 'I understand that demolition work on the hotel is due to begin on Monday, and I would very much like to inspect the ballroom before then.'

'Ah,' said the little man confronting her. 'It's the murder, isn't it?'

'It is.'

She decided to say no more. Mr Newcomen wants, Pansy Balfour indicated, the investigation to be kept secret until, with a blaze of publicity, the work of Greater Birchester Police under its dynamic new Chief Constable gets maximum publicity. Right then, I'm not going to be the one to let the news get abroad. Little point though there is in keeping it under cover.

'Well now,' the little man said, 'I can tell you all you want to know about it. I was here at the time. General manager. Name of Popham, Charles Popham. No more than the caretaker nowadays. Came out of retirement and took on the job when the old place was finally closed. A bingo hall, I ask you. But that Sunday evening— No, I must give you the facts. It was the Monday evening. For some reason the Boy Preacher's meeting had had to be postponed from the date originally chosen. But the ballroom did happen to be free next day, and we were able to give it to them. Always ready to oblige, if we can. And so I was at the centre of it all, supervising the occasion. Indeed, I was the one who actually went and telephoned the police. I had the pleasure of telling Detective Chief Inspector Kenworthy, a very fine officer, a very fine officer indeed, everything he needed to know about the ballroom and about its foyer, where they were all assembled when it happened. Yes, indeed. But come in, come in.'

Right, a piece of luck, Harriet thought. Provided this chap's all that he says he is.

'And the ballroom, where I believe the Boy Preacher was strangled,' she said, 'is it still as it was thirty years ago?'

23

'Ah, there you're going to be unlucky. The old hotel has gone down in recent years. Sadly down. I don't know what the youngsters they brought in when I retired thought they were doing, but they let the place go down and down. You ought to have seen it in its prime. There wasn't a hotel to get near it in the whole of Birchester, in the whole of the Midlands, I might say. Everyone would tell you that. The city's finest. Its finest by far.'

He was scuttling along in front of her across what seemed to be, in the dim light, the hotel's reception area. Impressive it may have been once, but now all Harriet could make out were strips of reddish embossed wallpaper dangling down where they had come away from the walls. A long mahogany counter that must once have gleamed with daily polishing was now dimmed by layer on layer of dust.

Then they entered a wide corridor, the carpet along it in places dangerously holed.

'Yes,' little Mr Popham prattled on, 'the cream of Birchester society would come to our ballroom in those days. The cream. The grand balls that took place you wouldn't believe. There's nothing like that nowadays. Only what they call raves. Raves, I ask you. It's through here, through here.'

He took a turn to the right and trotted ahead of Harriet into yet deeper darkness. But he knew exactly where to find the switches, and after a series of heavy clickings the place they had reached was, if not dazzlingly illuminated, at least fully visible.

It seemed to be the entrance foyer to the ballroom itself. Harriet remembered from Michael Meadowcraft's elaborate, if hazy, description of the scene that it would have been here that his Seven Suspects – invariably capitalized – had waited for some two hours while, in the ballroom beyond, the Boy Preacher had sat in deep meditation. And, yes, in the middle of this long, narrow outer room there was a large cushioned circular bench, in the centre of which there must once have stood, if Michael Meadowcraft could be relied on, a tall clump of pampas grass in a large brass planter. So it seemed that during the two hours' wait there would have been opportunity for any one of the Boy's so-called Clique to take advantage of the cover the tall foliage must have provided and, after a hasty look round, to slip unobserved into the ballroom itself.

In the gloom, Harriet realized now, they had passed through a narrow entrance to the foyer with, beside it, what must have been a ticket-collecting desk. She looked over to the far end of the room and saw, as she had expected, that there was no way out there. So, again, what she had gathered from the bulked-up pages of *Who Killed the Preacher?* seemed right enough. No one other than the seven people entitled to be waiting outside the ballroom could have entered it unnoticed.

She turned to the hotel's former general manager.

'Tell me,' she said, 'what access to the ballroom is there, other than those three sets of double doors over there?'

'Aha, I thought you'd ask me that,' Mr Popham proudly replied. 'It was the first question Chief Inspector Kenworthy put to me. And I was able to give him the answer he required straight away. Yes, there is an emergency exit at the far end of the ballroom.

But it was my practice then, in order to make sure we got no unwanted intruders, to keep it securely locked until the ball, or whatever other event the ballroom was to be used for, had actually begun. I saw to that myself. Invariably.'

Harriet turned right round now to look more closely at the four small doors spaced at intervals along the opposite side of the long foyer.

'Where do those go?' she asked.

'Well, as you can see from the signs on them, dreadfully obscured as they are – I don't know what my successors thought they were doing, I really don't – the two at either end are the Ladies and the Gents. The middle two lead to small rooms we used to hire out for meetings when the ballroom was not in use. There's a table in each of them. Or there used to be. And chairs. As many as were required. But there's nothing beyond them, nothing at all.'

'I see,' she said, thinking that here again, if some of the seven had made use of these smaller rooms at various times, the opportunity for one of them to enter the ballroom itself would have been all the greater.

She looked back at the three sets of wide doors that gave access to where the Boy Preacher had been strangled. Each consisted of a pair of double doors, in all some eight feet across. Easy enough to imagine, in Mr Popham's heyday, the crowds of men in evening dress and women in floating silks and trailing brocades making their way towards the spirits-raising music of a big band. And it had been through one or the other of these doors that someone had quickly thrust themselves, prepared out of sheer vindictiveness, or so

26

Michael Meadowcraft claimed, to end the meditating Boy's life.

Yes, some good has come out of ploughing through all that Meadowcraftian verbiage. I do now have a reasonable idea of what the situation was on that evening so long ago.

'So,' she said, 'can I go in?'

'Yes, yes. To where the murder actually took place, though who that murderer was has never yet been found out. So, yes, go through any one of the double doors there and you'll see it all. But, if you don't mind, I won't come with you. It may be silly of me, but I've always felt the place has— Well, an atmosphere. I used to go in often enough while dances were still taking place, of course. But— But somehow, now that it's all deserted, I don't quite like . . .'

'I understand,' Harriet replied. 'Don't you worry. I shan't be long in any case.' She gave him a smile. 'I don't suppose I'll find the vital clue lying on the floor, not after all this time. If it ever was there.'

'No. No, you won't find anything like that, that's for sure. Chief Inspector Kenworthy was a remarkably efficient officer. If there'd been anything worth noticing in there then, you can be sure he'd have picked up on it. Yes, you can be sure of that. But, no, I won't come in. You'll find me waiting here outside when you've seen enough. I've not got much to do these days, only wait.'

The sight of the ballroom struck Harriet the moment she pushed open one of the leaves of the middle set of doors – it gave a screech of agony – as altogether extraordinary. The whole enormously high room was lit from a long tunnel-shaped glass roof, through which the strong sunshine of this bright May day was pouring unimpeded. Only here and there did some windblown piece of debris make a black shadow on one of the hundreds of panes.

Under this in-pouring of light the elaborate decoration of the walls all round stood out clearly. Thirty years earlier the light would have come from huge chandeliers hanging from bars across the foot of the glass tunnel above. But now just one was still in place, its long fall of glass slivers glittering in a ray of sunshine that just caught its edges. But sunlight now illuminated scores of tile-pictures of luscious nymphs and lusty gods twined together in amorous, but still decorous, writhings, of distant dancing maidens and shepherd boys playing their pipes. And each picture – they rose one above the other to the very top of the walls and stretched from one end of the long room to the other – was surrounded by tree or column shapes in colours of light blue and light yellow tangled over by swathes and swags of every sort of flower and foliage.

I wonder, Harriet thought, that all this tumbling, absurd stretch of decoration hasn't been, like those missing chandeliers, ripped out and sold off. To America even? But perhaps such fantastically ridiculous decor is no longer wanted anywhere, not even in the palaces of Central European dictators. Art nouveau, I suppose it is. All those curvaceous tree-trunk pillars supporting nothing and merging here and there into semi-human figures, equally serving no discernible purpose. Made of earthenware of some sort, I imagine, twisted and twirled into those curls and coils and then painted and fired with glossy yellow and blue.

C'est magnifique, mais ce n'est pas my taste.

But enough of that. What I need to see is the exact scene of the crime, dust-thick and obscured though it may be.

She strode rapidly down the length of the huge room towards the small dais at the far end. If what Meadowcraft had said was right, it had been there that the Boy had sat, cross-legged and oblivious of all the chairs that must have been ranged in front of him, while – What was that purple passage? – *with secret dread steps his killer had approached, in their mind the worst thought that any human being can have about another, their hands already claw-like, gripping in imagination the throat they were intent on choking into eternal oblivion.* Something like that.

With steps clacking loudly out Harriet in her turn advanced on that little platform. She halted at its foot.

So this was where it happened, the murder thirty years ago that I still can't really get into my mind as anything other than an event from the past. Yes, Mr Newcomen told me about it, preached his DNA sermon on it. And, yes, I read about it as a thrilled schoolgirl. And, yes, again, no doubt when I'm established in this office I've been promised at Headquarters I'll be able to read the Crime File which DCI – what was his name? – yes, Kenworthy compiled. Solid facts. But only facts on paper, and perhaps some of them, for all Mr Popham's praise of the DCI, distorted by prejudice and misconceptions. And, yes, if Mr Newcomen has it right, there'll be a fact to be gained from the DNA analysis of one of the garments preserved in the Headquarters evidence store. A fact that will, so Mr Newcomen asserted, state unequivocally that a certain one of the seven suspects was showered with spittle as they leant over the Boy to throttle the life out of him, saliva that could have come only from the mouth of their victim.

But still the scene doesn't come to life.

Yes, the Boy must have sat, probably cross-legged indeed, at just the centre point of the dais here. And, yes, it is the very spot where he was strangled. A process that, unless his murderer managed to hit at once on the carotid arteries, would have taken possibly two long minutes, even more.

But there's nothing to be seen here that means anything to me. Here's a low dais, a now tattered carpet still on it, and nothing more.

She turned away.

Walking slowly back up the length of the huge room, she let her gaze wander once more over that once dazzling, now dust-obscured setting. All those corkscrewing pillars serving no purpose but to frame clumsy tile-work scenes of locked-together lovers and arm-waving dancers in a supposed age of antiquity.

And yet . . . And yet . . . she thought. However appalling the taste of the designers here in – what? – the early years of the twentieth century or the last years of the nineteenth, there was about the whole huge room a magnificent confidence. This is how it should be, the man – almost certainly a man in those days – who had conceived the decor of this extra-ordinary room had stated. He had stated it in twisty pillars, in horrible unlikely tile-pictures, even in the huge expanse of polished floor at my feet.

Into her head then, willy-nilly, there came the music of a waltz. And in her imagination she danced all the way along the remaining length of the huge room. Until, with a sudden shock, she came to those three sets of double doors, through one of which . . .

Cautiously she tugged at the right-hand leaf of the middle one, only to create again the long, horrible screech it had made as she had entered the room.

And there, standing puffing at a cheap-smelling cigarette, was Mr Popham, caretaker now, but holder of a far grander post at the time the Boy Preacher had been killed.

Then, swiftly as a searchlight flicked into life, the rank smell of that cigarette brought back to Harriet the odour that had been so familiar to her in her sixties and seventies schooldays: the smell of men smoking. Gardeners, handymen, tradesmen, the school doctor, happily puffing, as well as such masters as the school employed. Every male she had encountered during her life within privileged boarding-school walls had smoked. And with that sharp, nostril-irritating smell there had come, by what mysterious process of the mind she could not say, full belief in that murder thirty years earlier.

Yes, she said to herself. Yes, this is my case now.

Chapter Four

Right, Harriet said to herself, standing outside the great gloomy bulk of the Imperial, I'm damned now if I'm going to hang about all weekend doing nothing. Time to get down to it. I don't know what Pansy Balfour was making such a hoo-ha about. Surely I must be able to get into that Headquarters office I've been allocated. And, once there, I can get those garments that DCI Kenworthy took from the seven suspects and send them over to the Forensic Science lab at that place near Lincoln. Come to that, there's no reason why I shouldn't get hold of Kenworthy's notes from Records. A police officer's account of the murder should be a good deal more down to earth, and accurate, than the purpler-than-purple ramblings of *Who Killed the Preacher?*.

Yet she found herself, as she waited to cross over to her car, recalling the words Michael Meadowcraft had spattered out in describing the very scene now in front of her at the hour he supposed the murder took place. *Imagine what different thoughts were in the heads of that group of Sunday-night young men, most of them over-eager disciples of the god Bacchus, as they went rolling past the great hotel singing the popular ditty 'You'll never walk alone'. But inside the Boy Preacher had just walked, all too alone, to his horrible death.*

Which is all very well, she thought. Except that Mr Popham told me the Boy's meeting had been postponed from the original Sunday to the Monday, for some reason or other. Meadowcraft, though he does his best to pretend he was there, must actually have been far away. Only when he realized that here was a chance to add yet another over-heated volume to *Cold Steel and Spilt Blood* or *The Men They Asked Inside* or to *Death in Pale Pink Pyjamas* would he have hurried to the Imperial to begin acquiring, or imagining, the juicy details.

But, she thought, taking advantage of a gap in the traffic to dart across, what I was looking at just now was the real world of today, dull, grimy twenty-first-century Birchester. But a Birchester where it's possible that the killer of the Boy Preacher is walking the streets, untouched. And, like any other criminal, they should be brought to justice.

My job.

Harriet got into the car and drove off towards the Headquarters building at the edge of the city. She found herself in her eagerness going rather faster than was perhaps wise.

As soon as she had managed in the becalmed Saturday afternoon atmosphere of Headquarters to get hold of the key to her office, she realized why Pansy Balfour had been in such a state about it. Quite obviously the place had been, until the Big White Chief had re-allocated it, no more than a small store room, hardly a step up from a broom cupboard. It did possess

33

a window, though it was very small and looked as if it was sealed fast with encrusted dirt, and it had been marginally equipped as an office. There was a small wooden table, one hard wooden chair behind it and in front another, a dangerously leaning typist's cast-off. Mercifully, there was at least a telephone. But no computer.

Damn it, damn it, damn it, she thought. This is Newbroom's doing. The man has deliberately deprived me of the investigative tool no detective nowadays can manage without. Does he mean me to go to him and beg?

I'm buggered if I will, though. I'm simply going to forget about his notion of what a doomed-to-fail senior detective deserves as accommodation. I'm going to get to work to resolve this case he's thrust on to me, with or without the equipment I ought to have. If I need something a computer will tell me quickly, I'll just get the DC who's going to be attached to me – whenever they appear – to go and use someone else's.

So, right, a word with the Evidence Store. Get the bags of clothing that Newbroom told me are there off to the Forensic Science lab.

She picked up the tatty, stapled-together internal directory that had been left beside the phone, scrabbled through its greasy pages and stabbed out the number.

No answer.

She let the phone ring and ring. At last she put the handset down and carefully jabbed at the buttons again. Still nothing.

All right, try Security.

Success here. But, no, the man on duty stolidly

informed her, bar exceptional circumstances, the Evidence Store was always closed at weekends.

'It's the cuts, ma'am.'

The cuts. It always was the cuts. Except in criminal activity.

So, what next? Yes, right, Force Records. At least get hold of DCI Kenworthy's files and see what he made of the case. Unless Records, too, shuts down from Friday night to Monday morning.

Buttons jabbed. Then – hooray – a voice answering, if a faint one.

She identified herself, and asked if the Boy Preacher murder files could be sent up to her.

'Well . . .' the quavering voice replied, with a discernible trace of worry. 'Well, you see, that might be a bit difficult.'

'Will it, indeed? And why is that?'

'It's not that the files aren't here all right. I happened to turn them up last Saturday, as a matter of fact. There's not often a lot going on here at weekends, and I've always been interested in that case.'

'Then why can't I be sent them? Now?'

'I'm here on my own,' the voice almost wailed, 'and I can't leave without getting the whole store locked up.'

'Right, I'll come down.'

Slightly regretting her sharpness – the man in Records had seemed pretty ancient, probably a part-timer – she made her way down to the basement. And, after all, the old chap had said the case interested him. He might even have some useful memories of the time. The time when I was still at school, eating Tennis Court cake and chattering about the latest sensation in the newspapers.

Her guess about the clerk proved right. He was a shrivelled-up fellow, who could even be into his eighties. A full head of white hair, but no better shaved than Mr Popham had been at the Imperial. A big pair of tortoiseshell-rimmed National Health spectacles kept slipping down his fleshless nose.

'We're looking into a few of these old cases where we never got a result,' she said to him, conscious of Mr Newbroom's security ruling. 'Just to see if any of them might benefit from the advances in DNA techniques these days.'

'Well, I hope this is one of 'em. It was a bad business. A very bad business.'

'You remember it then, do you?' she asked, as, with hands that trembled a little, he pushed the bulging files across the counter towards her.

'Oh, yes. Yes, I remember it well.'

'You said it was a bad business. The victim not one of those who perhaps deserved it?'

'Oh, I don't know about that. No, the case caused a lot of fuss but that's not why I still believe it was a bad business. Don't know why people got so excited about that Boy Preacher at the time. Perhaps just because he was young, and foreign with it. I don't hold with preaching myself. Not a lot of use in telling people to be good. What you've got to do is stop them when they're bad. That's what the police are for, isn't it? I served my thirty on the beat, and reckon I know what's what.'

'So why is it then,' Harriet asked the long-retired constable, a spark of curiosity flicking through her, 'that you said the case was a bad business?'

"Cos that killer was never brought to court, that's why. He was never found guilty, and he was never hanged for it.'

The old man glared at her through his dulled-over glasses.

And, good heavens, yes, she thought. Back in those days, the death penalty had not long been abolished. A die-hard like this old fellow would still be thinking *bring back the rope*. And perhaps the Hard Detective, if I'd been a serving police officer then and not an idealistic schoolgirl, would have echoed that. And what about the officer who had tried to find out who the murderer of the Boy Preacher was? Would he, too, if he'd made his arrest, have felt it wrong that hanging no longer existed?

'Tell me,' she said to the old fellow, 'did you see anything of DCI Kenworthy when you were still in the force?'

'Oh, yes, I did. Dead and gone now, of course. But he was a fine officer in his day, a fine detective. We all knew that. If he was never able to put his finger on whoever strangled that silly young man, then no one else could have done.'

Harriet felt that as something of a body blow.

If a detective as good as everyone tells me Kenworthy was failed when the case was fresh and evidence was there to be found, what chance have I got so many years on? Very little, unless bloody Mr Newbroom's wonder-working DNA gets a result.

Nevertheless she examined the tabs on the files stacked on the store counter and, finding the one that looked likely to hold DCI Kenworthy's personal notes – what nowadays would be his Policy File – she wrapped her arms round it, lifted it up and headed for her broom cupboard of an office.

Back there, after an unsuccessful wrestle with the jammed-up window, she got down to the aged buff folder that contained DCI Kenworthy's running commentary on his investigation.

Briefing Notes: Murder of Krishna Kumaramangalam, 20 years, of 17 Lower Church Street, Birchester. At or about 1900hrs, Monday, May 22 1969.

So, one thing made clear straight away: Meadowcraft had indeed got the day of the Boy Preacher's death wrong. Thank you, Mr Newbroom, for your loan of that informative book.

Giving the file a rapid survey, she soon realized Kenworthy was as conscientious a detective as both the old man on Saturday duty in Records and, for what it was worth, fat little Mr Popham had claimed. Conscientious, she came to think, but not perhaps as quickly intelligent as he might have been.

Yes, he records here, for instance, urgently having fingerprint checks made on the unlikely surfaces of the Boy's neck. But, when there proved to be nothing there of evidential value, why hadn't he had the ballroom doors dusted? They probably would have turned out to be so blotched with varied prints that there would have been no sorting them out. But it was also possible that someone intent on killing as they slipped through one of the doors might have put a sweat-damp hand somewhere unexpectedly high up on it.

So does this mean there's a glimmer of hope for a more imaginative approach now? Despite those thirty-plus years?

But, by God, I'm certainly going to be every bit as conscientious as ever Kenworthy was. All right, if in the end the result comes from the lab over in Lincoln-shire, and Mr Newbroom's faith proves justified, I'll still deal with the case with total efficiency. Or, if from any interviews I'm able to have with any of the sus-pects still alive something emerges, I'll see that goes into its fully attested place. Whatever opinion New-broom's acquired of me, I'm not the sort of dash-at-it idiot that finds their case in court sunk by a clever defence counsel picking on a weak spot in the con-tinuity of evidence.

She replaced Kenworthy's Briefing Notes in the bulging cardboard file and picked out the first sheaf of documents she saw. As she did so, the perished rubber band round them snapped and fell like a discarded snake-skin on to the table. A bundle of photographs fanned out from her grasp in an untidy sprawl. She began gathering them together again, wondering if she might possibly find in the drawer in the table some newer rubber bands. Glancing at one of the faded black-and-whites as she placed it on top of the others, she saw again, with a little shock, the low dais in the

Imperial's ballroom which she had stared at not much more than an hour earlier.

Does it look any different thirty years before I inspected it for anything that might tell me what exactly had happened? Hard to make out. Almost impossible. Perhaps the carpet on it is glossier than the wretched thing I saw, if that was the one there thirty years ago. And, yes, there do seem to be some pressed-down patches on it where the Boy's body must have been lying. Pity they weren't using colour film back in those days. It's not really very clear. But then nothing I've seen in Kenworthy's notes indicates he was able to deduce anything of value from his own inspection of that carpet.

Ah, shots of the ballroom itself, four or five of them. Not telling me much. But even in the faded black-and-white it's easy to see what a magnificent, if wildly over-the-top, sight all those twirly columns and bright tile-pictures must have presented to ball-goers in the days just before the Boy was strangled. Strangled perhaps while he looked at them. The last things he saw.

Oh, and this is better. This lot, held together separately, surely they're mug-shots of each of those seven who had access to the ballroom that Monday evening. Okay, let's see if I can identify them from Michael Meadowcraft's lush profiles.

She eased away the rusty paperclip at the top.

Right, two women. Which is the schoolteacher, Priscilla Knott, which the dubious Bubsy Willson? Easy. Bubsy must be the really appallingly ugly one. Her flat, suetty face is clear enough, and the pic must have been taken under strong lights. I can even see the wiry black hairs protruding. And, something Meadowcraft didn't mention, her body, even in this head-and-shoulders view, looks distinctly ungainly. Poor creature. And Meadowcraft came crashing down on her as his Number Two suspect.

Something DCI Kenworthy pointedly refrained from doing in his notes. A man I feel an increasing respect for. If he had in fact pointed the finger, he wouldn't have been the first investigating officer to pick out a suspect and tell his team 'Find me the evidence'. An even more frequently used method, I suspect, thirty years ago, when a hunch must often have been preferred to the cruder science of those days.

Right, so this must be Priscilla Knott. Not quite a glare at the camera, but certainly a challenge. Surely as much as to say how dare you suggest I would commit a murder. An attractive young woman? Well, features certainly good. But I rather feel that not many men would find themselves drawn. Perhaps, though, when I see her, if she's still alive to see, I'll change my mind. Black-and-white shots of thirty-odd years' age tell very little.

But now, the men. Not so easy to sort out. Who've I got? First, at least on the social scale, let's find Undersheriff Lucas Calverte. Ah, easily spotted, every inch the gent. And, yes, this must be Barney Trapnell; even if the photo doesn't show his callipered leg, his bent-forward posture's a giveaway. Now, try for something more difficult: Marcus Fairchild, the mysterious figure, long ago killed in a traffic accident. No, can't be sure.

Yes, though, that one must be him, nondescript though he appears, because, no doubt about it, here's Sydney Bigod, street trader. Looking properly shifty. So, finally, this dark, wide-eyed, trusting face must belong to my favourite, Harish Nair, and, yes, it's plain even from this head-and-shoulders shot that he was, as Michael Meadowcraft described him so viciously, a little fellow.

I wonder why, subconsciously, I came to him last of all? Was it because deep down I don't want to find out that he killed the young man who lodged in his house? Better watch myself, or I'll find I'm doing the exact converse of what I was castigating old-time officers for doing a moment ago. First pick your prime suspect, then scrabble together the evidence.

Wait, damn it, there are names on the backs. Of course there are. Silly of me. So, yes, this is Trapnell, and here's the oddly-named Sydney Bigod – got that right – and, after him, really looking a little pathetic—

Stop. Harish Nair may look pathetic to my eyes. But, just as much as any of the others, he could be the person who strangled his distant cousin.

So, yes, this is Undersheriff Lucas Calverte, and this is the mysterious Marcus Fairchild, that long face and blank give-away-nothing eyes. But why did he abruptly appear in Birchester just before the murder? And how was it that he managed to insinuate himself into what Meadowcraft calls the Clique? And why did he need to do that?

So there they are, the famous Seven Suspects. And, as soon as I can get to the Evidence Store and have their clothes sent off to the lab at, what's it, Cherry

Fettleham, the sooner the answer will come back. And what will it be? Spittle with the DNA of Krishna Kumaramangalam present in quantity on the garment worn by— Worn by whom?

Chapter Five

Harriet, arriving home to find John back from his day's shooting and a pair of rabbits hanging over the sink in the kitchen, was still feeling a trace of exhilaration at the way her investigation had begun. Three further trips down to the aged ex-constable in Records had delivered into her hands the whole mass of ancient files on the case. And she had learnt a lot.

'I'll deal with the gutting in a bit,' John said from the depths of his favourite chair, as she came in from the kitchen. 'It's just that I'm temporarily exhausted.'

'Snap.'

'Oh, why's that? You're not the one who's been tramping Mr Markby's fields all day, trying to prove you're a better shot than your junior colleagues.'

'No. But I have been shut up all afternoon in the sort of big cupboard that friend Newbroom's allocated as my office. Further proof, incidentally, that he's got his knife into me.'

John chuckled.

'Newbroom's what those seventeenth-century writers used to call your *maggot*. As I told you last night, it's a great mistake to allow an idea like that to obsess you just because, in all likelihood, Mr New-comen doesn't happen to have a very high opinion of you. Though why he shouldn't I can't imagine. The Hard Detective's a good detective.'

'Oh, please, not the Hard Detective, not from you.'

'All right then, Detective Superintendent Martens is a good detective. But she'll be less of a good detective if she lets herself be bugged by what's surely a fanciful notion, a maggot.'

'Well, I don't think it is a maggot.'

For a moment she wondered whether she should tell John about her devil and the deep blue sea dream. But she decided it would only confirm his notion of her as being in the grip of a totally false idea.

Yet she was sure the idea was by no means false.

Mr Newbroom wants to sweep me right out of his force. And he's given me this task with just that object in mind. If all I do is see to the despatch of the suspects' outer garments to Cherry Fettleham on Monday, and they in due course come up with definite, go-to-court evidence, Newbroom'll take the credit. Then I'll be relegated to a series of dogsbody jobs. Skids under the career. If, on the other hand, the lab finds no reliable evidence and my investigation, as is only too likely, fares no better than poor old Kenworthy's, it'll be the same result. And next Mr Newbroom will expect me to go looking for pastures new. But who can't go to a decent post in a major force without causing havoc to her life as Mrs John Piddock? John can't move very far away from Birchester. He really needs to be on the spot, especially with his career in the Majestic on the up-and-up. All those frequent calls to go off abroad at a moment's notice. All those boardroom conferences, first thing in the morning or far into the evening. So how can he say—

But now he broke in on her grutchety train of thought, which she realized must have produced an equally grutchety expression on her face.

'No, tell me more about this business you feel's been foisted on to you. You could be right about it, after all. You don't generally chase after totally absurd notions.'

A sense of warm relief at this sudden showing of sympathy.

'Thank you, kind sir.'

So she gave him a fuller account of her interview with the Chief the evening before, and then pulled from her briefcase that wildly inaccurate copy of *Who Killed the Preacher?* which Mr Newbroom had given her. Further evidence of malicious intent.

'Well, I tell you one thing,' John said, leafing through the book. 'Gift or loan, this remarkable work is going to find its eventual home on my crowded shelves, if I have to displace Homer's *Iliad* to get it in. I see many happy hours ahead plunged into these pages. Listen to this. *Under the glittering chandeliers of a ballroom that in days gone by had seen pirouetting dancers with royal blood flowing in their veins . . .* How about that?

'All right, all right. Keep it for when I'm not here. I had a basinful of it when I was trying to get the outline of the affair into my head this morning. But now, thank goodness, I've managed to read the notes made by the investigating officer thirty years ago.'

'And he's – I suppose it is a *he*. A murder inquiry wouldn't fall to a woman at that time.'

'You're only too right. Things were very different thirty-odd years ago.'

'But is the chap whose notes you've read as good an investigator as the Hard— As Detective Superintendent Martens?'

'No, actually I don't think he is, unless I'm crediting myself with powers I haven't got. No, Detective Chief Inspector Kenworthy was an extremely efficient investigator. I certainly give him that. But what I do think he lacked is— Well, what shall I say? What shall I claim for, if you must, the Hard Detective? Not hardness, though there's no harm in that. But something else. Call it the ability to produce jump-thoughts out of nowhere. What's that expression?'

'Lateral thinking. Man called Edward de Bono coined it.'

'Right. And I think that happens with me. Sometimes. But I didn't see any signs of anything similar as I worked my way through DCI Kenworthy's stuff this afternoon.'

'But what did you learn?'

'Oh, a good deal. I'm not saying I didn't. First, that the murder took place on a Monday. Monday, May the twenty-second, 1969, to be precise. Not on the Sunday, as your delightful Michael Meadowcraft states. Then, there really were no other people except the ones Meadowcraft calls the Seven Suspects able to get into the ballroom where that poor young man was strangled. But, while they were, all seven of them, waiting outside for the Boy Preacher to finish his customary period of

47

pre-meeting meditation, any one of them, Kenworthy believed, could have slipped into the ballroom unobserved.'

'And did he have a favourite?'

'Not at all. That's one of the reasons I said he was – he's dead now – a good investigator. Mind you, I wouldn't put have-a-guess police work past his Number Two on the case, Detective Sergeant Shaddock. From what I read of his reports he was a regular pick-your-own-murderer detective.'

'But dead now, too? You might find him worth talking to, if not.'

'Oh, dead almost certainly. Kenworthy mentions in his personal notes somewhere that the fellow is a much older man, on the point of retirement. He distrusted some of the arguments Shaddock put forward on those grounds.'

'Too bad. But, talking of what you call bag-carriers, didn't you tell me yesterday that Mr Newcomen was going to let you have a detective constable to assist you? Has he or she appeared yet?'

'No, they haven't. I haven't even been given a name. Another thing in favour of my maggot, as you like to call it.'

'But DCI Kenworthy is dead, and probably Sergeant Shaddock too. So how many of your delightful Meadowcraft's Seven Suspects are dead as well?'

'One is, certainly. Meadowcraft's book states in a footnote that the journalist Marcus Fairchild was killed in a traffic accident in London just before *Who Killed the Preacher?* came out. He announces that this clears him of suspicion, without attempting to say why. But the death is confirmed in the report on the first statutory check on the evidence after the investigation was put on file. I'm sorry to say for the efficiency of Greater Birchester Police, however, that this was the last time such a check was properly made. Afterwards those files have simply been marked *NFA*. So—'

'*NFA?* Some police jargon I'm not up to.'

'Sorry. *No Further Action.* But, of course, any of the other six remaining suspects could have died in the last thirty years or so.'

'And do you agree that the chap who was killed in that road accident can't be the murderer?'

'No, I don't altogether. All right, Kenworthy interviewed him at some length. But then he let him go back to London, where he worked. He was a journalist for *The Times*, Kenworthy says. I suppose that may account for how, suddenly arriving in Birchester, he wormed himself into what Meadowcraft calls – time and again – the Clique.'

'You don't seem altogether happy about this Fairchild. Have you had a piece of lateral thinking pointing to him?'

'No. No, I haven't. I dare say he was perfectly above board. But I don't know.' Harriet laughed. 'Perhaps it's just that I've been somehow impressed by old Meadowcraft's repeated references to him, before he knew about the accident, as *mysterious*.'

'So he still could be . . .?'

'Any one of them *could be*. Kenworthy says so in his summing-up. He said it had been impossible to establish the movements of the seven in the foyer to the ballroom at the time before the murder. It had even been, in the confusion there, impossible to be certain who it was who actually found the body. So there it is. All to play for still. But little hope, really, of a result. Unless the DNA turns up trumps, and it can't do that if it so happens there are no traces from the Boy on what the person who strangled him was wearing. Something Mr Newbroom certainly knew when he gave me the investigation.'

'Now then, I've told you before, that's a maggot you shouldn't try to fish with.'

'And you've also told me,' Harriet said, hoping to score in the familiar happy-marriage war, 'that you were going to deal with those two rabbits dripping blood all over my kitchen.'

'All right, I'm going, I'm going. But I really meant what I said. And I tell you one thing. You're going to take Sunday off. It doesn't sound as if there could be anything more for you to do, if you do go in. So, Doctor Piddock prescribes twenty-four hours' rest.'

Harriet glared at him.

Then she laughed.

'Okay. So long as it's the doctor prescribing and not the prelate preaching.'

So Sunday morning saw the two of them getting into the car to head for the Majestic Insurance Social and Sports Club for an early swim, before the unusually warm May weather brought out a crowd of other privileged employees. Then, feeling full of new vigour, and with Harriet not having a single thought about the devil and the deep blue sea, they headed for Aslough

Parade. There in Birchester's 'Bond Street' a shop sold out-of-the-oven croissants to vie with the best in France. Which brought them back eventually to chairs in the garden and the Sunday papers.

But neither of them found much in their wordy pages, nor in the innumerable glossy extras that had tumbled out on to the lawn. So, soon John picked up the book he had presciently also taken out with him, not *Who Killed the Preacher?* but his current reading, a biography of *Dong-with-the-Luminous-Nose* Edward Lear. Harriet simply contented herself with lying back and letting the sunshine pour on to her.

Except that before many minutes had passed she found herself churning over the circumstances of that murder thirty years and more ago. What, she asked, would those seven people, waiting just outside the Imperial's ballroom when the Boy Preacher was strangled, have been doing on that May Sunday, one day before the Boy's meeting?

Bubsy Willson, the ugly girl, for instance, would she have been lounging at home in a frowsty bed? And in it would she have been thinking about the Boy's injunction as recorded by Michael Meadowcraft, not to *bring children into the world without the care of both mother and father* or, in the doubtless more accurate Indian expression DCI Kenworthy had meticulously noted, *Do Not Bring into World Whatsoever Child Without Ma-Bap?* Or would the lumpy creature be day-dreaming about the sorts of adventures that had brought her, as Kenworthy's checking of the suspects' records had revealed, into court on fourteen separate occasions on charges of soliciting for immoral purposes? Another

thing Michael Meadowcraft had been inaccurate over.
It was not on charges of indecent behaviour that Bubsy
Willson had somehow always escaped fine or prison.

Right, zip up the social scale. To Mr Lucas Calverte,
barrister and Undersheriff for the county of Birrshire.
What about his Sunday morning? Not very likely he
would still be in bed at eleven o'clock. No, more probably at church in the village where he had a house. I
wonder whether, on that day so long ago, he found the
sermon improving? Or unnecessary? But perhaps he
was no church-goer, and had spent the morning doing
a little gardening while Mrs Calverte— No, this was
the sixties – while Cook prepared a roast-beef Sunday
lunch.

But, as he uprooted an unruly dandelion, had
he been thinking that, for some yet-to-be-discovered
reason, the Boy Preacher had also to be eliminated?
Yet for what reason? What possible reason could a
man who was chairman of the Birchester Immigrants
Welfare Council have to kill a harmless young preaching Indian?

And zip down the scale again. To Barney Trapnell,
crippled watch repairer. Difficult to see why, lying in
bed that Sunday morning or perhaps already busy at
his bench, he should have had murder in mind. All
right, apparently his connection with the Boy lay in
his having great strength in his arms, enabling him,
despite his callipered leg, to hoist the young preacher's
slight form here and there when needed. And, incidentally, why should that office have been required? What,
if anything, had been wrong with the Boy? Kenworthy's
notes don't ever indicate what it was. Room for a

famous lateral leap here? Can't see there really is, though.

No, the only possible, and highly unlikely, reason for rough-and-ready Barney Trapnell to strangle the Boy would be the envy of the unsuccessful and the crippled for the suddenly tremendously successful preacher he sometimes had to carry in his arms. And, to me, that hardly holds water.

All right, the wild card next. Marcus Fairchild, feature writer for the mighty London *Times*, according to Kenworthy's interview notes.

All unaware that he had less than a year to live, was he lying in bed with the Sundays in whatever Birchester hotel he had booked into? Hah, had the *Times* put him into the Imperial? And had he chosen to make a bit on his expenses by staying somewhere more modest? Meant to be the journalist's way of life. But as he lay there – hope the mattress was as lumpy as the ones we had at school back then – what could he possibly have been thinking about the Boy who was to die only shortly before himself? He could, I suppose, have been wondering about the preaching youth he had, presumably, been sent to Birchester to write about? Well, he might have been. But I don't see a journalist, however good his description of aspects of the life of the day might be, devoting every idle hour to polishing his prose. So, what? So, nil, nothing, zilch.

On down the list. Right, can't dodge it any longer. Little Harish Nair, whom Meadowcraft blatantly lined up for the dock. But it was DCI Kenworthy's balanced interview notes that made me . . .

' . . . like him. And I do. I just like him.'

'What's that?' John said, looking up from *Edward Lear*.

'Oh gosh, did I say that out loud?'

'You did. Whatever it was.'

'Well, it was just that I like one of my suspects.'

'The Hard Detective eliminates one out of seven? Were you asleep and dreaming, or actually awake?'

'God knows. Betwixt and between, I think. But no, of course not. I haven't even in a dream decided who cannot have killed that poor Boy. No, I was just thinking, or dreaming, that I liked the sound of the Boy's cousin, Harish Nair, as a person. He comes over as a nice, nice man, even in DCI Kenworthy's solid notes. And since Meadowcraft manages to get his knife into the poor fellow, I've all the more reason to think he's a really decent chap.'

'Picking favourites without any evidence? You want to watch out for that, or you'll lose the title of Hard—'

'Get back to the *Dong with the Luminous Nose*, damn you.'

John, with a little smirk, returned to his book in silence.

And Harriet thought.

Right, Harish Nair has undeniably made his way into my affections. A man of such simplicity and good-will, so modest in his claims on life, can he really have strangled his lodger, Krishna Kumaramangalam, there in the empty ballroom of the Imperial Hotel? Would he, small as he is, actually have hands physically capable of the swift act? If Kenworthy did look at them with that in mind, he certainly made no note of his observations. So, is that one of the things an investigating officer with the ability to employ lateral thinking would have done? And that Kenworthy did not? Right, if Harish Nair is still in the land of the living, I'll take a damn good look at his hands. Even after thirty or more years it should be possible to see whether they were once strong enough to effect rapid manual strangulation.

And if they were, what would have been the motive that drove the little man – Kenworthy had put his height at five foot four – to dig them into the boy's neck and hold them there till he could no longer breathe? Leaving on whatever garment he was wearing on that warm May evening the spittle the boy had spewed out as his life came to its swift and ugly end? Certainly nothing that leaps to mind. But there may have been circumstances in that small household at – what's it? – 17 Lower Church Street, that no one knew about. Were they what caused Harish Nair to change from an outward lamb into an inward raging lion? Could the outlandish idea suggested to Kenworthy by DS Shaddock be right? That Krishna could have attempted to make love to Mrs Nair? Could it really have been something like that? Kenworthy had, conscientious as ever, probed the possibility when he was interviewing Mrs Nair, and had come to the conclusion that there could be nothing at all in it.

But there might have been something else. Anything's possible when two human beings come into close contact. But beware of liking little Harish Nair too much.

Who's still to come? Right, the other woman who was there walking up and down that ballroom foyer for two long expectant hours, perhaps going into the Ladies once or twice, perhaps going to sit for a while in one of those two little meeting rooms. Miss Priscilla Knott, teacher. Right, May is in term time. So, on a Sunday morning would she, as a conscientious young woman, be busy preparing for her next day's teaching, cutting up coloured paper for her children to make into little lanterns, or whatever? And certainly, from what Kenworthy says about her, and Meadowcraft echoes, she seems to have been conscientious. But church for her first, I think, nodding away in agreement with any pulpit denunciations of contemporary behaviour. By this time of the morning, though, perhaps she'd be sitting with a pile of exercise books. *No, wrong*, her pencil would jab down in a margin. Or, *How many times have you been told how to write BED?* Or, worse, *See me after class.*

All right, say, lifting her head from imposing a particularly fierce red-pencil mark, she finds herself, whether she wants to or not, thinking about the Boy. Why would her thoughts be of murder? Surely, if she found anything gravely amiss with his conduct, she would simply have preached him a ferocious sermon, in return for all the mild ones she must have heard from him. A good woman, to judge by Kenworthy's notes. If an unyielding one. So what motive for murder could she have had? Answer: you never can know the secrets of the human heart – if that doesn't sound too much like the author of *Death in Pale Pink Pyjamas*.

Okay, last man up, and hop from the good to the bad, or at least the regularly presumed to be bad. To Sydney Bigod, street trader. And no difficulty in finding a motive here, or a motive of sorts. Money. And, yes, Kenworthy found there was money awash in the Boy Preacher's wake, and not all of it easily accounted for. A good head for figures, old Peter Kenworthy. But all his work, aided by the small Greater Birchester Police fraud team of those days, had not been able to show how much of that, if any, had got into Sydney Bigod's hands before he decided to return to his native Norfolk.

And his Sunday morning thoughts on the day before the murder? In bed, very likely. Unless there was a penny or two to be made in some Birchester side street, which wouldn't have been anything so likely as it would today. The Lord's Day Observance Society was in full career back then. No universal Sunday openings, and probably precious little other commercial activity. So, plotting and planning? That'd be it. Sydney Bigod plotting how to make a few extra bob, all unconscious of the fact that in twenty-four hours' time his life was going to be dramatically changed by murder. Unless he himself had some reason to shut the Boy Preacher's mouth, and was working out how to get away with it.

'You know,' John said, suddenly looking up from his book, 'there's a lot I never knew about dear old Edward Lear.'

Harriet came to with a start.

Jesus, she thought, what have I been doing, on what's meant to be a Sunday without any thoughts of the task I've been landed with? At least I wasn't thinking about Mr Newbroom. Name never crossed my thought-lips, John, dear.

'Oh,' she managed to say, 'there's something you actually didn't know?'

He smiled.

'If you're not the Hard Detective,' he said, 'then I don't see why I should be the Walking Encyclopedia.'

'Right, truce from now on. And what was it you didn't kn— What was it you found interesting about "pleasant to know" Mr Lear?'

'Well, right at the beginning it emerged that he wasn't quite so pleasant, for one thing.'

'Oh? I always thought that that was the thing about him, what a nice man he was. You're not going to tell me he had thoughts about committing horrible murders, are you?'

Her mind flipped back at once to the notions she had been pondering when John had interrupted her.

'Well, as a matter of fact,' he said now, 'the lady who's written the book, Vivien Noakes, who seems pretty acute, says, with good backing from Lear's diaries and correspondence, that there was a mysterious figure in his childhood days. He wrote of whoever it was as a "particular skeleton" who had done him some evil affecting him for all the rest of his life. I think he might well have wished a nasty fate on whoever that was. But, no, what I really didn't know about Lear was that he was an epileptic and had fits throughout his life, though he felt he always had to conceal them. Epilepsy was not to be spoken about in Victorian days. Any more than homosexual yearnings, which he also suffered from.'

'But however did he manage to actually hide those fits?'

And what similar secrets, she said to herself, might Meadowcraft's Seven Suspects have had to hide?

'Oh, you get some warning of the fit's onset, apparently,' John replied. 'I looked it all up, as a matter of fact. You get what's called the *aura epileptica*. It gives you time to go somewhere out of the way, hide in Lear's case, and have your short spell of rigidity and then your convulsive jerking about before you pass into a coma and then into a brief sleep.'

'Poor old Lear. What a wretched life it must have been for people with something like that, in those tuck-it-away times.'

'True enough. Not that all times don't have their horrible aspects. Look at the period you're busy investigating right now. One of those people who could have got into the ballroom at the Imperial must have been going through an appalling time, for some well-concealed reason or another.'

But which of them, Harriet said to herself in a swift blaze of fury. Which? Which? Which? And if I do learn a name from the lab at Cherry Fettleham, my troubles will have just begun. After all, it'll need more than a report on some DNA work to bring a defence-proof case to court.

Chapter Six

Arriving at her office at exactly nine on Monday morning, Harriet found that things were looking up a little. There, standing a few yards away from its locked door, was a short sturdy man in his late fifties with a pointed snow-white beard and head of tufty hair. A fawn linen jacket and light-green cotton trousers both showed signs of age. But an air of alertness in his bright blue eyes made her guess at once that here was her promised DC.

Responding to her look of assessment, the fellow made a sudden little rush towards her.

'Detective Superintendent Martens?' he jerked out.

'That's me.'

'I— I'm— I'm the DC attached to you for . . .'

His voice dropped away.

'The inquiry into the Boy Preacher murder,' Harriet snapped, thinking the fellow could hardly have been allocated to her without being told about the investigation.

'Yes. Yes. I suppose— I mean, I imagine even after the DNA lab gets a result there'll be inquiries to make.'

'If they get a result.'

'Oh, I understood— Well, I understood there wasn't going to be much doubt about that.'

'Then you've more faith in forensic science than I have. It could be, you know, that the people down there will eventually tell us there was nothing for them to find.'

'So what— what, er, then, ma'am?'

'A lot more interviews, unless all the supposed suspects turn out to be dead. And then a good deal of disappointment for Mr Newcomen.'

'Yes, I suppose so.'

The little white-bearded detective looked as if he would like to say more. Harriet turned to her door, unlocked it and waved him inside.

'You haven't told me your name, DC,' she said.

'Oh, no. No, I haven't. I— It's Steadman, ma'am. Steadman.'

'Spelt S-T-E-A-D or S-T-E-D?'

'S-T-E-A . . . The first way, ma'am.'

'Well, I suppose as the two of us will be working together I'd better call you by your forename. When I don't call you DC. What is it?'

'It's— er— Phillip, ma'am. Phillip. But— But, well, I'm generally called Pip. Pip. I've always been that. Pip. Pip Steadman.'

She was beginning to find this perpetual hesitance more than a little irritating. Perhaps, she thought, a degree of informality may reduce it. Provided it didn't make him get above himself.

'All right, Pip,' she said, sitting herself at the room's wretched wooden table and indicating to him to take the lurched-over ex-typist's chair. 'Tell me about yourself.'

It was a mistake, if the object had been to eliminate the hesitant manner.

'I, er, I— Well, ma'am, perhaps I ought to tell you that I'm only just back from— From sick leave.'

'Oh, yes? And what was that for?'

A gulp. And silence.

What the hell have I been landed with? Is this another of Newbroom's little exercises in tyranny?

'Ma'am, it was a— Well, a nervous breakdown, actually.'

Right, a nutter. Thanks very much.

'I— Well, let me tell you a bit of my history, and then you'll perhaps understand.'

His two bright blue little pippy eyes looked up at her, as if they ought to have been big, deep brown, pleading dog's eyes.

'You see, I haven't been in the service all my working life, er, ma'am. I was in advertising to begin with. I'm— I used to be something of a dab hand with words at school and the job appealed to me, and— And— Well, I thought that by doing it I'd be also doing some good in the world, telling people what were the best products at their disposal. And I did quite well in the job, down in London actually. But—'

He came to a slap-bang halt.

But. But. Oh, yes, bound to be a but. Harriet allowed the thought to rip out in her head. But kept it in bounds.

'But then— Then one day I, I, er, thought about what it was that I was actually doing. I was telling people what they should eat or drink or wear, but not because I believed it was in their b-best interests any more. Oh, no. No, I knew by then that it was only in the best interests of the people manufacturing the food, or drink, or clothing. I— I was the devil's preacher.'

Going it a bit. The devil's preacher. Though I suppose . . .

She remained silent.

'So I quit. I quit, ma'am.'

'And then what? Did you go straight away and join the police?'

Pip Steadman looked wounded.

Oh God, Harriet thought, I'm going to have a fine time working with this idiot if he looks like that whenever I bark at him.

'Well, yes. Yes, ma'am. I suppose that's what I did do. You see, I always believed one ought to do something that was for the good of one's fellow human beings, and I— I thought a job in the police back in my home town would give me opportunities to do that. Helping people in trouble, putting young offenders back on the right track, that sort of thing.'

He broke off, apparently ashamed at his spate of words.

Harriet looked at him in as pleasant a fashion as she felt she could manage at that moment.

'I suppose it was naive of me,' Pip Steadman said.

'Right, so how did you get on after you'd taken the oath? I don't think I've come across you before.'

'Yes, yes,' the little white-haired DC replied, evidently encouraged. 'I was posted to A Division, so I never took part in the Hard Detective's "Stop the Rot"

campaign in B Div. I— I thought it was an excellent
thing. If I may say so.'

'All right, you may say it, once. But not more. And
I don't ever want to hear the words *Hard Detective* pass
your lips again. Yes?'

'Oh. Oh, gosh. Sorry. Sorry, ma'am.'

'And you still haven't told me why you had your
breakdown.'

'No. No, but, you see, I thought you might understand better if I told you about— About my leaving the
advertising profession, and why I did it.'

'So, go on, DC. Go on, Pip.'

'Well, it was like this. I was doing well as a police
officer really. I turned out to be good at the job— Quite
good. And, I actually did feel that at the same time I
was helping my fellow man. So, after a bit, thought
I might do well in the CID. I thought it was really the
life for me. Something I would be good at, and . . . But
then—'

A full halt.

Harriet waited a little and then, suppressing her
impatience, prompted him.

'And then?'

'Yes. Yes. Well, and then— Then something rather
awful happened to me.'

Going to need another gentle prompt? No. Seems
not.

'It was like this, ma'am. I'd been on a murder
inquiry— It was— It was— It was a man accused of
battering his wife to death. And I'd thought— I'd— You
see, he was a fellow I rather liked, and I thought he was
getting something of a raw deal. Not from Prosecuting

Counsel, of course. It's their job to paint black blacker than black. But from our own side. Some of the evidence my boss put in disproving the alibi was a bit loaded. Well, a lot, really. He was dead keen on getting a verdict, his last case before retirement. And so—'

Flow abruptly stopped.

'Go on, DC.'

'Well, so, ma'am, when it came to my turn in the box, with what was really a pretty crucial bit of evidence to break that alibi, I— Well, I contrived to muff it up. And in consequence the fellow got off.'

'And you were reprimanded? You should have been, you know.'

'No. No, it wasn't that. Of course, I came in for a bit of flak. But my boss – I'd better not tell you his name – was demob happy, and I got away with no more than a cheerful bollocking. But, no, it was a lot worse than that.'

'Explain.'

'You see, ma'am, about a month later the chap who'd been found not guilty went and killed both his two kiddies.'

Harriet at once recognized the case. It had been less than a year ago.

'So you had the breakdown?'

'Yes, ma'am.'

He sat there, blinking furiously.

'Ma'am,' he said. 'Do you mind if I have a cigarette?'

Harriet looked at him.

'No, DC, I don't mind. But let me point out to you that the Chief Constable has had notices posted reminding everybody that the Headquarters building was declared a smoke-free zone more than a year ago, and that there will be severe repercussions if any officer is found breaking that rule. So, go ahead.'

Pip Steadman looked at her cautiously. And then pulled from his pocket a much-squashed pack of Marlboro Lights and lit up.

'It all got to be too much for me, thinking about what I'd done. In the box. And I got to the point where I couldn't sleep for going over and over it in my mind. My work went to pot, too, of course. And— And I started shouting at people for no reason at all. And then, well, everything sort of went blank. And it was the psychiatric ward.'

He leant forward across the little table, a look of desperate earnestness in his pippy eyes.

'But I'm over it now. I really am. I— I'm ready— Ready for work. Really.'

Harriet looked at him.

'Right, you're back,' she said. 'And still a DC. You're damned lucky, you know.'

'Yes. Yes, I am. I do know it. In fact I was luckier than perhaps you realize. You see, my sick leave came to an end just before Mr Newbr— Mr Newcomen was appointed. Everybody said, despite what his predecessor had decided, that if I hadn't actually been back in the CID, he'd have had me on the beat before I knew where I was.'

And so, Harriet thought, old Newbroom, young Newbroom, has scored a double here. Sending me a detective like Steadman, the sort of man, as that old redneck Superintendent Froggott used to say, *you wouldn't use to send shopping*, has made my life extra difficult. And at the same time he's demonstrated his contempt for Sir Michael by showing that he thinks the man he allowed back into the CID is only fit for a half-cock job like this.

'Right,' she said. 'First things first. There's only one key for this bloody little cell of an office, and I can't have you locked out if I ever have to be away. So see about getting me a lockable cupboard of some sort, and then we can leave the door open. Right? And, when you've seen to that, I want you to make your way down to the Evidence Store and obtain, first, the clothing taken from each of the possible Boy Preacher suspects straight after the killing. Sign for it. Make absolutely sure it's the right evidence, and that it was properly accounted for back in 1969. And then get hold of the specimens from the post-mortem on the victim, which they'll also need down at the Forensic Science lab in Lincolnshire. Take every precaution to see that nothing from outside is introduced into any of them. Bring them all up here for me to see, and then you can pack them off to Cherry Fettleham.'

She found, when Pip Steadman brought back the evidence bags of clothing taken from the suspects and the PM specimens, that he seemed to have carried out his task with efficiency. Questioning him sharply, as she peered into the sealed transparent bags, she could find no fault in the way the vital continuity of evidence had been preserved.

But then something struck her. She had looked at

only six bags, and there were seven people whose clothing ought to have been taken.

'There are six bags here,' she said sharply. 'Did you leave one behind? The seventh bag?'

'No, no, ma'am,' he jabbered out. 'No, there really ought only to be six. You— You see, there was a note down there. A note with the missing bag's tab. It said that the garment taken from it belonged to a Miss Priscilla Knott. It was a blouse, pink with pearl buttons and, and a scalloped neck. It, the tab said, had been returned to her when Fingerprints back then had finished with it. She had asked for it. But she was the only one to claim her rights.'

'Very well.'

All right, she thought, jittery though my beardy friend still is, he seems after all to be capable enough. But Priscilla Knott and her pink blouse, that needs a little thought.

'So, let me tell you what I want you to do when you've seen these bags on their way. I want you to find out which of our suspects are still alive, and where they're currently living. Marcus Fairchild is off the list, safely dead these thirty years. But I need to know about the others, so I can decide whether it's good policy to see them now or to wait till the Forensic Science people produce their answer. If they ever do.'

'Ma'am.'

'I've made a list of the last known addresses, which may put you on the right lines. But I imagine even those that are still with us aren't very likely to be where they were thirty years ago. So take all the time you need. The lab down there is hardly going to come up with an answer tomorrow.'

'Very good, ma'am.'

He began gathering together the bags cluttering the little table.

Helping him, Harriet gave each bag a parting look.

Will this one with the colourful blouse, nylon by the look of it – nylon, the great sixties mainstay – will it prove to have the long-ago dried saliva on it that matches the Boy Preacher's DNA? It must be Barbara Willson's, Bubsy's. Much the same splodgily patterned, cheap and cheerful affair she was wearing when those black-and-white police photos were taken.

Or – she picked up another bag – will this dark grey waistcoat I see yield the right specimen? Waistcoat on a warm evening in late May? Or that white shirt? And is that a tie? A club tie? Must be. They did things differently, all right, thirty years ago. Or, at least, Undersheriff Lucas Calverte did, because that waistcoat can only be his.

She gave the bag to Pip.

Just as this bright blue shirt here, nylon again, can only be that belonging to Sydney Bigod. I can see him behind the trestle of a street stall, wearing just such a shirt as he shouts his wares. And in the pauses between was he, in the days just before the murder, asking himself in twisted anxiety whether the fact that he'd helped himself to large amounts of the Boy Preacher's funds was about to come to light? Unless the Boy was no longer there to denounce him.

But what about the collarless shirt in the bag here? Didn't collarless grandad shirts come back into fashion

69

recently? This'll be Barney Trapnell's, most likely, though possibly Harish Nair's. Either of them, thirty years ago, could have been wearing this sort of greyish shirt with the faint red stripes. But, no. No, look at that thick cotton one, with a collar. Only a man who was Indian would wear that design of little yellow daisies on a pale green background. And, damn it, I can't help thinking it indicates a nice happily smiling temperament. But, yes . . .

She shook the bag.

Yes, Harish Nair surrendered a tie, too. That horrible red one. Clashing appallingly with his charming shirt.

So what sort of temperament does Trapnell's grey-white collarless shirt indicate? A sort of dull response to life? A not caring one way or the other? Could be. And if anyone's as careless about their own life as that, would they also have been careless about others' lives? Would they be the sort of person who'd drown a kitten without a second thought?

So, this last bag must contain whatever outer garment Marcus Fairchild, somewhat mysterious journalist, was wearing at the time of the murder.

She peered through the thick transparent cover, dulled to a yellowish shade now after more than thirty years in storage. But whatever was inside was so wrapped up that it was unidentifiable. The mystery man keeping his secret still.

'Oh, and one thing more,' she said, as she passed the bag over. 'You might just check on a DS Shaddock, DCI Kenworthy's bagman. He was at the end of his service during the investigation, but I suppose it's just possible he's still alive. If so, it could be worth having a word with him.'

Pip left, staggering a little under his load.

Chapter Seven

Harriet sat staring at the door the nervy DC had closed behind him, a long oily black streak all down one edge, asking herself whether it had been wise to have entrusted him with his task. What if, making inquiries, he allowed his tongue suddenly to run away in the way it had when she had been sharp with him? Would he then, under some pressure or other, blurt out that the Boy Preacher's murder was being investigated again thirty years afterwards? The investigation Mr Newbroom wanted kept confidential until he could reap the full benefit of a successful outcome?

And, if he did, who would find coming down on to her the whole weight of a Chief Constable's displeasure? Detested Detective Superintendent Harriet Martens. That's who.

She sighed heavily.

And then what about that empty seventh clothing bag? What had Pip said was in it? Yes, a scallop-edged pink blouse. Fits in well enough with what I've learnt about Priscilla Knott, prim little primary school teacher. But did that blouse all those years ago have on it some traces of spittle, of no evidential value back then, but vital to my inquiry now? Was there a secret hidden in the heart beneath the pretty pink blouse? And there, in the realm of sexual fears and fantasies, had murder been inching its way forward?

Steady. Steady on. Meadowcraftian prose casting its lurid light.

No, enough speculation, though speculation had its place resolving crimes. No, nothing else for it now but to get on with acquiring every possible fact that may help, and hope that somehow, if DNA turns out not to be the great answer to everything, sheer hard graft will be. With, in the end, credit going to Detective Superintendent Martens rather than new broom Mr Newcomen.

Right, over to the offices of the *Birchester Chronicle* and let's see what its reporters had to say about the murder in 1969. They certainly ought to be a great deal more down-to-earth than the bejewelled pages of *Who Killed the Preacher?* And perhaps they'll prove to have indulged occasionally in some more imaginative, less evidence-bound writing than efficient but stodgy DCI Kenworthy.

At Newspaper House she found the *Chronicle* had an excellent printed index. Conscientiously she sat down with the volume for 1969 and checked every entry under *Boy Preacher, murder of,* from the staid *Suspicious Death at Imperial Hotel* onwards day by day, through *Preacher's Death, Police Statement* and *Senior Police Officer Given Charge of Imperial Murder* to, many weeks later, *Boy Preacher's Death Remains A Mystery.* Weary from going over to the ancient bound copies of the paper, hauling down the staggeringly heavy leather-bound volumes from the racks, and then tracing her way down column after column of thick black print, she had at last to confess to herself she had not really learnt anything new.

All right, for what it's worth I've got an even better idea of what went on thirty years ago in and around the Imperial Hotel – how magnetically the paper had swung back again and again to that then familiar proud Birchester building – but really I'm no wiser. The same events seen through different eyes, but nothing more revealed than I've already taken on board.

Except . . .

Her mind flicked back to one odd little index entry which she had decided, when she first saw it, was not worth bothering about. *The Trufflehound Looks at Birchester.* She had thought that whatever that odd headline referred to must have slipped in error into the *Boy Preacher, murder of* column. But the index's compiler hardly seemed to be someone who made errors. He, if he was a *he*, had scrupulously entered, after all, dozens of tiny items with just the slightest bearing on the murder. So why was this reference there?

Blinking-eyed with tiredness though she was – it was long past lunchtime – she decided to lift down this one last back-breaking monthly volume.

Okay, it's most likely nothing. And if it is, I can go off with a good conscience, find the nearest pub and give myself a decent drink. And, if it turns out to be more than some meaningless reference to the murder . . . Right, you never know.

When, flipping through the dried-out pages of the paper, she came across the item at last, she saw it was a short paragraph in *Birchester Day by Day* written by *Looker On*, whoever that had been. It turned out to be not quite one thing, not quite the other. In that curious prose style such columnists had used in those days, it read: *Birchester was honoured last week, I learn, by the attentions of that most ironic of observers, the man who writes under the sobriquet* – sobriquet, would anyone now dare to put such a Meadowcraftian word in the news columns? – *of the Trufflehound in that gossip and guesswork periodical which glories in the curious title* Time Will Tell. *We gather Trufflehound has been here to write about Birchester's much-hailed young preacher Krisha Kumara* – not the most accurate of journalists, Looker On – *and he is to write again in next week's issue of the magazine after he has attended the special meeting the Boy Preacher is to hold in the ballroom of the Imperial Hotel on Sunday to celebrate the hundredth time he has preached his message of peace and purity, sermons that have attracted such enormous audiences up and down the country.*

That and no more.

Harriet wondered whether she really need do anything about it. The whole paragraph could scarcely have been less informative. No doubt Looker On had not even troubled to get hold of the copy of *Time Will Tell* that someone must have mentioned to him. Or, if Looker On had managed that, Trufflehound's assessment of the Birchester where the Boy Preacher was soon to be murdered must have been so dull that it had yielded nothing to quote.

No, the item had plainly found its way into my section of the index only because it mentioned the Boy

Preacher's next meeting, even if, in the event, it got caught out by the change of the day. So, yes, the pub and—

But, no. Or, rather, yes, the pub and that drink, but, all the same, that paragraph may have some link to my inquiry. Isn't it possible – even very likely – that Marcus Fairchild, Michael Meadowcraft's mysterious intruder into the Boy's inner circle, was, not a feature writer from *The Times*, but that 'most ironic of observers', Trufflehound of *Time Will Tell*. He must have used the name of the august newspaper to gain his entry. And, if that's so, dead though he's been these thirty years, it might well be worth finding out more about him. After all, he certainly failed to tell DCI Kenworthy that he had, presumably, only pretended to be from *The Times*. And might there even be something in what he wrote here in Birchester about the Boy that could be worth learning? Surely he must in that promised second piece have said something, perhaps even a lot, about the dramatic event that had occurred in the Imperial's ballroom. I've an idea *Time Will Tell* may have ceased publication though.

Back in her Headquarters office – all the better for a glass of wine and a sandwich – Harriet found Pip had already got hold of the cupboard she had wanted. A narrow, green-painted steel affair it stood now in the corner nearest the door, with Pip standing beside it, a look of proud achievement on his white-bearded face.

'Good work,' she said. 'I thought it'd take at least a week to get anything.'

Pip produced a slow, even sly, smile.

'I sweet-talked the Stores people, ma'am,' he said. 'All those advertising techniques I learnt still pay off sometimes.'

'Right. I see you're going to be more use to me than Mr Newcomen perhaps thought.'

'I, I, I hope so, ma'am. And— And— Well, I have managed, actually, to track down all but one of the six remaining suspects. I haven't had any luck with that fellow Sydney Bigod. He left Birchester shortly after the murder, you know. Went back to Cromer, I gather. But, when I phoned Norfolk Police, they told me they'd lost all trace of him.'

'Right. Then we must just hope our DNA wizards down in Lincolnshire don't find he's the one with traces of saliva on that awful shirt he wore. Otherwise we'll have a lot of thankless work digging our Sydney out of wherever he eventually went to ground.'

'Yes, ma'am. Though I suppose . . .'

'Yes, what do you suppose?'

She could see Pip positively nerving himself up to give her a contradictory reply.

'Well . . . Well, I was thinking that really— Really with a name like Bigod he shouldn't be too difficult to trace. I mean— well, not really, should he, er, ma'am?'

'Unless he's changed that rather unlikely name, DC. Or, rather, unless he's changed back from the unlikely name, which, by the way, I think you don't actually pronounce as By God.'

'Oh. Oh, I'm sorry, ma'am.'

'What for, DC?' Harriet could no longer refrain from snapping out. 'For not realizing a name can be changed? Or for mispronouncing it? It's actually a Norfolk name, I happen to know. I spent a sightseeing weekend there once when my husband was in Norwich for his work. All the early Earls of Norfolk were Bigods, though in those days they seemed to spend most of their time rushing about fighting whoever it was the King wanted fought.'

By the end of her little history lesson, she noted with relief, Pip seemed to be beginning to regain his composure. But she thought it better to plough on a bit.

'Yes, I gather from Mr Kenworthy's notes,' she said, 'that, although he saw no reason to detain Bigod, he did put the fear of God into him over his borderline legal activities. So, no doubt, he was all too ready, when he was let off the hook, to skedaddle back to Norfolk and report to the police there.'

Now, she saw, Pip was on an even keel again, all twitching gone.

'Right,' she said, 'so let's have the list of people you did track down. Remarkably quickly, too, let me say. They all still alive?'

'Well, no. No, ma'am. I mean, not Harish Nair. Nair's dead.'

Harriet felt a jolt of dismay. Poor little Mr Nair, the man who had been, as DCI Kenworthy had noted, a Christian non-conformist lay preacher before he had generously given way to the much more charismatic talent of the young relative who had come to lodge with him. He was someone who, from all I've learnt about him, seems to have been as nice a man as you could hope to meet. All right, I've recognized that prejudice of mine, and pledged myself to discount it. But somehow, although I knew any one of those people in that ballroom foyer might well have died in the intervening years, I've thought all along of Harish Nair as being a person I was going to meet. I'd even looked forward to it.

But, now, dead.

Dead, and possibly having taken with him the secret of why he strangled his young cousin.

'And have any of the others gone from us?' she brought herself to ask.

'No, ma'am, no. All still alive, and actually all still living in Birchester. Except—'

Another of those awful disconcerting up-against-the-buffers pauses.

'Yes, DC. Except what?'

A little blush appeared on the knobby cheekbones above the pointed white beard.

'No, no, ma'am. It was just— Just that I meant Mr Lucas Calverte actually lives a little way out of Birchester. Near a village called Westholme.'

'Right, I know Westholme. What's the name of his house there?'

'It's called Travellers, ma'am. Travellers. I don't know why.'

'Never mind that. But, if I go to see any of these people before we get a report from the Forensic Science lab, I think someone like Undersheriff Lucas Calverte, a barrister—'

'Retired, retired,' Pip Steadman broke in unstoppably.

'All right, retired barrister. You do seem to have

turned up a lot of facts this morning. Nevertheless I think a former barrister is the one most likely to be able to tell me anything useful about that two-hour wait outside the Imperial's ballroom thirty-odd years ago.'

'Yes. Yes, ma'am, I'm sure—'

'Never mind that. You got all their addresses, you said. Are all of them actually still where they were living at the time of the murder? Except Bigod, of course.'

'Well, Bubsy Willson isn't at her former address, the one on the list you gave me. It turns out she's married now. But still called Bubsy, I understood from the witness I asked. She's Mrs Barbara, or Bubsy, Brownlow. But she's here in Birchester all right.'

'Good. And Priscilla Knott, of the hurriedly reclaimed pink, scalloped-neck blouse. Is she married? I doubt somehow if she is.'

Pip blushed again.

'But— But— I'm afraid you're wrong there, ma'am.'

'All right, all right. I'm not God Almighty, you know. I can make a guess that turns out to be incorrect. And I don't mind being told I've got it wrong, either.'

'Yes, ma'am. Or, no. Well, yes.'

'So Priscilla Knott did get married, you say. What's her name now, then?'

Yet another blush rising up on the knobby cheek bones.

'It— It's Knott, ma'am.'

'I'm not going to ask *Not what*, DC. But I'd like to hear why, though married, she's still Patricia Knott.'

'It— It's quite simple, ma'am. She did get married,

to a Mr Joseph Johnson, a fellow teacher. But they're divorced now, and she's reverted to her maiden name. She's a head teacher, actually, much respected. At St Peter's Primary in the Boreham area.'

'Now that doesn't surprise me. Mr Kenworthy's notes on his interview with her actually complained that the lady – in her early twenties then, remember – kept trying to tell him how he should be doing his job. So, yes, a head teacher, married but divorced. Then that just leaves the cripple, Barney Trapnell. Is he married?'

'No. No, ma'am. And he's actually living at the same address that he was thirty-odd years ago. It's a shop. Of sorts. Watch repairs. But he must be different from what he was at the time of the murder. He's very, very crippled now. I saw him at a distance. He— He— Well, poor devil, he goes about looking like— Like— Well, some sort of awful three-legged table, if you know what I mean.'

Harriet thought, lips pursed.

'Yes,' she said, after a little, 'I do think I know what you mean, DC. You draw a vivid picture.'

'Yes, well, yes, I sort of— Well, I sort of felt for him. I mean— I— Well, I hope those DNA tests don't prove he was the one.'

'Charitable, Pip. But not to be encouraged. You may yet have to question him, and a purely objective approach is the only possible one.'

'Yes. Yes, ma'am. Yes, you're quite right. It's a fault, I know that. I mean, that was why— Why I made that mistake before.'

Perhaps it's a good thing, though, Harriet said to

herself, that little Harish Nair is dead. If I'd had
to question him, would I have succeeded in being – a
wry smile – the Hard Detective I warned Pip here
never to call me?

Then, yes, she answered herself. Yes, I would have
been as objective with him as I would be with any
other suspect in front of me in an interview room. No
point in putting myself down. Yes, I'd have been hard
with little Harish Nair, whatever I felt about him.
There's some truth, after all, in that wretched tag the
media plastered on me. As a police officer I am hard.
I believe I ought to be, never mind what soft, senti-
mental thoughts I indulge in when off duty about
people who seem as nice – Yes, that's the soppy, sloppy
word, *nice* – as that little Indian tailor.

She sat up straight on her hard wooden chair.

Right then, I'm going to see barrister Lucas
Calverte.

Chapter Eight

Harriet found Lucas Calverte, grey-haired, scrawny of neck, dressed in baggy corduroy trousers and an open-collared check shirt at work this sunny May afternoon in the garden of Travellers, his large cottage a couple of miles outside the village of Westholme.

Lucky, she thought, to have caught my ex-Under-sheriff in an informal moment, and a good idea to keep things as casual as possible. That way it'll be easier to stick with Mr Newbroom's plan to keep the inquiry strictly hush-hush till his hour of glory arrives. If it does.

'I've risked finding you at home, sir,' she began after she had introduced herself, 'because we're looking at any unsolved crimes where the recent advances in the technique of DNA analysis might make it worth going into again.'

Abruptly Lucas Calverte straightened up, with a sharp little groan, from where he had momentarily stooped to tug out a stray clump of grass from the well-kept flower bed beside him.

'The Boy Preacher murder,' he said. 'That's it, isn't it?'

He looked at her with an expression she found hard

to analyse. Was it simply an outward reflection of what was obviously a decidedly acute mind? Or was there in it a touch of suspicion? Even the tiniest hint of fear?

'But,' he added quickly, 'it must be thirty years or more since that terrible day. Are you sure, Superintendent, there'll be anything more to learn now than the police at the time managed to find out?'

Harriet gave a casual shrug.

'It would be a long shot,' she said. 'But the case is one of the ones where the possibility of new evidence exists, though, as I say, we're doing no more at present than look into the prospects.'

'Well, Superintendent, I'll certainly tell you anything I can. But I doubt if I'll be able to help. I should have thought, you know, that the Greater Birchester Police would have had more urgent matters in front of them. The sights one sees in the streets, on the rare occasions I still visit the city in the evening, are, frankly, disgusting. One cannot go anywhere without seeing drunken youths rioting about, and girls, too, girls who ought to know better. Those appalling short skirts and naked midriffs. Can't you do anything to keep them under control?'

In his gnarled old man's hands the clump of long grass he had pulled from the bed was twisted and twisted.

Harriet thought for a quick, bitter moment of the efforts she had once made in her 'Stop the Rot' days to keep at least the worst of Birchester's streets *under control*. But evidently the former Undersheriff had taken no notice of the campaign, or had forgotten it. He must, after all, be well into his eighties, though

Michael Meadowcraft's pen pictures of his Seven Suspects had failed to give any details of his early life.

She gave a somewhat dramatic sigh in reply to the old boy.

'We do our best, sir,' she said. 'But the spirit of the times is against us. Life today, as you must know, is very different even from what it was at the time of the Boy Preacher's death.'

She had hoped, in this way, to steer things back to what she wanted to hear, whatever Lucas Calverte might have to say about that long-ago time. But again she was to be balked.

'Oh yes, yes, I know all about that. I dare say you saw my letter in the *Chronicle* a few months ago. I took advantage of it being the true start of the twenty-first century, not that Year 2000 nonsense, to make a number of observations about the decline in moral standards we're witnessing. And to make some suggestions about how to enforce better ones. In my young days you could be birched for the sort of behaviour you see everywhere now.'

Harriet snatched at all this huff-and-puff preaching to bring things back to where she wanted them.

'Yes, indeed, sir,' she said with deliberate ambiguity. 'How much better life would be if people heeded the message Krishna Kumaramangalam had for the country back in those days.'

And it worked.

'Indeed, indeed. You know, Kumaramangalam was a truly remarkable young man. I came across him first through the Birchester Immigrant Welfare Council, of which I was chairman at the time. I have always had

a particular interest in India. I was out there in the
Indian Army in my younger days. And so I went once
to hear the boy preach, frankly as a matter of duty.
But I was, well, absolutely bowled over. And, as you
perhaps know, I interested myself thereafter in the
administration of his affairs, which, I may say, were
being grossly neglected. Grossly. The people who had
insinuated themselves into his entourage were, to
speak plainly, a pretty wretched lot.'

The bundle of mangled grass was tossed aside into
the nearby hedge as if such a fate was the least the
people in the Boy's inner circle deserved.

So, Harriet thought, would a man who had been so
'absolutely bowled over' go on to kill the preacher he
had admired and supported? And, yes, she answered.
If Lucas Calverte was, in fact, the person who had
strangled to death the Boy Preacher, then he would,
thirty years on, still be portraying himself as someone
who could not in any circumstance be guilty of the
Boy's murder. And addressing me as if I were a public
meeting.

What was it Michael Meadowcraft had said when
writing about him? Yes. *Who can probe the depths of the
human heart?*

But the public meeting was still being addressed.

'No, Superintendent, a great deal of work had to be
done to see that Kumaramangalam's message reached
the very widest audience. His preaching would have
affected, I don't hesitate to say it, the well-being of
the whole country. A message of such simplicity and
purity. And, until I joined those people round him,
there was certainly a grave danger of that message

being lost for lack of a few elementary steps being taken. Yes, a feeble lot. The only one of them I gave tuppence for was Kumaramangalam's cousin. You know about him?'

'Yes. Yes, sir.'

Harriet wanted nothing to halt the flow of information, wrapped up in Mandarin-speak though it was. But, all the same, she waited with some apprehension to hear the Mandarin's verdict on her *nice* Harish Nair.

'Yes, nothing much wrong with him. A thoroughly good-hearted little man, with all the right ideas about life. Yes. But— But, you know, a certain lack of personality.'

Which, by implication, is not your failing, Undersheriff.

However, now's my chance to get a different view of that entourage of the Boy's.

'That's very interesting, sir. And I'd appreciate, actually, having your considered opinion of each of the other people who clustered, as I understand, round the Boy.'

The old man's lips puffed out in an expression of angry suspicion.

'I don't know ... I don't really know, Superintendent. It was— It was all a long time ago, you understand.'

'Yes indeed, sir. But, if we do find the case is suitable for DNA analysis, that is likely to be my difficulty, too. I shall need, if it comes to it at all, to make my assessments of each of those people who, it seems, were the only ones who could have entered the Imperial Hotel ballroom at the time the Boy was strangled. So any assistance I can get will be, if you look at it this way, a matter of public duty.'

The appeal to tell the public what it ought to be told proved as hard for Lucas Calverte to resist as she had intended it would.

'Very well. Whom do you want to hear about first?'

Harriet made a small daring leap.

'Shall we say the person you yourself think must have been that murderer?' she said.

The old man's tanned face seemed to grow a degree more sternly fixed.

'I, I, well, no, Superintendent, I do not think it would be right for me to make any sort of accusation. No, no. I might be opening myself to an action for slander. No, I don't think I could do that.'

All of which means, Harriet thought to herself, that there is a name you could produce. Unless it's your own that I shall eventually have to reveal. However, there's no chance I'll get a killer's name out of you now.

'Very well, sir,' she said. 'Let me list those people with access to the ballroom in, shall we say, alphabetical order?'

Lucas Calverte nodded stubbornly reluctant agreement.

'Right then, Bigod. Sydney Bigod.'

'Yes. Well, I dare say a man of that sort might well commit murder, though let me hasten to say I don't accuse him of this murder, any more than I accuse anyone else. I hope I have made that clear.'

Of course you have, you pompous old idiot. Or

gasbag. That's what we would have called someone like him when I was at school. A gasbag.

'Of course, sir,' she said. 'Quite clear.'

'Very well then. I had reason to believe the fellow might well have been making away with the funds that the Boy's mission had caused to accrue. Reason to believe, but, no, nothing that I could prove. And I understand that when the police looked into that aspect of the matter later, they too failed to uncover any provable defalcation.'

'Yes, sir, that's so. But have you any other comments you would like to make about Mr Bigod?'

'About a person of that sort, Superintendent? Well, no. Frankly, no, I paid him as little attention as I could.'

Harriet felt a strong wish to extend that answer into what the gasbag had seen of Sydney Bigod in the foyer of the Imperial's ballroom on the evening of the murder. Had he paid any attention to Bigod's activities as the seven of them prowled about waiting there? Would he remember now something he had not been able to bring to mind when DCI Kenworthy had interviewed him? But, no. Asking as precise a question as that would show only too plainly that a new investigation of the thirty-year-ago murder was actually under way. Out of Newbroom bounds.

'So, F for Fairchild,' she said hastily. 'Mr Marcus Fairchild of, as I understand, *The Times.*'

'Ah, yes. Yes, that not very prepossessing gentleman. An odour of alcohol permanently on the breath, you know, and indeed a glass of, I believe, Guinness very often in the hand. You know, I had my doubts about the fellow at the time. Not altogether what I should have expected of a representative of *The Times*. I had intended, if I remember right, to look into the gentleman's antecedents. Yes, indeed. But then— Then that terrible thing . . .'

Yes, I've acquired a little more knowledge than I'd gathered from Kenworthy's notes about Marcus Fairchild, whom I now believe also to be one Trufflehound, gossip-sheet writer. And a lot more than friend Meadowcraft told me, for all his attempts to blacken his mystery man in the days before that footnote in *Who Killed the Preacher?* recorded his death.

'But Mr Fairchild is not your choice as the Boy's murderer?'

'Choice, Superintendent? I don't think this is a matter for picking and choosing, as if—' He looked all round. 'As if I were looking at plants at the garden centre.'

Rebuked. From above. And justly, as a matter of fact.

'An unfortunate word, sir. But what would be your answer.'

'No, really, Superintendent, though I am willing to respond to your request for my assessment of those individuals, I cannot go further than I have. In any of their cases.'

'Very good, sir. So, alphabetically, we come next, I think, to Miss Patricia Knott.'

'Yes, Miss Knott. A perfectly worthy young woman, of course. Perfectly worthy. But young. Young and— And, if I may say so, rather too forward in giving her opinions on whatever was the subject under discussion, regardless of whether more informed views had been put. Yes, altogether too forward.'

'Thank you, sir.'

And, yes, confirmation of Kenworthy's opinion, though his was less pompously stated in his personal notes. *Pert little piece, tried to tell me what I should be doing.* It had been something like that.

'Harish Nair you've already spoken about, sir. So what were your feelings about Barney Trapnell?'

But again came a magisterial rebuke.

'Feelings? I trust that anything I tell you, Superintendent, is based on more than feelings. No, I had no particular feelings about that fellow Trapnell. He was, as far as I could see, good-hearted in his rough way. No, he was useful in that poor Kumaramangalam was afflicted with occasional weaknesses, the nature of which I never understood. But when that made him too feeble to get about easily, then young Trapnell had his uses. His arms were certainly strong enough, despite the calliper he had to wear on one of his legs. Yes, he had his uses.'

Dismissed.

'Then finally we come to Barbara Willson.'

'Yes. Well, I said Kumaramangalam's entourage were a pretty doubtful crew, and that young woman was more dubious than any of them. Frankly, I think she was a prostitute, Superintendent, or that she had been a prostitute. I suppose when she fell under the Boy's spell she must have reformed. But that type of gutter girl can never be relied upon to go straight, you know. Never, never.'

Not exactly the sort of view that's likely to help me

when, and if, I come to assessing each of the people who could have got into the Imperial's ballroom at the crucial time. Among whom I include, of course, Mr Lucas Calverte, former Undersheriff. But which of them one day will I have to interview hour on hour till I get a confession? Will it be Lucas Calverte himself? Or his 'good-hearted in his rough way' Barney Trapnell? Or that 'frankly I think she was a prostitute' Bubsy Willson? Or, the very opposite, 'perfectly worthy' Priscilla Knott? Or the man Lucas Calverte would certainly like to see found guilty of the murder, street trader Sydney Bigod? Or would it have been dead-and-gone Harish Nair?

Driving back into Birchester, sights set on home at the end of a not unproductive day, Harriet was disconcerted to hear the sharp burble of her mobile.

'Wrong number. Bound to be another bloody wrong number,' she said aloud.

But, senior police officer as she was, she felt obliged to pull over on to the verge before having a conversation, however brief and bad-tempered.

Bad-tempered she certainly felt when she answered. But brief the conversation was not going to be, she knew. It was the Chief Constable calling.

'Yes, sir. Is there anything new?'

For a moment a jab of exultation rose up in her, despite her reply having been designed to express her discreet fury at this prodding from on high. Could it actually be that Mr Newcomen had changed his mind? That the murder of the Boy Preacher was going to be left lying quietly in the files?

'New, Superintendent? No, there is nothing new. Not unless you have some progress to report. I should have thought that by now you would have had something to tell me.'

'Well, no, sir. The clothes taken from those people thirty years ago have, naturally, been despatched to the Forensic Science laboratory. But I don't think we can expect to hear anything for some time to come. The rule there, of course, is that current murders take priority.'

'Murder takes priority, Superintendent. I think you'll find that's simply the rule. And, may I remind you, this is a case of murder, a case of murder that has attracted considerable public interest. I want you to make that clear to those people down in— Where is it? In Lincolnshire. Get on to them first thing tomorrow.'

Harriet felt a wave of pure astonishment rise up in her.

Newbroom, new broom, how avid for publicity can you get?

'Yes, sir, understood,' she answered stolidly. 'I am fully aware of the importance of the case you've tasked me with.'

'I'm glad to hear it, Superintendent. And perhaps in future you'll keep me fully briefed. I don't want to learn at some later date that steps that ought to have been taken were neglected.'

'No, sir. I quite understand.'

She ended the call, too abruptly to show respect.

Yes, she thought, I do quite understand. You could

hardly have made it more plain. You're sitting there poised to swoop the moment you can find something to my discredit. God, what's got into the man? How has he possibly got it into his head that I am somehow a menace to his new-come authority?

Oh yes, my subconscious was all too right in sending me that blatantly obvious dream. The devil and the deep blue sea.

Right, the devil's just advanced one long step towards me, trident at the ready. So how am I going to push back the deep blue sea of a case thirty years old?

Chapter Nine

Harriet found next morning, lying in bed for a few extra minutes after John had quietly left to get an uninterrupted hour or so at the towering Majestic Insurance offices, that the rage she had felt as she was driving home the previous evening had by no means left her.

Christ, she thought, how can a man who's had a good career in the police, a very good career in fact, how can he, once he gets into a Chief's chair, run amok in this way? I can hardly believe it myself. I couldn't have convinced John last night, if I tried for half an hour, that he had said what he did on the phone.

It's incredible. But it happened. It really did. For whatever reason, the new Chief Constable of Greater Birchester Police has become paranoid.

And what am I, the poor bloody object of his paranoia, to do about it?

Mind blank.

Then – had she dozed off for a second or two? A momentary dream? – then she knew. The dream had told her.

Damn it, what I'm going to do today is to follow the most absurd lead I've got. I am not going to let myself be dragooned by that man into doing whatever he thinks I should. I'm going to do precisely the opposite. I am going to go down to London and at *Time Will Tell*, if it still exists, I'm going to investigate Marcus Fairchild, the least suspicious of Michael Meadowcraft's Seven Suspects, the man who allowed DCI Kenworthy to believe he was from *The Times* and just happened to be on the scene at the time.

Even, an hour later, in her cubbyhole office – Mr Newbroom's poisoned chalice – she did not for a moment waver in her decision. She took a few minutes to give Pip Steadman tasks to carry out in her absence. First, he was to find out whether dead Harish Nair's wife was still alive and, if so, where she could be found. Then he was to make inquiries about DCI Kenworthy's bagman, Detective Sergeant Shaddock.

'It's no use just assuming a man who was on the point of retirement thirty years ago must be dead by now,' she said. 'Never assume anything: it's the first rule. I dare say, if you do track him down, you'll find he's gaga and no use to us at all. But tracked down he must be. All those years ago he may have seen something or done something that didn't get into Mr Kenworthy's notes, and that something might be the one small thing that will lead us to answer the question the DCI couldn't!'

From Pip's pocket a battered pack of cigarettes, Royals not Marlboros, appeared. And was shoved hastily back.

'I'll do my best, ma'am.'

When Pip had departed, however, she took care at once to obey Newbroom's phoned instruction about getting in touch 'first thing' with the lab at Cherry Fettleham, fool though she knew she would feel passing on his message.

She was careful, in fact, when she got through to Dr Passmore, who had been given the six bags of clothing for analysis, to make it clear that it was a message from her Chief Constable she was giving him.

'Your Chief?' The tone of almost flabbergasted surprise came down the line as unmistakable as an amber traffic signal.

'Yes. Yes, he's most anxious for a quick result in the case.'

'Well, if he is, he is. But I'm afraid I've got material from a current murder inquiry in front of me, and, as you know—'

'It has total priority, of course. I absolutely understand that.'

Then she felt free to behave in an altogether responsible way about her irresponsible dream decision, if dream it had been. She telephoned *The Times* and made inquiries about the man who, thirty-plus years ago, had told everyone he was a feature writer for the paper.

Whoever it was she eventually got through to asked to be given time to find her an answer.

So she had waited patiently, going once more through DCI Kenworthy's files to see if there was anything about Marcus Fairchild amid the realms of paper that she had missed. There seemed to be nothing recorded other than that Fairchild was in Birchester for *The Times* and that he had no apparent reason for murdering the Boy Preacher.

So, the unmasking of the Trufflehound. Another small coup for the Lateral Detective?

Her phone rang. The young woman from *The Times*.

'Superintendent, I have gone through all the employee records for the period you asked about. Luckily they've been put on the computer. But it's quite certain that no Marcus Fairchild was a full-time member of staff. Of course, he may have been a contributor. We used to have some pretty odd pieces under the byline "by a correspondent". But I'm afraid it's unlikely we'd be able to trace any one particular writer of those – not all that way back.'

All that way, Harriet thought. It wasn't so far back into the mists of time when I was at school.

'No, I understand,' she said. 'You've been very kind, and I think what you've told me will be enough. I suppose I can always get back to you if the matter turns out to be absolutely relevant to my inquiries.'

'Oh, yes. Yes, of course,' the distant voice said, sounding as if she scarcely meant it.

Harriet picked up the phone again and rang Birchester Central station about trains to London. There was one she could just catch that would get her there by eleven o'clock.

Standing in a dingy street on the edge of the City, Harriet looked across at the tall narrow old building which had once sheltered the London office of *Time*

Will Tell, 'gossip and guesswork periodical' as the *Birchester Chronicle* had sniffily described it. She had hoped that there would be some remnant of its existence at least. But there was nothing, not even its name on the dusty plaques listing the various enterprises the grey, aged building now housed.

Jesus, she thought, have I been a total fool? Going off on something of a wild goose chase like this on the strength of a dream. A dream, damn it. To allow myself to be led away, with not much more than an hour's consideration, by something I just for a moment dreamt. But, of course, it wasn't really that. It was Newbroom. If I hadn't been in such a rage all evening, all night while I slept, all this morning, I would never have set off in that absurdly impulsive way.

So what now?

Only one thing for it, of course. Back to Birchester as quickly as possible, tail between my legs, and hope that Newbroom hasn't been on to me in the meantime.

She turned away in the direction of the Underground station she had just come from. And an odour of frying sausages swept into her nostrils.

Damn it, I'm hungry. It must be getting on for midday. At least I'll get a snack here. I deserve it, even if I did leave the house breakfastless so as to chase after my ridiculous hunch.

Me, a senior detective, with a bloody good record, following a hunch, a dream.

Blame Newbroom again.

In a moment she had tracked down the source of the delicious frying smell. It was a small, old-fashioned cafe. Very old-fashioned, to judge by the sign painted in curly letters above it, *Mack's Sausages Are the Best*. No early twenty-first-century clamour like *Great British Breakfast Served All Day* or *Super Traditional Fish and Chips*. This place must have been here, just as it is, back in the days when the Boy Preacher was drawing crowds up and down the country to listen to his simple message of peace and plain living.

She pushed open its door, hearing with pleasure the ding-dong of a real bell clanging out over her head.

There were a dozen tin-topped tables, a little the worse for wear if truth be told. Only one of them was occupied, by an elderly man with a drooping moustache, head down, chewing away at a plate of sausage and egg. A counter stretched across the far end of the long narrow room, and the ceiling, once white, had turned a yellowish brown from years of tobacco smoke.

And, for all the newish statutory notice on one wall saying *No Smoking*, that smell still lingered.

Harriet forgave every sniff of it, little though she usually liked having to eat in such an atmosphere. And into her mind once again there came the stale cigarette odour from the past that, as little Mr Popham had greeted her coming out of the Imperial's ballroom, had taken her suddenly back to the time of the Boy's murder and fired her with the determination to resolve it, however many years ago it had taken place.

'What can I do you for, love?' the man behind the counter boomed out.

He was all of a piece with his surroundings, and must indeed be Mack whose sausages were best. Robust, bald-headed, red-cheeked, a blue and white striped apron across his considerable tum.

'You can give me a plate of your delicious-smelling sausages, if you will.'

'Right here behind me, me dear. And a nice cuppa?'

Harriet, who in truth preferred coffee, and straight from the cafetière at that, decided on the spur of the moment that, yes, tea, good, strong tea, was what should accompany that plate of sausages.

She watched while Mack scooped them out of his wide frying pan.

'There's something else you could perhaps help me with,' she said on an impulse. 'I've been looking for the office, over the way, of a magazine called *Time Will Tell*.'

'That lot,' Mack roared out. 'All been gone this many a year. Rum, they were. A right rum lot. Communists and all sorts. All right, mind. All right when you got to know them. But it was the old duck as used to come to do their typing as I really liked. And she really liked my sausages, she did. Got it out of me one day where I get 'em from, and for years she'd come back every now and again and buy herself a half-pound from my butcher round the corner. Always came in here when she did, say good morning. But a half-pound only, mind you. Won't go having no good guzzle, old Ma Wetherleaf. Enough's enough, that's her motto. Enough's enough, and a bit too much. But I liked her. I liked her, for all her mousy ways. One of the old sort, that's what she is. One of the old sort.'

Harriet stopped him as he was opening the hatch in his counter to take her plate to one of the tables. A thought had occurred to her. A wisp of an idea.

'No, no, I'll carry them over,' she said, taking hold

of the plate and the mug of tan-brown tea. 'But, tell me, Miss Wetherleaf, was that her name? It's one I've never heard before.'

'Yeah. Yeah, that's it she is. Miss Wetherleaf. Funny old name. Known her for years.'

'And you say she used to be a typist at *Time Will Tell*?'

Mack smacked his forehead with a huge, meaty hand.

'No, no,' he boomed. 'I tell a lie. I tell a lie. Not a typist. No. Something else. Told me all about it once. Yes. Yes, that's it. Copy typist for those recording machines. No, she used to come up, once a week, twice, and collect the big reels their writers used to send 'em with their stories. All different now, of course. My little grandson got one of them mini things you can put a message on, and he sends me them sometimes. No bigger than a packet of fags. 'Course I can't hear them, haven't got the whatsit. But he likes to do it, he likes to do it, and I never lets on.'

Harriet set down the fragrant plate, which was beginning to burn her fingers, on the nearest table.

'Bread and butter, love?' Mack inquired. 'Comes with the order.'

'No. No, thank you. This will be more than enough. But, tell me, does Miss Wetherleaf still come up to buy her sausages? How often does she look in on you?'

'Oh, she don't come here no more. Journey too much for her, I expec'. She'll be getting on a bit. She weren't no chicken back in the old *Time Will Tell* days. No, it's been a year – two – since I seen her.'

'You wouldn't know where she lives, by any chance, would you?' she asked.

Standing by the table, she waited with more anxiety than she liked to show for the big cafe owner's answer.

'Gawd bless you, no,' Mack said cheerfully. 'Only known the old bat thirty or forty years, but we weren't never on what you call intimate terms. Oh, dear me, no.'

'No? Well, never mind.'

She sat down, feeling the suddenly aroused hope fizzle out of her as rapidly as air from a punctured tyre.

And found all her appetite had gone.

My wonderful piece of luck, she thought, when Mack turned out to know someone who had worked for *Time Will Tell*, has run out. The luck that, in an instant, justified my stupid dash down to London.

And with its disappearance, it seemed, her initiative had run out too.

But I can't not eat these, she said to herself, looking down at the three still sizzling sausages Mack had ladled out for her. He's so nice, so enthusiastic about everything, it'd be a miserable thing to do, to get up, pay, and leave the plate where it is.

She jabbed her fork, its tines a little splayed from long use, into the first of the sausages and cut off a piece.

But I was so near. So near. And surely old Miss Wetherleaf would have been able to tell me things I need to know. Am I right in my guess that the Truffle-hound was actually dead Marcus Fairchild? She could

103

confirm it in a moment. And, if I am right, I might learn that Meadowcraft's mysterious journalist had, somehow, a stronger motive for killing the Boy than any of the others. That was one of old Kenworthy's difficulties, after all – that none of them had any obvious motive. And I might have learnt from this former *Time Will Tell* copy typist that Fairchild had had some particular reason which took him to Birchester, and eventually into the ballroom foyer in the hours before the Boy was strangled. At the very least I might have learnt how many pieces he had written about Birchester for *Time Will Tell*, and then I could have got hold of copies – the British Library newspaper collection would do it – and perhaps hit on some fact about one of the other six which Kenworthy never knew.

But, no. No, Miss Wetherleaf is— Wait. No, no, no. *Wetherleaf.* That altogether unusual name. She could be traced, surely. Telephone directory, Register of Electors, something.

No, better than that.

She tugged her mobile from her bag and called her office back in Birchester. A roundabout way of finding out what she wanted to know, but probably quickest in the end. And she was fired again with hope.

Pip Steadman was there. She stopped him from reciting the success or otherwise of his morning's inquiries and got him to go as quickly as he could and find a computer terminal such as the one her office ought to have had, and to search on it in the London phone books for the name Wetherleaf.

'W-E-T-H-E-R-L-E-A-F. Probably spelt like that. But

try any alternatives. Anywhere in London. And call me back. Straight away.'

The sausages tasted even more delicious than they had smelt. The tan-brown tea was sharp on the tongue, sharp as it ought to be. She ordered another cup.

Chapter Ten

Good Lord, Harriet thought, I'd no idea a place like this existed. I thought in my Met days I knew central London, but I was absolutely unaware of this.

She looked round her once again.

The Peabody Trust Wild Street Estate. An enclave. An extensive courtyard surrounded by a dozen or more six-storey blocks, starkly flat-faced in yellowy London brick. Saying *Private* at every lace-curtained window. A village, inward-turned, self-sufficient, and respectable.

Into her mind came the forbidding notices she had seen on the estate's locked, black-painted outer doors as she had made her way towards the arched entrance, beyond which, Pip Steadman had told her, lived one Wetherleaf, Miss M. *DO NOT Dump Rubbish Here!!* and *Don't be LAZY!! Use the BINS PROVIDED!!* Real hellfire preaching. Cleanliness next to godliness.

And, she thought, standing there, the whole sturdy village-like community is settled here within a stone's throw of the West End's temple to pride and wealth, the tower-topped marbled bulk of Freemasons' Hall.

Right, now where's Block M?

Another sweep round and she had located it. Rapidly she walked across to where she had seen that incised letter above its stone doorway. There was a row of bellpushes at the entranceway. A steady pressure on the one marked simply *11*.

From the microphone grille above the buttons came a voice, prickling with suspicion.

'Who is it?'

Harriet gathered herself together.

'Detective Superintendent Martens, Greater Birchester Police. I am making inquiries in connection with a case some years ago, which we are currently investigating. And I have reason to believe, Miss Wetherleaf, you may have some information concerning the time you were employed by *Time Will Tell* magazine that might assist us. May I come and talk to you?'

A long pause.

But then at last the tetchy voice emerged again from the grille.

'Very well.'

The lock of the black-painted door in front of her clicked open. Cautiously she pushed the door wider. In front of her she saw right-angled flights of bare stone steps, a plain iron railing leading upwards beside them. She began to climb.

The door of Flat 11 was open when she reached it, and standing formidably upright within the frame was a lady of some eighty years of age, white hair drawn back ferociously from her head, face deep-cut with wrinkles, spectacles glinting in the dull light. She was wearing, despite the warmth of the day, a woollen dress in a shade of reddish purple. It came down almost to her ankles.

'What exactly is it you want?' she demanded of Harriet.

Harriet took a mental step backwards.

This was it. The moment she had with such difficulty reached, and on what had seemed the flimsiest, dream-directed grounds.

'I am anxious to learn as much as I can about a writer for *Time Will Tell*, a journalist, Marcus Fairchild, who was killed in a traffic accident some thirty years ago.'

'Mr Fairchild's death can be of no interest to the police in Birchester. He was killed here in London in perfectly ordinary, if disgraceful, circumstances. If you wander the streets in a drunken condition it is to be expected that you will meet with an accident.'

Harriet, with an inward sigh, persisted.

'We are not inquiring into the circumstances of the death. We understand, however, that shortly before he died he had an assignment in Birchester for *Time Will Tell*. I believe at that time you were engaged by the magazine as a copy typist?'

'I was.'

'Then could I perhaps come in and ask you if you knew anything about what he wrote during that assignment?'

She could easily refuse, Harriet thought to herself. A cantankerous old person of her sort could quite easily take it into her head to decline to say anything at all about someone who had been working for the gossip and scandal magazine. Very likely she is ashamed of her own connection with it, however marginal it was.

But, to her surprise, Miss Wetherleaf took a step back, turned and led her inside.

The room she stepped into was small but not oppressive. Its ceiling was high which, coupled with the light that came in through the two narrow but tall windows, was enough to give it a feeling of some spaciousness. But countering that, in the exact centre of the room, there stood on heavy carved legs a large table with, massively present on it, a big, sit-up-and-beg typewriter. This altogether dwarfed, just behind it, the room's one concession to the twenty-first century, a small TV perched on a wooden stool in the corner.

A black-and-white set, I'll bet, Harriet thought. We're far removed here from the computer era, further back even than the day before yesterday's little electronic typewriters.

Opposite the looming yesteryear typewriter there was a plain oatmeal-coloured place mat with a green embroidered border. Two knives, a fork and a spoon were meticulously laid for lunch, with a napkin, matching the mat, in a thin silver ring on the side plate and a plain tumbler for water at the top right-hand corner.

'Oh, dear,' Harriet said, 'I'm afraid you were just about to eat.'

Miss Wetherleaf looked across to the clock – it read ten to one – on the low cupboard under the room's two windows. To either side of it there were Staffordshire figures, a shepherd and a shepherdess. Beside the shepherd, a black telephone with a dial stood where it must have rested year upon year, its surface greyed with age. Beside the shepherdess, Harriet could not help noticing, with a momentary twinge of pity, there was a glass dish of prunes in their deep brown juice.

To be taken every day. Regularity of the bowels.

'No, no,' Miss Wetherleaf answered. 'I do not eat until half-past one. But I like to have things ready earlier. Please sit down, and I will endeavour to answer whatever questions you may have.'

On each side of the fireplace, which now housed the pipeclay white pillars of an ancient gas fire, there were well-worn upholstered chairs, one narrow and with arms, the other low and armless. Harriet made for that one.

But when Miss Wetherleaf had seated herself in what must be her own familiar chair, Harriet sat for a moment or two in silence. It might be better, she thought, not to fire out my questions about Marcus Fairchild, otherwise known as the Trufflehound. A roundabout approach may produce a more sympathetic atmosphere.

'This really is a remarkable place to find tucked away in the very centre of London,' she said at last.

A tiny flush of pleasure appeared on the deep-wrinkled face opposite her.

'Well, yes. Yes, it is. To tell you the truth, I am quite proud of living here. Of having lived here, indeed, for nearly fifty years. It is not, of course, the first of the dwellings that Mr George Peabody, that excellent American philanthropist, caused to be built. That was, I believe, in Spitalfields in 1864. However, this estate is one of the oldest, and, I think I may say, one of the most established. There have been children born in these flats who have then lived all their lives here and, indeed, died here.'

'Remarkable,' Harriet murmured.

'Of course, things have altered over the years,' Miss Wetherleaf went comfortably on. 'I dare say you saw all the motor cars there are in the courtyard now. They were none of them there thirty years ago. Then there were just swings and little roundabouts for the children to play on. But times change, times change. If not always for the better.'

Harriet saw this harking back to a different past, a past in fact of thirty years ago, as her opportunity to steer the conversation into the waters she wished it to swim in. It had arrived sooner than she had expected.

'Yes,' she said, 'I'm afraid the days I have come to talk to you about have gone, and they were, in many ways, pleasanter and, indeed, better than today.'

'You say *in many ways*, er, Superintendent. And you are right to do so. But I am well aware that life thirty years ago as well as its pleasures had its unpleasantnesses. And among those, I may say, was the publication my circumstances constrained me to be associated with. A deplorable periodical, I acknowledge that. However, I found after some consideration that working for it did not go altogether against my feeling for what is proper, provided I confined myself to visiting the office once a week and taking away recorded material to type.'

A sudden full blush on the withered cheeks.

'But I must confess there were times when the words I heard on the machine they lent to me were such that I was happy to think no one else was present to hear them.'

Harriet wondered for a moment just what terrible words Miss Wetherleaf had dutifully typed on the ponderous machine still on her table. But she had been given an unexpected way in to what she needed to know. And she took it.

'And, tell me, did you ever type out articles Marcus Fairchild had recorded?'

'The Trufflehound,' Miss Wetherleaf said with plain scorn.

'Yes, I believe that was the pseudonym he used. And you typed his work?'

'I did, almost all of it. I was contracted to do so. But, let me say, there were occasions, not a few occasions, when I realized all too clearly why he needed to record his work. There were the slurred sentences and the muddled repetitions. And interruptions. Interruptions I prefer not to enlarge upon.'

'Yes, yes. I understand. But can you remember anything about what he wrote during the visit he made to Birchester? I have learnt from the *Birchester Chronicle* of the time about one article he wrote, but was there a second one? You see, if you remember that there was, I could perhaps find it in the British Library newspapers collection at Colindale.'

'I can do better than that,' Miss Wetherleaf said, a touch of pride in her voice.

'Yes?'

Without another word she pushed herself up out of her chair and went over to the mantelpiece above the unlit gas fire. From a small yellow enamelled box she took a key. With it she went over to the low cupboard under the windows, stooped in a series of little jerky movements, inserted the key, turned it with difficulty – a harsh little squeak – and opened the cupboard doors wide.

Harriet, with a feeling of incredulity, saw inside row upon row of big reels of recording tape, such as she had not encountered since they used to be inserted in the state-of-the-art machines of her schooldays.

'Are— Are those,' she said in wonder, 'really the reels *Time Will Tell* supplied you with? Are they all there? Really?'

'Every one.'

Miss Wetherleaf stood upright again, with the same series of painful jerks.

'I think, however,' she added, 'that I will ask you to look for the ones you may want to hear. I labelled each one as I received it. The people at *Time Will Tell* were appallingly careless. But I find bending down that far rather awkward nowadays.'

'Of course, of course,' Harriet hastened to say. 'Even at my age I sometimes find stooping unpleasant.'

'And you will have to take out the recording machine,' Miss Wetherfield said. 'I'm afraid it's altogether too heavy for me. Dear me, it must have been in the cupboard there for more than twenty years. Ever since *Time Will Tell* suddenly ceased publication. I waited then for someone to come and collect the machine as well as the reels for it, which I had, after all, only on loan. But no one came, and in the end I thought I had better put them all away.'

'You must have had some difficulty finding room

for them,' Harriet said, seizing her chance to demonstrate some sympathy. 'Did you have other things in this cupboard?'

'I did. I used to keep my bedlinen there.'

A note of censoriousness. Directed, Harriet hoped, at *Time Will Tell* rather than her intrusive self.

'And did you find somewhere else for that?' she asked.

'They are in a large suitcase, under my bed.'

A fact about her personal life, Harriet guessed, that would not have been told to a male detective.

She saw the machine now. It was stowed in the furthest corner of the cupboard's lower shelf. And she recognized it. In the music room at school there had been its counterpart, the latest thing on the market. Kneeling down, she managed to tug it out, not without grazing two knuckles.

'Thank you,' Miss Wetherleaf said. 'Perhaps now you could put it on the table. Just next to the typewriter. The wire on its plug will reach the electric socket if it's put right at the edge.'

So, Harriet, still kneeling by the cupboard, said to herself, am I really going to hear coming out of this relic of the past the very words dead Marcus Fairchild uttered, all that time ago, about Birchester? And possibly too, just possibly, what he had to say straight after the night of the murder?

'*Like any other reasonable person . . .*' To Harriet's astonishment words were emerging from the long outdated machine, miserably hard though they were to make out under the spittings and crackles on the ancient tape. *'I have always distrusted, and indeed disliked, the people who take it on themselves to preach to their fellow men, whether from the pulpits of long-established churches or from the hustings seized upon by the itinerant hot gospellers who from time to time undertake to crusade among us, many of them from that land of we-know-best America.'*

Here's something about Marcus Fairchild I hadn't realized, she thought. Something, too, that I suspect DCI Kenworthy hadn't taken in. Fairchild is plainly a man who can hate. There's a vindictive side to him. *A vindictive side?* Purple-prosed Michael Meadowcraft's sweeping conclusion about the Boy's killer came back into her mind. *There can be no possible doubt that sheer vindictiveness lies at the heart of this atrocious crime.* Something like that.

Don't tell me that awful man got it right. Marcus Fairchild with some injury done to him that so hurt him he had felt compelled to kill the Boy Preacher? No, it just isn't on. It isn't. But then, it's obvious even from these first words that he was capable of a good deal of viciousness, at least with a pen, or a symbolic pen.

But listen to this stuff. Listen. Damn it, the machine may cease to work if we run the tape again.

' . . . went to Craven Cottage football stadium to hear the latest recruit smother us in pious flannel, one Krishna Kumaramangalam, a young, an exceedingly young, preacher of, as I had gathered, a brand of mystical flim-flam even more excruciatingly banal than the wild war-blings of the flatulent gurus India has long delighted in

exporting to bloat the ever open ears of the credulous westerner.'

Right, he lets his readers have it, no holds barred. But . . . But do I detect, coming up, a *however*?

Ah, yes.

'*However, imagine my feelings, as amid a crowd of several thousand I lent half an ear to those warblings, when something about the Boy Preacher struck me. It was hard at first to analyse just what it was. Was there something in the total stillness he had achieved as he had waited to speak and as he spoke? Or was it the tone of voice he used, or rather the voice that issued from him? Certainly, it was hardly the content of his message, which in truth was little less banal than the ferociously earnest mouthings of his American predecessors on the credulity circuit. But, as I paid him more attention, I realized that, simple as his exhortations were, they had in them a core of plain truth. "Do not be one friend to Mammons." Quaint enough words. Yet it's true after all that many of the ills of this nation today can be squarely put down to being "friends to Mammons".*

'*And hearing those words delivered in that pure fluting voice, which yet seemed to be the only way they could be delivered, with the impetus of Truth, no less, behind them, I found myself, professional cynic that perhaps I am, saying Yes. It was one of those sickening moments, no, more than sickening, mind-shattering, when the beliefs of a lifetime are all in a single moment turned topsy-turvy. Yes, I said to myself jammed tight in that mass of sweaty, unthinking humanity waiting to be offered the pleasure of wailing and gnashing their teeth, yes, there are men and*

*women occasionally making their appearance upon earth
who stand out from all this.*

'*I thought of the prophet Mohammed, of Mahatma
Gandhi, of Winston Churchill, of, in quite another way,
that extraordinary person, the cellist Jacqueline du Pré.
Only for the last of these have I any personal liking. But
I recognize in the others the presence in our world of
human beings of super-human status. And so yesterday I
came to Birchester where the young preacher is to hold
what, I gather, is the hundredth meeting he has conducted.*'

So, Harriet realized, all this must have been
written, or rather spoken into the microphone of his
own recording machine – with, yes, at least one unmiss-
able belch breaking in – in the piece about Birchester
published in *Time Will Tell* before the postponed
meeting when someone – which of them? Which? –
put their urgent hands round the meditating boy's
throat and choked the life out of him.

And, yes, now he's moved on to his reflections
about the city in general. Interesting enough, but not
what I want to hear. No, what I must hear now is the
reel – it's here on the table – that Miss Wetherleaf
conscientiously labelled all those years ago *M. Fairchild
– 24 May, 1969*.

Chapter Eleven

'No,' Miss Wetherleaf had said. 'No, Superintendent, I am sorry but, as I told you earlier, I eat my lunch at half-past one. There is no time now to listen to this next reel.'

Harriet had felt a plunge of disappointment.

'Yes, I understand,' she had replied, fighting to make herself sound truthful. 'After all, you have your life to live, and you must find at your— And, when one is getting on, it's important, I know, to have as regular a life as possible. So I'll leave you. I'll leave you now, but may I come back this afternoon?'

'Yes, of course. If you want luncheon yourself, you will find there is an Indian restaurant just across into Great Queen Street at the top of Wild Street. I do not care for that sort of cooking myself, but I know many people these days seem to enjoy it. Perhaps you would care to return in about an hour?'

Harriet, relieved and still comfortably full of her late breakfast sausages, hardly wanted another meal, Indian or not. But she found somewhere to have a cup of coffee, and at two-thirty precisely she was ringing Miss Wetherleaf's bell once more, possessed of an entirely irrational feeling that something would have happened to prevent her hearing Marcus Fairchild's second tape. Altogether irrational it proved when, entering Miss Wetherleaf's sitting room again, she saw at once that the new reel from thirty-years-ago Birchester was already loaded into the creaky old recording machine. She saw, too – she could not help it – that the level of dark-brown liquid in the bowl of prunes had been reduced by a good half-inch. All well within, then.

'I have just witnessed a murder. The Trufflehound, though in his time he has scented out more than a few crimes, even if the powers-that-be have almost invariably looked the other way, has never yet been faced with a brutally inflicted death. But last night I was. And it was a death we all could well have been spared. The death of young Krishna Kumaramangalam, otherwise known as the Boy Preacher.'

Witnessed? Witnessed the murder? For a moment Harriet felt the blood racing through her.

Did Marcus Fairchild, almost prototypical journalist, deliberately keep his 'story of a lifetime' from DCI Kenworthy's ears? His scoop? Am I going to hear now who it was he saw strangling the Boy? But, no. No, of course not. If Fairchild's a typical journalist it's only in the way he puffs up whatever it is he writes.

So, no, all I'm hearing at this moment is his account of his own feelings there on that evening thirty years ago.

' . . . of last Monday's events will be known to almost all my readers before this appears. But I cannot refrain

from telling you of my reactions to what was, as it happens, my first encounter with a murdered body. I had been waiting in the foyer of the ballroom at Birchester's Imperial Hotel for almost two hours while the Boy, as I learnt was his custom, stayed inside preparing himself by meditation. I was among a motley, even dubious, crew who had collected round the Boy during the time of his crusade, if that pretentious word fits those preaching tours of his, always modest despite the vast crowds who attended.

'Just as some hotel staff were about to pass through the closed barrier into the foyer to make the final preparations for the meeting, which had been postponed because the Boy had had some minor illness, one of the sets of doors leading into the ballroom was violently thrust open. I turned at the loud screeching sound it made, and on the far side of a hideous clump of pampas grass planted in a huge pot I heard one of the women in the entourage – I could not see which exactly – shouting at the top of her voice some totally incoherent words. It was not long, however, before I gathered their purport. Krishna Kumaramangalam was dead. Killed, it soon emerged as questions were shouted to and fro, by strangulation.'

So, far from being a witness, Harriet thought, Marcus Fairfield didn't even see who had come out of the ballroom shouting. He implies it was one of the two women present in the foyer. But it could have been any one of the others who had thrust open that noisy door, that still made its screeching sound when I opened it on Saturday. The woman he heard yelling out might simply have heard someone – But who? Who? – say in a quiet voice that the Boy had been strangled. No wonder poor old Kenworthy had to admit defeat at last.

But listen to the tape. If I have to run it back, I'll be lucky, ancient as it is, if it doesn't snap.

' . . . *my way into the ballroom, ran down the aisle between the ranks of red plush chairs up to the dais. And there I saw that small body, already seemingly shrivelled yet smaller, the deep red marks of the throttling fingers that had killed him all too plain to see on his neck. I am not ashamed to say I turned and ran back into the foyer where in the lavatory I was comprehensively sick.'*

Yes, I suppose DCI Kenworthy, or one of his detectives, will have obtained proof of that vomit having been there. But was it proof that Fairchild did no more than go into the ballroom, look, turn away and, sick at the sight he had seen, run for the door, the door I saw myself on Saturday, the one labelled *Gents*. Or had he vomited only after he himself had come racing out of the ballroom where it had been his hands that had been round the Boy's throat? And was all that talk about hearing someone come out and announce that the Boy was dead no more than an alibi for himself, made with all the pseudo-authority of print?

But listen. Listen. There may be more.

'But before I go on to describe my somewhat pusillanimous reactions, I must offer one exception to that description "dubious" with which I have labelled all the Boy's inner circle. It fits all but one of them well enough, but the Boy's much older cousin, Harish Nair, I found as I got to know him, is, despite having once stood Sunday after Sunday in a pulpit, by no means tarred with the particularly odious preacherly brush. No, if the word "decent" has any meaning in these indecent times, then it altogether suits the little Indian tailor. He may be no great intellect.

He may have little head for figures. But I am as certain as I can be that he is an honest man and a man filled with simple goodwill.'

Hooray, I'm right. Harish Nair, now dead these many years, was, as I thought, a decent fellow. But . . . But, what if, when I see the report from Cherry Fettleham, it states with full scientific authority that the shirt of his which I had Pip Steadman send down there yesterday is impregnated with the spittle that sprayed from the Boy's mouth as he died?

'Filled with goodwill is not something I can say, however, about any of the others in the Boy's entourage, and if my words bring this journal yet another action for libel, so be it. The Trufflehound is there to nose out the truth.'

Oh, excellent, at least I'm going to hear now a different assessment of the five suspects who are, as it happens, still alive. Even if it's through Trufflehound's cynical eyes. They'll certainly be better than Meadowcraft's gooey ones. Better, too, perhaps than DCI Kenworthy's police-blinkered ones. And even better, again, than my own imaginative ones on Sunday morning as I lazed and pondered out in the garden. Perhaps now I'll get some idea of what motive one of the Clique, as Meadowcraft delighted to call them, could have had to kill that simple young man. Because, unless I have that, I'll have more than a little difficulty getting together a watertight case for Birchester assizes. DNA evidence alone, however convincing it is to Mr Newcomen – and to myself, to be fair – is hardly going to be certain to convince a jury. Not after a good defence team has done its worst.

'So, who to snuffle into first? Let's take some prime hypocrisy material. The Undersheriff for the county of Birrshire, Mr Lucas Calverte. Let me tell you straight away that there is something to be dug out about that gentleman. What it is I have not yet had time to discover. It may be something perfectly innocent. But I have seen in my time too many people high up in the world who have a secret in their past not to know the signs. And on the face of Lucas Calverte, of the distinguished title and the distinguished name, the signs are there.

'But at the other end of the scale – I almost said down at the other end of the scale, but where's up and where's down? – there is one Sydney Bigod. Odd how the two ends of the social scale often prove very much alike under the skin. Sydney Bigod is another man who, I'm willing to bet, has a shady past, as well as a shady present and, no doubt, a shady future. I am willing to bet, too, that he has not always gone by the name of Bigod.'

Yes, I won't offer you odds on that, Trufflehound. I said as much yesterday to little Pip.

'But Bigod, or Bydevil, here's a fine specimen of what you might call the honest cheat. I have also watched him at the street stall he stands behind. I noted there the quickly moving eyes in his head. And I know that whatever he was selling was not what he claimed it was. However cheekily honest-sounding his claims may be, "Straight off the back of a lorry, ladies and gents", they are designed to conceal a sharper dishonesty. Those goods, as likely as not, were the whole of the lorryload. I would not be at all surprised to learn that, within two or three days from now, Sydney Bigod will no longer be seen in the markets of Birchester, and a Sydney Whoever, a good deal richer *than he ought to be, will be shouting his wares somewhere else.'*

Yes, but did you have proof of that, Trufflehound? Mr Kenworthy thought he could safely let Sydney Bigod go back to his native Norfolk, and he would hardly have done that, old-style detective that he was, if he had had any hard proof that Bigod was milking the Boy Preacher's funds.

Miss Wetherleaf, Harriet noted, had now gone over to the nearer of her two windows and was looking out at the block opposite as intently as if she had spotted a cat burglar making his way up its blank face. None so deaf.

'Or take the entourage's representative of the moral incompetents who surrounded me as I first listened to the Boy preaching. "Do not be drinking any wines," that limpid voice had exhorted me. Well, I still am, if Mr Guinness's brew can be called "wine". But, believe me, if I had heard the Boy preach once more I'd have abandoned the habit of years, knowing full well that I'd be all the better for it. So what is it, I ask, that Barney Trapnell has abandoned at the Boy's behest? And for how long will he stay away from whatever vice, whether genuinely wicked or merely deplorable, that he formerly clung to?'

All right, before long I'll see, thirty years later, how well Trapnell did manage. And I wonder what that vice was. Could it have led him, for some reason, to throttle the voice that had preached at him to give it up?

'The Trufflehound has had no opportunity to nose away at that little secret, and, to tell the truth, not much inclination. Not even now when, I suppose, it may lead to a discovery of which of the seven of us prowling up and down that wretched foyer, grimly decorated in the worst

of taste, was the one who succeeded – it would not have been difficult – in slipping into the ballroom and strangling the Boy Preacher. I'm happy to leave that sort of fact-finding to the police, who are good at it, if not so good at many other things.'

A thunderous belch out of the machine. At the window Miss Wetherleaf's bony shoulders rose and fell.

'But here is one fact I have unearthed about another of the seven of us, though it did not require a very long nose to get at it. Miss Barbara Willson, Bubsy to all her friends (of which she has many in the lower reaches of the Birchester proletariat), is not a prostitute. You might well have thought that she was had you been there in the ballroom foyer during those two weary hours, watching her in that appallingly blatant multicoloured nylon blouse she was wearing, open far enough down to put before the world the better part of her breasts, sweat-glistening and powder-caked, that she made a living working the streets of Birchester. But that notion could only have occurred to you if you had contrived to avoid looking at her face because, alas, that face is as ugly a mug as it has ever been my pleasure to see, and if you were also prepared to ignore the stains and splashes decorating that fearful blouse. Even while we were all pacing up and down out there she had succeeded in spilling most of the cup of tea from the urn we had been provided with all down her front. Nevertheless many kind voices around the Boy were quick to confide in me that prostitution was her profession. But I think not. No, Bubsy Willson may be a dubious member of the dubious circle round the Boy, but a working prostitute she is not. She is, to put it frankly, too unsavoury even for the lower depths of that profession.'

A little too ready, Trufflehound, to believe in his own judgments, if you ask me, though he may be right about Bubsy. A man, after all, would be a better judge of sexual attractiveness. And how many of his comments on Bubsy, and on the others, eventually survived the blue pencil at *Time Will Tell*? Perhaps listening to these clicks and crackles will have given me, after all, an advantage.

And Miss Wetherleaf there, I do believe she's blushing now. Yes, she really is, and after she has actually typed all this out word for word, though it was so long ago. And, also, after what she can hardly help knowing, with that TV set there in the corner if nothing else, about the willingness of young women today to put themselves about.

'And so to the last, the seventh wanderer to and fro in that dreary foyer, one you would think was as far from being dubious as could be. She is a primary school teacher, Miss Priscilla Knott, a young woman who radiates, at first glance, purity and light. But glance again. She radiates those two virtues but she directs them, two piercing rays, into anybody and everybody she meets. Be pure, she instructs us. Do as I say. Follow the light when I tell you what the light is. Oh, yes, if the Boy is a preacher, Priscilla Knott is ten times, a hundred times, more of a preacher. What she thinks you ought to do, she tells you that you must, and she needs no pulpit to do it. The world would be much, much better off without persons of that sort. But the preachers we have always—'

With a sudden loud click the tape did now break.

*

Miss Wetherleaf, touchingly eager to help the police, had fretted away wondering how the two ends of the tape could be joined together. She had suggested Gripfix – 'But you can't get that nowadays' – and going round to one of her neighbours 'who is very good about repairs'. But Harriet had firmly stated that what she had already heard had been enough.

Marcus Fairchild, plainly, had not seen which of his six fellow members of the Boy's entourage had succeeded in getting into the ballroom without calling attention to themselves. The faint hope she had possessed had been extinguished with the snap of the breaking tape. And, she thought, each one of the six who were with him in the foyer of the Imperial Hotel ballroom had been put through the harsh mill of his judgements. What he had said about one of them might, one day, prove useful in getting together subsidiary evidence for the court. But there could hardly be anything more on those lines that would be worth hearing. So, with effusive thanks to still twittering Miss Wetherleaf, she had left.

'Are you quite, quite sure, Superintendent?'

'Yes, quite sure.'

No, little to do now but wait for the Forensic Science lab report. To go back to Birchester and talk to the still-living suspects would risk giving warning to whichever of them the results from Cherry Fettleham were going to point to. Then, when it came to the interview room, there could well be, by their side, a solicitor skilled in prompting them to profusely repeat *No Comment*. Or even, as with someone like Sydney

Bigod, otherwise Fairchild's Sydney Bydevil, there could be no suspect to be found.

One piece of better news Harriet did find when she got back to her poky, ill-equipped office. Pip Steadman, unable to refrain from stroking his neat white beard in glee as he spoke, told her that he had located Harish Nair's widow.

'She's in an old folks' home, ma'am. It's called Restholme. It's out in Boreham, a nice-looking place. I've asked and you can see her there whenever you want.'

'Good work,' Harriet said.

But she had some difficulty in sounding as enthusiastic as she should. She had seized on Fairchild's summing-up of little Harish Nair as 'decent' and 'honest' to cross him mentally off her list. But, since that moment of elation listening to the crackly tape, other thoughts had moved in on her. All right, Harish Nair had seemed to Fairchild, who must have talked with him at some length, not to be a man who could have murdered the Boy, and she had been quick in her mind to echo that. But how many times in her life had she repeated to herself the always-to-be-remembered detective's adage *assume nothing*?

So should I, she thought, just sit and wait? Possess myself in patience. Wait for that report, and hope that the message from Mr Newbroom which I relayed as tactfully as I could has not put someone's back up over in Cherry Fettleham? Or should I go to see Mrs Nair in her old folks' home and, perhaps, find some evidence that supports my feeling about her long-dead husband? Or will I find the opposite?

Chapter Twelve

When Harriet saw next morning that there was no bulky report from Cherry Fettleham waiting on her desk, she wondered for a moment what to do next. But at once she found her mind had been made up for her. She would go and see old Mrs Nair. One way or another she was going to settle the question of Harish Nair's likely responsibility for the death of Krishna Kumaramangalam.

'All right,' she said to Pip Steadman, as he stood there quivering with puppy-dog eagerness, 'I may not be able to get anything at all out of Mrs Nair. She may, heaven knows, be totally gaga, but—'

'No, no, ma'am. They told me at the home. No. No, she's perfectly *compos mentis*, very good for— She's very— Very alert for her age. No, if we go to see her—'

'Not *we*, DC. This isn't going to be any sort of formal interview. I shall just be trying to see how the land lies. The last thing I want is—'

And then she noticed the utterly crestfallen look on Pip Steadman's face.

Damn it, I've knocked him off his perch. There he was, all agog to go crusading away to find the truth and rescue poor dead Harish Nair from the evil thoughts people will have about him when news of the inquiry breaks, and what have I done? I have stamped right down on all his delicate idealism.

But bugger that. This investigation is about finding who killed the Boy Preacher thirty-odd years ago, and I'm not going to let even the frailest line of inquiry be compromised by soft feelings for a half-recovered subordinate.

'No, I'm sorry, Pip, but I don't want the old lady to feel in any way pressured. So it's a solo operation, absolutely.'

'Very good, ma'am.'

But the crestfallen look had hardly disappeared.

'No, when I come back, nothing will have pleased me more than to be able to put Harish Nair's name on my list of dead ends in the inquiry, alongside Marcus Fairchild's. Because, after what I learnt in London yesterday about why he was actually at the Imperial on the evening of the murder, I can't see that he can have had any reason to strangle that poor boy.'

'You're sure, ma'am?'

Plainly Pip was not going to crusade to rescue the reputation of a dead journalist, however much he wanted to save that of a decent little Indian.

'Oh, yes, you have to recognize in an investigation of this sort, of any sort, that there will be lines of inquiry that end up nowhere, and the Fairchild one falls into that category. But the Harish Nair line hasn't reached that point yet. Assume nothing, Pip. It's a rule always worth having in one's mind. So, make me an appointment, please. For as soon as possible.'

Restholme was, as Pip Steadman had said, a nice-looking place. Harriet, going up the path to its front door, suppressed a tendency to shudder.

God, imagine if one day, well into the future I hope, I end up somewhere like this. Everything as it should be. Neat flower beds to either side of the path, all the external woodwork crisply painted, brass knocker on the door glinting with polish in the sunlight. And, no doubt, as well organized and sanitary inside. Including the people who have ended up here. Ruled and regulated, told what to do and what not to do at every hour of their lives.

What was it John was saying the other night? How the one thing we all really want is to be in control. And how, on the other side of the coin, what a good many people also want is to be in control of the lives all around them. That's what preaching's about, he said. Making other people do what you want them to do, behave in the way you think they ought to. And I dare say he's right. Even if he was exaggerating a little, as he usually does. Poor John. Dear John.

She rang the well-polished bell beside the door.

And, the moment it was opened, by a girl neatly wrapped in a standard light-blue polyester overall, a waft assailed her of pine disinfectant mingled with floor-polish.

But, yes, she was told. Mrs Nair is expecting you. She's in her room.

A brisk walk then behind the girl's clicking heels, with just one glimpse through a wide-open door of the row of chairs facing the television – already, at this hour of the morning – sunken-cheeked faces goggling and open-mouthed.

Me one day? It could happen. A long-retired police officer, widowed, the Hard Detective gone irretrievably soft.

Up the stairs, pine floor-polish smell and pine disinfectant ever present. And then a brisk knock, and the door of Mrs Nair's room thrust open.

'Your visitor, dear.'

Mrs Nair was every bit as old as her fellow residents mesmerized by the TV down below. A little hunched-up Indian woman who could be any age from eighty to a hundred. But surviving. Something in the shining brown eyes set in the brown-skinned face, withered almost to nothing, told Harriet that much. Tenacious of life, and preserving, despite all the ravages of time, an outward-going intelligence.

'Mrs Nair, I'm Detective Superintendent Martens, Greater Birchester Police, and I have asked to see you because we are looking into the possibility, thanks to recent scientific advances, of re-opening the case of the death of your cousin, or cousin by marriage.'

'It wasn't my Harish.'

The words came almost spitting out of the toothless, shrunken lips.

Harriet wished she could echo them whole-heartedly. But *assume nothing*.

'I am glad to find you know so quickly what I am talking about,' she said.

'Of course I do. What do you think is in my mind, day in, day out in this place?'

'But it seems quite a pleasant place to me,' Harriet

said, not quite ready to cope with such an unexpectedly strong view.

'Oh yes. Very nice, very nice. I'm lucky to be ending up my days here. It's thanks to one of the people there outside that ballroom with my Harish, you know.'

Now, is she wandering? Or what?

'I'm afraid I don't quite understand.'

A look of contempt in the shining brown eyes? Yes, it was. Plain contempt.

'Mr Lucas Calverte. When I was so ill after Harish was dying he was still the big man there, and he arranged for some funds to pay for me at this place. You don't think we live here for nothing, do you?'

'No. No, I suppose not. To tell the truth, I hadn't thought how it was that you came to be here. Your husband was not a particularly well-off man, I believe.'

A spark of resistance.

'Harish did very well. You know, when we came to Birchester not many people wanted an Indian to be mending their clothes. We had very much of hard times. But in the end business was doing well. No, my Harish left me with a good sum in the bank. Yes.'

'But not quite enough to let you live here?'

'Yes, not quite enough. So Immigrant Welfare Council was making up the amount.' An abrupt cackle of a laugh. 'And they have had to do it much, much longer than they were thinking.'

Harriet smiled broadly. She could hardly help it.

'And you have kept the memory of your husband alive all this time?'

'I must. I have to. If I am not doing it, there will

be people even now who will be saying Harish, my poor Harish, was strangling Krishna in that place. You know they are knocking it altogether down? I was reading that in the paper. Specs I need to do it, but I can still read. If the print is proper.'

'That's very good. Very good. But are you really sure people, after thirty years, would say that about your husband?'

'They do. Go downstairs and ask. If they will stop watching those silly programmes. For children, you know. For children, and they watch them. But they are not so much of child as all that. They can be wicked, very, very wicked, in talking about my Harish.'

'But what is it they say? Is it any more than just making out your husband must be the one who— Who killed your young cousin?'

'Oh, no. There is not any more to what they say than that. It is just only malice. It is that. Malice. Because I am an Indian, because Harish was Indian, because poor, good Krishna was Indian.'

'Yes, I suppose so. Things are meant to be better these days, but with the very old prejudices die hard.'

Mrs Nair gave her a quick, shrewd look.

'And what about you also? Are you believing, Miss Police Officer, that Harish did that murder?'

What to answer? Easy enough to deny it. Easy enough to let my feelings about nice, decent Harish Nair come pouring out. But it is possible, possible in strict logic, that he did kill his cousin. He could have had some reason, deep-buried even from his wife, for needing to bring the Boy's life to an end. So how do I answer?

Answer. I answer with a question. The old technique when interrogating any hostile, challenging suspect.

'Mrs Nair, how much do you remember about that day Krishna Kumaramangalam was killed?'

'How much am I remembering? All. Everything. What else can you think?'

'I am glad to hear you say so. If there is any hope of clearing up the mystery of Krishna's death, then we in the police need to know as much as we possibly can learn.'

'So, ask. Ask.'

'Very well. Where were you yourself at the time?'

'Where I was? At home, of course. When the men are going here and there preach-preaching, the woman must stay at home, quiet-quiet. For cook-cooking. Whatever important things are going on, men and women must always eat.'

'Quite right. So Krishna and your husband set out to go to the Imperial Hotel together?'

'They must. Krishna was not always well, you are knowing. Just only the day before that meeting he was having one of his what they are calling funny turns, smelling sweet smells in air when there was nothing whatsoever there to smell. So, yes, yes, Harish was going with him in the bus in case another funny turn was coming.'

'I see. And that was the last you saw of them? Until – was it – your husband came back and told you what had happened?'

'No. No, he was not telling.'

'Not?'

'Yes, yes, not. Police were keeping and keeping all in that hotel. They were questioning and questioning. Who was entering that ballroom? Who were you seeing and when also? Taking away all their shirts and blouses, ties also. Giving out horrible ones instead. Harish was explaining all to me, but not till late, late that night when a police car was at last returning him home.'

'But you said he did not tell you that Krishna had been killed? Yes?'

'Yes, that is a hundred per cent correct. It was Mr Lucas Calverte who was informing. The police were allowing a big, big man like him to go to telephone, and he was ringing me up. I was ironing Harish's shirt for next day. He had insisted to wear the one he had already put on for Sunday, when the meeting was going to be held, except for Krishna's funny turn. I was putting down electric iron and going to the phone. You are never knowing when a customer will ring with some order. And then, Mrs Nair, it is bad news, Calverte sahib was saying, and afterwards he told.'

'And did he say anything more than just that, that Krishna was dead? Did he perhaps tell you who he thought must have strangled him?'

'No, no. He was not saying one thing about that. He was not even telling me Harish could not have done that thing.'

'But you had expected him to?'

'Yes, yes. At once he must say it. It was impossible that it could be Harish. It is impossible-impossible still. I will fight and fight for his good name till I have not one more breath in body.'

*

Harriet had continued asking questions, but from that moment on Mrs Nair had, it seemed, been unable to say anything but that she was going to fight and fight for her dead husband's 'good name'. Eventually Harriet had left her, stopping on her way out to see the matron and tell her that perhaps someone should look in on the old lady.

What did I learn from all that? she asked herself as she drove away through the sedate, leafy suburban streets of Boreham. Precious little, despite her telling me to ask, ask. No, I did learn that, beyond doubt, Harish Nair's aged widow believes he cannot have killed his young cousin thirty years ago. And that's something I would like to believe about such a decent, unassuming man myself. But I shouldn't do so. Not when I am the investigating officer tasked with finding out who did kill Krishna Kumaramangalam.

Tasked, she thought with a sharply wry smile, by the new Chief Constable of the Greater Birchester Police, who for some crazy reason wants me to fail ignominiously in the task.

And I am not going to. The answer must be there somewhere, however locked behind the iron gates of time. Perhaps it will become clear, quite simply, when the report from Cherry Fettleham lands on my desk. Perhaps then it will be only a matter of going to one of the suspects and telling them that now we know. Then with a confession at once pouring out, breaking down the dam of all those years, it's done. All right, Mr Newbroom will then make sure he gets all the sweep-clean credit. But I can put up with that, if I have to. At least the truth will have been brought to light. And isn't that, after all, what a detective is for?

But perhaps I can bring that truth to light without Mr Newcomen's latest in DNA techniques. I could. All right, the murder was investigated very thoroughly at the time. But it was investigated, as I have now realized, with blinkered eyes. So can a detective who prides herself on not being blinkered do better? Someone who's prepared to let her subconscious take its wild jumps, and is then prepared to look at where they've landed her?

Damn it, we'll see.

No more pussyfooting around in case word gets out that Mr Newbroom's newly polished police are tackling the case. No, damn him, what if the *Evening Star* does plaster that juicy rumour all over its front page? What if the new-broom thunder gets stolen? The truth is there, somewhere, to be found, and if there are possible ways of finding it ahead of the boys down in Cherry Fettleham, then I am going to probe into each one of them until I get there.

So, right, yes, get DC Steadman to locate the missing Sydney Bigod, if he has to stay up all night to do it. And me? What am I going to do? Yes, go and see whichever of the other suspects comes immediately to hand.

Barney Trapnell, crippled watch repairer. Why not?

There was a small swinging sign outside Barney Trapnell's little repair shop in one of the huddle of streets north of the Birchester–Liverpool canal. *Clocks and*

Watches Mended, it read. As, Harriet thought peering up at it, it had probably done thirty years ago in the days when the cripple had set out, time and again, to offer the use of his strong arms to weak and washed-out Krishna Kumaramangalam.

Approaching on foot – she knew better than to leave an unattended car hereabouts – she thought about what that 'True Crime' work *Who Killed the Preacher?* had said about Trapnell. Yes, one of its more flagrant guesses. What had it been? Something like *Can a cripple's twisted bitterness have led to a moment of terrible revenge on life?* Good old Meadowcraft, perhaps the wildest of his string of hope-to-hit nudging questions.

Right, we'll see now just how much that one's worth. Isn't it equally likely, after all, that years of crippled suffering can have led to a calm acceptance of the worst blows of fate? Or even that in the past thirty years medical science has found a way of dealing with the blow that polio, if it was polio, inflicted long ago? Pip's description of his state, however vivid, might not have been accurate.

When she opened the shop door – the bell above it rang with much the same old-fashioned clang as the one above the door of *Mack's Sausages Are the Best* – she saw at once from across the narrow counter that her rosy pipe dream had not got it right. The man working in the solitary pool of light at a bench on the far wall was yet more crippled than she had been led to believe. As he swung round to see who had entered, Harriet could not keep the thought out of her head that, yes, he looked like a human three-legged stool.

Both legs, not just one, were now grasped in callipers and above them the body was bent, it seemed, almost at a permanent right-angle. Nor did the expression on his frown-etched face show any of the calm acceptance she had imagined for him.

He glowered.

Harriet straightened her back, in unconscious repudiation of any such crippling effect time had brought to the watch repairer, and delivered yet another version of her standard introduction.

'Good morning, I am Detective Superintendent Martens, Greater Birchester Police, and I have come to you because we are considering re-opening, with the aid of recent scientific advances in the use of DNA, our investigation into the murder of Krishna Kumara-mangalam, known as the Boy Preacher.'

'Don't know nothing about that,' came a growled response, and the crippled body was swung round again to the bench.

'I think you do, Mr Trapnell,' Harriet replied with equal directness.

'I said, I don't. So you can get out.'

The words were delivered to the wall in front of the bent form of the watch mender.

'No, Mr Trapnell, on May the twenty-second, 1969, you were one of the seven people, the seven people only, who could have entered the ballroom of the Imperial Hotel and strangled the Boy. And I am the police officer in charge of the investigation into his death. So I have questions for you, and I warn you that you are bound to answer them.'

Into Harriet's head there came, in a sudden camera

shot, the sight of the ballroom as she had seen it for herself, ornate and ridiculous even under the layers of dust that had accumulated on all its surfaces. Now the cripple did ponderously shift himself round till he was facing her directly.

'And if I've forgotten?' he said. 'If after thirty years and more I have managed to put all that out of my mind, right out of it, how can I answer the questions you're so set on having answered?'

'Shall we try? For instance, can you remember who else was in the foyer of the ballroom while you were waiting for the Boy to complete his meditation?'

'No.'

'Come, that's nonsense. You must be able to recall some of the others, even though it's thirty years ago.'

'So I must, must I? But what if I can't? People forget, you know. People even forget the most terrible things that have happened to them. Do you think I can remember what I felt, when I was no more than a slip of a boy, when the doctors told me that with the ankylosis I'd have to wear a calliper on my left leg for ever more? Well, I can't. I can't remember that. I can't remember them fixing that first calliper on. It seems as if it, or the others they put on me, have been there for ever. So why should I be able to remember that day the Boy Preacher – Oh, I recall him from time to time – on the day he was strangled? If that's what happened to him.'

Can I believe all this? Harriet asked herself. Or is it the first line of defence that many a criminal has produced on the other side of the table in the interview room. Can't remember, can't remember, don't know, don't know.

Right, they've broken down in the end and come up with a full confession. Not all of them. But enough. So will this obstinate fellow crumble in the same way?

But he won't. Not here on his own ground, in this wretched hovel of a shop with its grime-stained wall, its ill-lit staircase, its tattered advertisements for brands of watches and clocks long forgotten. Here he'll feel he can defy the world with its alien commands and prohibitions. But one day, if he's to be had, I'll have him.

She turned to go. But in the narrow doorway underneath the old clanging bell she turned back and snapped out one sentence towards the cripple's sullen turned-away back.

'Let me warn you, Mr Trapnell, that if I find even the smallest piece of evidence that leads me to think you have not been entirely frank with me, I will come straight back. And I will not then take *I've forgotten* as being any proper answer.'

Chapter Thirteen

Harriet, as soon as she had stepped out into the narrow shabby street under the watch mender's swinging sign, felt a twinge of regret at her ferocity. But what's done is done, she said to herself with a faint shrug of resignation.

Time to move on.

'Right,' she said to Pip Steadman as she marched back into her cubbyhole office, 'have you located Sydney Bigod yet?'

A fierce blush appeared behind the white triangular beard as he rose from his chair.

But Harriet, the Hard Detective all set to beat to the post Mr Newbroom and his instant DNA expectations, ignored the all too obvious sign of nervous dismay.

'Well?'

'No. Er, no. No, ma'am, I'm afraid I— Well, I've had no luck. I've been on to Norfolk Police. In Norwich as well as Cromer. Er, twice. Twice, as a matter of . . . But— But they've lost all sight of Bigod.'

'Have they indeed? That's not much help, is it?'

By way of response the little detective extracted a cigarette pack from his pocket.

'Ma'am, may I?' he begged.

'All right, go ahead. If you must.'

'No, ma'am, I'm afraid I haven't done too well there,' he said, lighting up. 'But, well, there is one thing that I learnt from the station at Cromer. Bigod's name is not really Bigod. I got on to an old desk sergeant there, and he remembered him. He said— He said they found out thirty years ago, when DCI Kenworthy was making inquiries, that he'd only— That is, that Bigod had only taken that name when he left Cromer and came here. Here to Birchester, I mean. His real name, he said, was Vine. Vine. Sydney Vine. It was when he moved here – he'd made Cromer too hot to hold him – that he took to calling himself Bigod. Er, ma'am.'

'Right. Good. We could be on to something here. You remember I told you Bigod was an old Norfolk name, name of the Earls of Norfolk back in the time of King Richard and bad brother King John?'

At this friendlier tone, Pip subsided back on to his chair.

'Yes,' he said. 'Yes, ma'am. You were in Norwich when your husb—'

'Never mind that. The point is that, when things got too hot for Bigod down in Norfolk and he came to the big city here, he must have changed his name to the first one he thought of, that Norwich Bigod. So, when at the time of the murder he decided to go back to somewhere he felt happy, like Norwich, isn't it possible that, criminal as he is, he stuck to his old modus operandi and picked on a Birchester name to hide under?'

'Well, I suppose so. But, well, isn't that a bit of— Well, if you'll excuse me, ma'am, a wild guess.'

'Yes, DC. That's just what it is. A wild guess. But there's something to be said for wild guesses. If you find you can make thoughts that seem to come from the back of your mind, or from a dream even, fit into whatever investigation you have on hand you should go with them. All right, they may take you nowhere. Nine times out of ten they probably do. But there's always the tenth chance, and it's one worth following to the very end.'

She looked across at Pip sitting there twisting one hand in another.

'It's not just by being the so-called Hard Detective that I've clocked up such successes as I've had. It's by not immediately thrusting down, in the name of the great god Common Sense, the wild guesses that have sometimes come to me.'

'But— But—' Pip stammered. 'But, ma'am, even if your guess is right and Bigod has taken a Birchester name to keep himself out of the way of the Norfolk Police, how are we to find what that name is?'

He drew himself up a little, fighting to throw off the vestiges of the breakdown that had brought him as an extra burden to Harriet's side.

'Look,' he said. 'Look, I'm Birchester born and I can't think of any name, any name like Bigod, that sticks out here in Birchester. I'm sure I can't.'

'Can't you? Perhaps you've lost your trust in leaps of the imagination since your— Since you left advertising and joined the police.'

'Perhaps I have, perhaps I have. But I still can't see what leap of the imagination's going to produce a

Birchester name that Vine took to Norwich all those years ago.'

'Can't you? But it's simple enough. We don't try and persuade our imaginations to leap. To begin with you can't. It just has to happen. But what we can do is use a bit of plain hard work after they've made that leap. For instance, we can look on the Internet now at every page in the Norwich phone book till we find something that fits.'

She saw Pip's appalled look.

'Yes, DC. Hard work. But no case was ever resolved without someone doing some dull, plodding, sheer hard work.'

'Well, all right, ma'am.'

He heaved himself up from his lopsided chair. Harriet smiled.

'No, not you, DC. This plodding task, I rather think, should be carried out by the person who made the wild guess.'

But under the letter A, as she sat scrolling through the Norwich phone book on a commandeered computer, Harriet almost at once came across the name Aslough.

Bingo. Aslough Parade. Where we buy those perfect croissants. All right, it may yet turn out to be just an extraordinary coincidence, but Aslough's certainly as odd a name as Bigod. Didn't John tell me once it really should be *a slough* because the street, smart though it is now, was first made back in the nineteenth century to run across what had been a large patch of marshy land on the edge of growing Birchester? Of course he did.

And, of course, this entry for *Aslough Car Sales* could lead me to a man who has risen up from being a shady street vendor here in Birchester to— To the perhaps equally shady world of the second-hand motor trade in Norwich. I'd be surprised if there isn't a Mr Sydney Aslough known to the police there, though they may never have linked him to Sydney Bigod, otherwise Sydney Vine.

So, what a piece of luck. No sooner did I pontificate to poor Pip about the virtues of the wild guess, not to mention the dream, than up comes a splendid example.

Provided always that Sydney Aslough in Norwich does turn out to have been Sydney Bigod, just possibly involved in some piece of financial craftiness over the Boy Preacher's funds. A piece of criminality which, if it had somehow come to the Boy's notice, might have led Bigod to commit a spur-of-the-moment murder. Because, if he hadn't attached himself to the Boy for the purpose of getting at the considerable funds his preaching had brought in, then why had he become one of those Meadowcraft called the Clique? From all I've heard of him he's no good-hearted do-gooder.

So something to be found? Right, it's off to Norwich.

Glossy. That, Harriet decided, was the word for the Aslough Car Sales lot. The large forecourt, though fundamentally no more than an area of dusty tarmac, was decorated with bunches of bright balloons and flamboyant notices telling the world what bargains it was passing up by not coming in to look. And the premises beyond were every bit as alluringly smart, at least to the casual eye. The long fascia above them proclaimed in blazing red *Bargains! Bargains! Bargains! Aslough Car Sales – Bargains! Bargains! Bargains!* The windows below shone with polishing. Behind them, rather hard to see, three particularly smart cars gleamed enticingly, each presumably yet more of a bargain, if requiring a greater sum put down in cash.

But in much smaller lettering, under that *Bargains! Bargains! Bargains!*, Harriet spotted, next to the telephone number and website address, the words *S. Aslough Proprietor. S* is for Sydney, she said to herself. Right, let's have a word with Sydney Aslough, so-called, proprietor of Aslough Car Sales.

She marched through the crude scaffold-tubes entrance archway, heavily decorated with bunting, and threaded her way past cars of every shape and size, each bearing a bright red-letters notice saying how wonderfully cheap it was.

Inside the showroom a girl sat behind a smart light-wood desk, pretty and prettily dressed in a red low-cut cotton blouse with trousers to match. Lips, equally red, pouted.

'Mr Aslough in?' Harriet demanded. 'Mr Sydney Aslough?'

'D'you wanna buy a car? I can handle that.'

'It's a personal matter.'

'Yeah? Well, he is in, I suppose. Who'll I say it is?'

'Mrs Piddock,' Harriet answered, seizing on her married name. 'He won't know me.'

The girl picked up the phone on her desk.

'Lady to see you. A Mrs Piddock.'

Impossible to make out the voice at the other end. But it seemed that it had uttered some welcoming words. I wonder, Harriet thought, whether the response would have been the same if the girl here had said *Gentleman to see you* or, even worse, *Detective Superintendent Martens to see you.*

'It's through there. Door marked "private".'

Harriet immediately recognized the man she had seen in the thirty-year-old black-and-white police photograph which had fallen out of DCI Kenworthy's files. Sydney Aslough, though fuller in the face, was clearly Sydney Bigod, or Sydney Vine. He was sitting behind a much bigger desk than his receptionist's, the two telephones on it differently coloured, the computer terminal gleaming. Nothing else except a large glass ashtray in which a cigar butt still faintly smoked. A very expensive-looking open-necked shirt only partially hid Sydney's well-fleshed torso.

In garishness, Harriet thought, it might be fellow to the shirt I saw on its way to the lab on Monday, though that had looked a good deal less sail-like. So Sydney Bigod, street trader, has plainly prospered since he became Sydney Aslough, motor trader, proud possessor of this many-pocketed, multi-buttoned garment.

'Well, me darling, what can I do for you?'

Harriet paused for just a second before she delivered her puncturing thrust.

'You can answer some questions. Detective Superintendent Martens, Greater Birchester Police.'

Sydney Aslough grinned.

'Clever lady, ain't you, getting yourself in to see
me? Mrs— What did Maggie say your name was? Mrs
Something-or-other. Paddy? Piddy? Got it. Piddle. You
know, I must have a word with that Maggie. She's
meant to have eyes in her head. Not to let the boys in
blue – I beg yours – the pretty ladies in blue come
poking in here, not without giving me a word of
warning. Might have had the loot all spread out on the
desk, mightn't I?'

'Oh, I don't think you'd have needed a word of
warning about me, Mr Aslough. Or should I say Mr
Bigod?'

'Ah, so that's what we're on about, is it? Some bit
of trouble from my time in Birchester? Though I don't
know what it can be about. Kept my nose nice and
clean over there. Most of the time, anyhow.'

'Including the time, Mr Bigod, you spent looking
after a certain Krishna Kumaramangalam, known as
the Boy Preacher – the one who was murdered while
you were in the next room?'

'Ah, him.'

Yes, the cheeky tone vanishing away, water down
a drain.

'Yes, him. And the questions I want to ask you are
about that evening, there in the Imperial Hotel, when
the Boy's life was brought to an end.'

'Yeah, well . . . Well, long time ago, weren't it?'

'Yes, it was. More than thirty years ago. On the
evening of May the twenty-second, 1969, to be precise.'

'Yep, thirty years ago plus. You're dead right. So why're you coming all the way over here to ask me about it?'

'One simple reason, Mr Bigod,' Harriet replied, casting away, in face of this streetwise Norwich citizen, any pretence of this being a mere hunt for cases from the past suitable for re-investigation. 'Thanks to advances in the technique of DNA analysis, we are now in a position to know who it was who leant over the Boy, as he came out of a state of meditation, and strangled the life out of him.'

'Bully for you. Bully for those DNA techniques, whatever they are. But that don't answer my question. Why've you come to see little old Sydney, never did no harm to no one? Unless it was selling 'em something they didn't ought to have bought.'

Harriet gave him a grin. She couldn't help it. Cheek is endearing.

'Right, I haven't come to arrest you, if that's what you were afraid of. I've come, as I said, to ask you some questions.'

Sydney Bigod gave her a cautious look.

'Straight up?'

'Straight up.'

'Then fire away.'

'Right, the night or the evening of the murder. You were there in the foyer of the Imperial's ballroom with half a dozen other members of what's been called Kumaramangalam's Clique.'

'Hey, yeah. I know who called us that, chap what wrote that book. What was it called? *Who Knocked Off the Preacher*? Something like that. Read it, you know.

Saw it on the next-door stall in the market here, couple
o' years after it all happened. If I'd seen it earlier I
might have had a go at him, that Michael Mastercraft,
whatever. He was out of order, you know, right out of
order and not only about me. Said some right nasty
things about that little Harish, wouldn't hurt a fly. He
still around, old Harish? D'you know?'

Harriet sighed.

'No, no, I'm afraid Harish Nair died several years
ago.'

'You're not going to try an' pin it on him then, are
you? All nice an' dead, can't hit back? Wouldn't put it
past coppers, not anywhere, Birchester or Norwich.'

'No, Mr Aslough. We are not going to try to pin it
on Harish Nair.'

And then, a nasty second thought.

'Or, not unless we have evidence, good evidence.'

'That new DNA? Read about it in the paper. Don't
they use it in the States nowadays, fix the blame in
paternity cases? Screwing lolly out of all those sex-mad
billionaires.'

Yes, Harriet could not help thinking, some scientist
over in Cherry Fettleham may at this moment be
testing Harish Nair's shirt, the one with little yellow
daisies on a pale green background. I can see it now,
as Pip bundled it off to the lab. Just what I thought a
gentle, sweet man like Harish would have been
wearing. And it's not impossible the scientists there
will find a DNA match between the saliva on that shirt
and the specimens taken from the Boy's body. There's
no reason why they should not. If not today or in a
few days' time, then within weeks. After all, they may

have paid attention to the urgent message I sent on to them from Mr Newbroom.

But I haven't come all this way to sit musing about what a nice man Harish Nair was. I've come to find out, if I can, how nasty Sydney Bigod is, underneath all this happy cheekiness. Am I in fact talking to a murderer? A murderer who committed his crime thirty years ago?

'Right, enough about sex-mad billionaires. What I'm here for, Mr Bigod, is to ask you about that evening of May the twenty-second, 1969. You remember the ballroom foyer there, I suppose.'

'Yeah. Sort of.'

'Very good, tell me about the other six people in there with you.'

'Cor, that's a tall order. Can't hardly remember the names of some of 'em.'

'You remembered Harish Nair's.'

'Yeah, well, you don't so often come across a bloke as nice as him. Nice through an' through he was. An' that's not what you can say about everyone. Hey, yeah, here's another I do remember. 'Cos of that. That Mr Lucas Calverte. You'd say he was nice, first look at him. An' the second, an' the third. Gentleman of the old school, always polite even if it was plain he thought you were shit. But treat you as if nothing like that had ever been in his mind. What he'd been brought up to do. But – what was I saying? – get right down inside him, an' you see he's someone who just wants what he wants, an' bugger everybody else.'

'That's interesting. So, do you think, for some

reason, Lucas Calverte might have wanted Krishna Kumaramangalam dead?'

'The Boy, you mean? Never could get the hang of all that Indian. Did old Lukey want to get rid of the Boy, for some reason? Could be. Could be, I'd say. It's like I told you. Get below the skin, an' you find it's one for all and all for Number One.'

'But you've no more reason for saying that than – what? – mere dislike?'

'Oh, no. Sydney Aslough ain't so stupid as that, an' Sydney Bigod weren't neither. No, you could tell Lukey-boy weren't sweet as a flower from the way he ordered everybody about. Mind, it wasn't no *Do this, do that*. Nah, he was cleverer than that. But he was preaching to you, preaching to everybody, all of the time. But sort of subtly, you know. It was *I've always found it best if . . .* and *Don't you think we ought to . . .* But what we did ought to have done was just what old Lukey wanted done. For him.'

So, Sydney here is not quite the jokey, all-on-the-surface street vendor and car salesman he seems to be. No, an acute brain there, when he's persuaded to show it. Then where does that leave me? Thinking that Undersheriff Lucas Calverte's a more likely murderer than I'd believed. Certainly. But it leaves me, too, thinking Sydney Bigod is every bit sharp enough to be a calculating killer. If I could only get a line on why he would have needed to kill.

But I can't do that sitting talking to him here. No, what's needed is some hard digging back in Birchester, or some hard interrogation eventually in an interview room somewhere. Worth going on talking, though. I'm impressed by Sydney Aslough's insights.

'All right, so what do you remember about – shall we say? – Marcus Fairchild?'

'Marcus who?'

'Marcus Fairchild, the journalist who said he was from *The Times*.'

'Yeah, there was a guy there said that, or something like it. Never really took no notice of him. So he was there in that foyer place that night, was he?'

'Oh, yes. But you don't remember him from then, is that it?'

'That's it. Lot happens in thirty years, you know. Drives things out of your mind.'

'Has all that's happened driven, say, Bubsy Willson out of your mind?'

'No. No, not if that was what that ugly-looking tart was called. You should have seen that face of hers, flat as a pancake an' one what ain't been cooked either. And hairs. Dirty great black hairs sticking up all over it. Gawd knows why she'd got herself in with that lot. She'd got no interest in people like them, far as I could see. She'd have been happier opening her legs somewhere down by the canal. In the dark. They haven't filled up that old canal, back in Birchester, have they?'

'No, that's still with us. And so is someone who still lives near it. Do you remember Barney Trapnell?'

'Yeah. Cripple fellow, some sort of metal contraption on one of his legs. But strong. Strong, mind you. Don't remember much about him, though, only that he could lift the Boy up like he was a feather. Which, of course, he was. Sort of. Not quite here in this world, know what I mean? A feather floating in the wind. An', you know what? No feather ought to get theirselves scrunched out like that.'

'I agree. But, tell me, why was it that you came to be as close to him as you were? Full member of the Clique, Michael Meadowcraft said.'

'Ah, well, that's a funny story, that is. None o' my pals down here'd believe it for a moment. Not of naughty old Syd.'

'But?'

'Yeah, well, this was the way of it. It was right at the beginning of it all, matter o' fact. In them days the Boy didn't have no great big what they called mass meetings. Nah. Just took to doing a bit o' preaching at a chapel. Chapel where old Harish used to give out the good words, in fact. And one day I'd set up my pitch right opposite. Doing the old records, I was then. You remember 'em? Vinyl, big twelve-inch discs of vinyl. All the pop music was on 'em. Wasn't hardly nothing else then. An' it was a nice, hot day. So the customers was in a good mood. I remember that, doing good business I was. But the doors of that chapel had been pushed wide open. Give the would-be-goods inside a bit of air. And then the people round the stall began to go over an' listen to that voice coming sort of fluting out into the street, quiet like, but somehow telling you, going through an' through you. More an' more of 'em went. So in the end I went across meself. Just to take a gander, see what it was all about.'

He fell silent.

Looking at him across his desk, Harriet realized he

was sitting there, in his smart many-buttoned shirt, seeing once again that scene of more than thirty years ago.

'And that was it?' she said at last.

'Yeah. From then on I thought I'd better stick by the Boy, much as I could. Had a living to make, didn't I? But I reckoned he needed someone to look after him, the sort of hundred per cent innocent that he was. Someone to see no one was taking advantage while he told the world what they ought to hear. Because he did that, you know, he did that.'

Yes, another unexpected tribute to the power of that Boy's preaching to set beside that of his other unlikely adherent, Marcus Fairchild, the Trufflehound. But, no, *power* isn't the word. From what the two of them have said about the preaching it was more like a quietly embracing flow of— Of what? Of goodness, yes. Goodness it would have to have been.

Chapter Fourteen

'You seem to have been haring around all over the place,' John said to Harriet as they sat over the last of their supper. 'Aren't you paying rather too much attention to beating your Mr Newbroom? He's largely a figment of your imagination, you know.'

'No, I do not know. That man's real enough, Mr Newcomen, just appointed Chief Constable of the Greater Birchester Police. The interview I had with him was real enough, too. The bloody little cupboard of an office at Headquarters he's pushed me into is real enough. The DC he's attached to me is a real-enough officer, one hardly recovered from a nervous breakdown.'

'All right, all right. I dare say Mr Newcomen's taken a dislike to you for some reason. Probably, as you suggested, because he thinks you're some sort of a publicity hound. But all the same that doesn't really make it any more reasonable for you to have gone racing up to London yesterday and rushing over to Norwich today.'

'Oh, come. My trip today was well worthwhile, by any standards. One, I confirmed that the Sydney Bigod who was one of the seven people in the foyer of the

Imperial Hotel ballroom when the Boy Preacher was murdered is the same person as a Sydney Aslough, motor dealer in Norwich. And, two, he actually told me a lot about the others in that foyer with him. He's given me plenty of food for thought. He said, very shrewdly I think, that the former Undersheriff for the County of Birrshire, Lucas Calverte, is not exactly the decent English gentleman he purports to be. You know, when I went to see him on Monday, I felt at the back of my mind that there was something . . . something, I don't know, not quite right about him. Well, now I've got some extra evidence, if you can call it evidence. And before much longer I'm going to have another word with Mr Lucas Calverte.'

'Lady protesting too much?'

'No, she's not. I learnt a good deal more about Michael Meadowcraft's Seven Suspects today, a whole lot more.'

But on John's face there had appeared a big reminiscent grin.

'I read the whole of *Who Killed the Preacher?* this evening, before you got back,' he said. 'That final thunderous phrase is still ringing in my head. *So there we leave the Seven Suspects who alone could have committed what is perhaps the most mysterious murder ever to be laid to rest, unsolved, in the annals of British crime.*'

'Oh, gosh, that wretched book. I'd better have it back. If I don't return it to Mr Newbroom's Pansy Balfour, I'll find myself accused of stealing it.'

'If you really think so. But, in any case, all that luscious prose must have given you absolutely everything you could want to know.'

'Oh, have your joke. But the fact is I didn't learn a single thing from Newbroom's kindly and highly inaccurate loan, or not anything that's going to be of the least help. But I did learn things from Sydney Aslough. Not only about Calverte, but about Marcus Fairchild, confirming on the whole that he was up here in Birchester purely and simply because of the way the Boy had, despite himself, gripped his imagination. And I learnt something about that awful-sounding girl, Bubsy Willson. That she was always more interested in sex than in preaching. Trust a man like Bigod to see that. And, more, I found out from what he said about Barney Trapnell being a very strong young man, despite the calliper on his leg, that the Boy frequently needed to be lifted up. So I've been wondering if the Boy didn't have something wrong with him. Wrong in body, that is. Not that it's necessarily significant.'

'Okay, you've made out a case for whizzing off to Norwich so far, if a bit of a flimsy one.'

'Flimsy? You—'

'Wait, wait. It's just that I'd have been more impressed if you'd said to me that your facts-full informant had been able to tell you just what went on in the foyer of the Imperial's ballroom. I danced there once, before I knew you. And I'd especially have wanted to learn who was where in the foyer in, say, the quarter of an hour before the body was discovered.'

'Okay, I'd have liked that, too. Wouldn't I just. But I didn't get to hear. It was all a long time ago, don't forget, and it's hardly likely that Bigod or Aslough, call him which you like, would remember details. In fact, when I asked, he recalled just one thing, and that was pretty vague, something he said as he was seeing me out.'

'But it was . . .?'

'It was, as he put it, that the tart Bubsy came screaming out of the ballroom to say the Boy was dead.'

'Well, that's a piece of hard evidence for you. You never said your Mr Kenworthy got that out of him.'

'No. He didn't. You know what an interview between a senior police officer and a dodgy street trader's going to be like. Antagonistic. So Bigod wasn't giving anything away he didn't have to, then.'

'But with senior officer Harriet Martens it was a different matter?'

'It might have been, yes. I certainly wasn't hard on him, or not after the first few minutes. And besides a lot of time has passed since Kenworthy interviewed him, and perhaps now he has a more mellow view of the police. But, however it came about, I got even more out of him than that recollection about Bubsy, which, as I told you, was somewhat vague to say the least. There's also what he said—'

She came to a halt.

'Oh, and I've just remembered, I've got a nice joky little titbit from Norwich that should be right up your street. But be warned, you won't get fed it unless you're prepared to admit that my case, when you've heard it all, is by no means flimsy.'

'We'll see.'

'Right. Then from Aslough's happy chatter, and, you know, I do like him. He's—'

'Favourites again. I warned you about your nice Harish Nair the other day. Now you're doing it again.'

'No, I'm not. Okay, I liked Aslough, and I like the sound of Harish Nair from all that I've heard about him. But I'm not assuming anything about either of them. I'm a better detective than that, damn it.'

'If you say so. But let's hear the rest of what you learnt from your much-liked motor trader. I want my titbit, whatever it is.'

'Okay. But listen properly. If you put on your dismissive face, you'll get nothing at all. And I think you'll really like it, actually.'

'Proceed, Detective Superintendent.'

'Right. This is what Aslough told me about Bubsy Willson, or Barbara as Meadowcraft liked to call her. Aslough said, and I think it fits in well with Kenworthy's notes, that she wasn't really one of the Boy's inner circle, that she didn't seem to know why she was there and that she'd rather be having sex down by the canal than listening to him preaching.'

'Noted. If not fully accepted.'

'Your privilege, Judge. But listen to what he said about the last of them, Priscilla Knott. You know, on the whole everything that I've learnt about her has been favourable, to her as a person at least. But Aslough had a different view of her. He said she was the sort of lady who would do anything if she thought it was the right thing. She used to preach at them all, he said. To preach much harder than the Boy, and with . . . with something like venom. So I think it's not impossible she could have decided that some part of the Boy's preaching was wrong, and that in the end the only remedy was to— Right, to put him to death.'

'Tough talk. And I suppose it could all have happened. You've certainly not produced any better motive for any of them.'

He gave her a mockingly sly smile.

'So titbit time?'

'All right, I suppose you've earned it. So, this is what it is. In Norwich, just next to the premises of Aslough Car Sales there is a chapel, one of the evangelical or even charismatic sort. Outside it they have placed a big poster in stark red lettering saying just the three words, *God is Light*. And on that – it just caught my eye as I went past – someone has taken a thick felt pen and scrawled, *Then switch it off*.

John gave a long, loud laugh.

'But, you know,' he said, sobering up, 'all of what you've been telling me could fall away to dust.'

'You mean when the lab at Cherry Fettleham simply reports, on good DNA evidence, that X throttled the Boy to death and there's no evidence pointing to anyone else? But that won't be for two weeks or more, three from now.'

Next morning, however, Harriet found her supposition had been quite wrong. On her table when, a few minutes earlier than usual, she entered her poky, ill-painted office there lay a bulky envelope with at its top left-hand corner, plain to see, the printed designation *Forensic Science Service, Cherry Fettleham Laboratory*.

Oh, she thought as she walked over to snap it up, the voice of Newbroom is the voice of power, definitely. I'd never have thought, after my carefully presented message, that Dr Passmore down there would take the least bit of notice of that absurd claim for urgent treatment. Or has Newbroom telephoned them himself with all the authority of a much-praised Chief Constable? Because it seems that the death of the Boy Preacher in 1969 is, after all, 'a current murder inquiry'.

But what's this packet going to say? Whose garment was spattered with the Boy's saliva?

She ripped open the envelope, tugged the bulky sheets out, lifted them up and began flicking past the necessary opening bureaucratic notes and disclaimers.

Or – a momentary hope, or fear – will Dr Passmore finally state there is no reliable evidence from any of the specimens?

Then, at last, she found the paragraph headed in bold type: *Conclusion*.

Of the garments submitted for analysis only one showed identifiable traces of saliva corresponding to that of the victim. This was No. 5.

Blast him. Why can't he just say the name? The name.

Where's that list of garments? Turn back, turn back. Yes. No. Damn it. Yes. Yes, here it is.

She read.

5. Cotton shirt labelled as having been worn by Harish Nair.

No. No, it can't be. No, I don't believe it. I won't believe it. Not nice Harish. It's impossible. I know that man. Aslough knew him, knew him to speak to, day after day, and he thought he couldn't possibly have killed the Boy. Wouldn't hurt a fly, he said. Everybody who had had anything to do with him had only the nicest things to say about him.

But John. Didn't John warn me just last night not to have favourites? And didn't I say then, scarcely twelve hours ago, *I'm not assuming anything . . . I'm a better detective than that?*

Right, it seems I'm not. Because, whatever I said, whatever I thought I was doing, I was assuming that someone as nice, as good, damn it, as Harish Nair was not going to strangle a person like the Boy Preacher, the quiet youth who even that cynical Trufflehound, Marcus Fairchild, found himself constrained to compare with – who were they? – yes, Mohammed, Gandhi, Churchill and, odd addition perhaps, that marvellous cellist, Jacqueline du Pré.

But, here in my hands are the words of a report from the Forensic Science laboratory, no less, stating positively that garment No. 5, Harish's sweet daisy-covered, pale green shirt, singing, damn it, all the goodness of summer, was spattered thirty years ago with spittle forced from the mouth of that extraordinary boy. The boy whose preaching reduced a professional hard-case like the Trufflehound to compare him with those super-human beings.

And I cannot believe what those scientists have said.

She stood moment after moment looking unseeingly at the report clutched in both her hands and feeling nothing but that state of non-believing.

And then . . . Then a tiny gleam shot through the heavy cloud overwhelming her.

The speed with which Dr Passmore had worked on those thirty-year-old garments. Had he, in order to produce the swift response he had been asked for by a demanding Chief Constable, treated them with less than the scientific exactitude he would normally have employed? Can he be someone like that? What do I know about him after all? Nothing. He's just a name down there in Cherry Fettleham. So did he fail to understand as well as I had hoped my deliberately toned-down version of Newbroom's request? Is he the sort of bloody idiot who would take it as a distinct instruction from the Chief Constable of a major force?

Or . . . Or is it what I wondered about just now? Did Mr Newcomen personally telephone, say, the chief officer at the lab and repeat his request, not trusting me to pass it on? And was Dr Passmore then ordered to make it a rush job?

So, could there after all be a loophole in the conclusion here, however clearly it's been put?

Right, one thing. I'm not going to accept that conclusion without going into how it was actually arrived at. And I'm not going to let Mr Newcomen know the report's arrived. Not until I've been down to Cherry Fettleham and put that Dr Passmore through every hoop I can find for him. Harish Nair did not kill the Boy Preacher. I know that. And, damn it, I'm going to find proof that he did not.

Chapter Fifteen

Harriet took the lab at Cherry Fettleham by storm. She had made the journey across into Lincolnshire in a little over two hours, foot pressed hard on the gas pedal, furiously cursing any slow driver ahead. Resolutely she refused to let herself think about the report now locked in her cupboard back in Birchester. At last, when a pair of lumbering farm machinery vehicles blocked her on the lane leading to Cherry Fettleham itself and the laboratory just beyond, her fury was checked when she abruptly remembered the dream she had had of nearly being crushed by two huge oncoming fantastic vehicles.

Coming to a halt finally on the wide gravel forecourt of the lab, she marched in, flicked her warrant card in front of the receptionist in the entrance hall and demanded to see 'your Dr Passmore'. The girl almost grabbed for her telephone.

Two minutes later Harriet was at the door of the biology room. Glancing round the big, neon-lit laboratory, where in a far corner only one scientist – stained white coat, mass of blonde hair – was working at a steel-topped bench, she saw Dr Passmore smiling a welcome from the opposite end of the room. He was, she realized, rather older than the inexperienced man she had hoped to find, someone to be browbeaten into admitting he had not been as scrupulous as he ought to have been. Dr Passmore, however, might well be approaching his fifties. The short hair bristling on his head was touched with grey, the cheeks of his long, lean face had been rubbed by time into shininess, the eyes behind his large rimless spectacles were calmly quizzical.

'Detective Superintendent Martens? We spoke, of course, earlier this week when you passed on to me a rather odd request from your Chief Constable.'

Rather odd? So there hadn't been any misunderstanding about my adroitly worded message. Better go carefully after all.

'Yes, we did indeed talk. So, may I say, after what you told me about your priorities, that I was rather surprised to find on my desk this morning your full report.'

Dr Passmore laughed.

'I'm sure you were,' he said. 'But what you didn't know was that the Boy Preacher murder has always been something of a – what do they call it? – King Charles's head with me. You see, when I was still in my last term at school, the Boy Preacher murder was what first made me think I wanted to be a forensic scientist. I mean, I had a strong scientific bent, of course, and was all set to go to university and get my B.Sc. But I had no idea what particular branch of science I wanted to take up. And then one day I read about the murder. It made a great splash, you know.'

'I read about it at school too,' Harriet intervened.

'We all did. The big sensation of the day, and the Boy being scarcely older than some of us.'

'So you'll understand why the case intrigued me, and perhaps why I've been working privately on the evidence out of hours. Far into the night, in fact, far into every night. But perhaps, not being a scientist yourself, you won't see how a lad in his last year at school might have instantly thought how investigating the clothes worn by those seven suspects ought to solve the mystery within days.'

'But.'

'Yes. But, indeed. The science just wasn't there in those days. All right, the great Crick and Watson had laid down the basic theory of the double helix in – when was it? – 1953. But that, of course, was only the first step. However, there was young Passmore with the notion in his head that the science ought to be there and that one day it would be. More, I'm sorry to tell you, big-headed as that lad was, he decided he was going to be the one who discovered it.'

'And did—'

Dr Passmore laughed again, with more ease.

'No, of course I didn't. I haven't got a good enough mind to produce anything totally new. I'm more, if you like, the sure-but-steady type. All right, I've made one or two little advances in my time, but only by working and working away till I'd eliminated all the other possibilities and then was able to carry out enough experiments to obtain consistent results. No, nowadays my work is no longer experimental. I sit here merely making use of techniques others have discovered.'

Harriet, looking at the faintly rueful expression on

his face, could not help asking whether she was herself sure but steady as a detective. Or am I, as John said only a few days ago, a lateral thinker hitting from time to time on something really new?

The thought, she found, meant so much to her that she felt she must put it to Dr Passmore, on behalf of them both.

'But,' she said, 'aren't you actually knocking your own abilities? I mean, those one or two little advances, as you called them, were they in fact the result of something other than steady plodding? Weren't they, if you were to tell the immodest truth, the sort of sudden revelations that can come to a first-class scientist?'

Dr Passmore smiled.

'I know just what you want me to say,' he replied. 'You want me to say I've had the sort of heaven-sent revelation that came to a physicist called Leo Szilard some time in the 1930s. It's a well-known story. He was waiting to cross the road one day – the exact spot is even recorded, Southampton Row, in London – when, zip-zip-zip-zip, into his head came the idea of the nuclear chain reaction, something entirely new, one of the great discoveries of our times.'

'Yes. Yes, I suppose I was thinking of something like that, if not on quite such a scale.'

'I'm sorry to disappoint you, but, no, my discoveries were really achieved by no means other than steady plodding, as you kindly put it.'

'Oh, I'm sorry, I didn't mean . .'

'I think actually you did. But I'm not offended. I think it's probably not unfair to say that the actual discovery which, as a head-in-the-clouds schoolboy, I thought of making myself one day was arrived at more by hard work than sudden inspiration. Not easy to say. But it was Alec Jeffreys, working away at Leicester University, who, extrapolating from the recent discovery of the polymerase chain reaction, finally did the trick in 1985. He produced then what's been called genetic fingerprinting, and got his Sir for it.'

'But surely—'

'Yes, even his work wouldn't have provided the means for giving me the result I sent to you yesterday.'

'Ah, yes, that.'

Harriet felt a cloud descend. This was not going to be as easy as she had thought, racing into Lincolnshire. Dr Passmore was certainly not the tyro scientist she had envisioned, someone who could be knocked off a doubtful perch with a couple of penetrating questions.

She braced herself.

'Look,' she said, 'it's that conclusion you reached in your report that I want to talk to you about. I mean . . . Look, is it possible . . . No, let me say this straight out. When I read the name of Harish Nair as being the wearer of a shirt impregnated with Krishna Kumaramangalam's death-throes spittle I just couldn't believe it.'

A sharp frown appeared on Dr Passmore's hitherto friendly face.

'You didn't believe it?' he said. 'But the evidence was there. I detailed the steps that were taken. How could you not believe the conclusion?'

A sweeping sense of shame invaded Harriet.

Oh, my God, I never read the whole of that bulky sheaf. I was stupid. I was so shocked at seeing Harish

Nair named I just— Christ, I simply rushed straight off for Lincolnshire. Impulse. I rushed off on a stupid— But, no. No, I may have been a fool not to have gone painstakingly back through the report and traced how that conclusion was reached, but it would have done no good if I had. Of course, the work of a scientist like this man is going to be impeccable. I'd never have found a flaw there. No, that first thought of mine still stands. I cannot believe Harish Nair murdered Krishna Kumaramangalam. Okay, okay, it's what will derisively be called a hunch. But it's what I believe is the truth, the actual truth.

She drew in a deep breath.

'I'm sorry,' she said. 'I didn't mean to question the accuracy of your work. I've no doubt, from what you've been saying to me just now, if from nothing else, that your conclusion was arrived at on absolutely valid scientific grounds. It's— It's only that, on quite different grounds, though grounds which I feel perfectly happy about, I do not think that you can possibly have given me the right answer.'

'I have. How can you say otherwise? Are you one of those cranks who go about saying that science hasn't got all the answers, and then go on to imply we don't have any of them?'

'No, no. No, I'm a detective. I have to work on scientific lines too, although—'

'Then, Superintendent, I must tell you this: if you think you are working on scientific lines in saying that the evidence against this Harish Nair is flawed, then you are just not doing what you think you are.'

Harriet scoured her mind for an answer.

'No, look,' she said. 'Let's get this quite straight. I do not in any way doubt the science that has led you to state in your conclusion that the shirt worn by Harish Nair on that evening thirty years ago was impregnated with spittle that came from Krishna Kumaramangalam's mouth. But what I am saying is that, in a way I don't at all pretend to account for, there has been some error somewhere. And, yes, I base that belief on something as ridiculously insubstantial as my conviction that Nair – you know he's been dead for some years now – was not capable of committing that murder.'

Dr Passmore sighed. As much as to say *I'll be patient, at least for a few minutes more.*

'All right, shall we go through my report step by step?'

'Very well.'

Should I confess now that I haven't yet done so? No, he doesn't have to know how impulsive I've been. And I suppose, though I can't believe it will happen, that when he does go through it I will see that he's right after all. That I'm wrong.

Dr Passmore opened a drawer and pulled out a copy of the report. He laid it on the lab bench beside him and drew up a stool for Harriet. Then, painfully, page by page, he went through the whole process he had worked on or supervised. The checking of the garments against the specifications on the labels of the evidence bags, the examination of each particular one under ultraviolet light, the descriptions of the stains and smears revealed, the techniques that had eliminated anything other than saliva stains, and finally the sophisticated tests that had identified the traces of the Boy's DNA among the fibres of that green shirt with the daisy pattern.

Hardly once was Harriet suspicious of a logical gap in the process.

'You state here,' she said, 'there was a trace on one other blouse. But if there is, doesn't it mean . . .' But by now she had taken in Dr Passmore's mildly pained smile. 'Oh. You're going to explain that it doesn't at all mean what I— What I'd hoped?'

'I am. You'll remember from when I was pointing out how we could eliminate any stain that had been caused by something other than saliva that I had said this rather garish garment showed clear signs of having, thirty-plus years ago, had tea with milk splashed on it. Well, there might also have been minute traces of what might have been saliva in that tea-splashed area. But, even with the sophisticated tests we have now, there would never be go-to-court evidence of that. Those scarcely measurable traces could, after all, have come from a teacup that the Boy had drunk from earlier. It was much the same case, too, with the old-fashioned collarless shirt.'

'Barney Trapnell's,' Harriet said.

'Yes, Trapnell was the name on the evidence bag. Well, there were traces of saliva there as well. But the DNA we found in the saliva corresponded with DNA from the shirt's armpit stains. I imagine the traces were from dribble, or something of the sort. So the DNA there was, of course, Trapnell's own. And, yes, there may have been traces of DNA from another source, but they were altogether too minuscule for even our advanced techniques to make anything of them. Then, of course, when I found such evident saliva traces on the Nair shirt, and ones that clearly corresponded with the Boy's DNA, there was no longer any doubt.'

And, of course, there was no hint of any other flaw in the whole process. Nor was there, as far as Harriet could see, the possibility that there had been one.

She sat there on the high stool for a moment thinking it all over.

But, she found, there was still in her mind a solid conviction that dead Harish Nair could not have killed that exceptional human being, his young cousin and fellow preacher.

She made some sort of apology to Dr Passmore.

'Let me say again, I realize there's nothing wrong anywhere in what you've demonstrated to me. I'm sorry I've put you to so much trouble.'

'Not at all. It's always a pleasure to show anybody how a scientific procedure is carried out. So, may I ask, are you now happy that you have learnt the truth at last about what happened on that night of May the twenty-second, 1969, a night that's been vivid in both our minds probably for the past thirty-something years?'

She sought for an answer. And found one.

'Well, not exactly happy, but . . .'

Out in the forecourt she had only just, wearily, seated herself in the car and pushed in the ignition key when her phone rang.

Oh God, what's this?

It was worse even than she had somehow feared.

'Miss Martens, Mr Newcomen here.'

'Oh, yes, sir. Yes?'

'Where are you, Miss Martens? I've been down to your office, twice, and on neither occasion were you there.'

What to say? That I'm in Lincolnshire and have been trying to persuade a senior scientific officer at the Cherry Fettleham lab that his work was entirely wrong?

'I've been out on inquiries, sir.'

'I see. Well, what I want to know is whether the report from that place Cherry-whatsit has come yet? You did pass my message on to them, didn't you? I mean, it's perfectly plain that this is a matter that should have their most immediate attention.'

'Yes, sir. Yes, I emphasized your view when I telephoned.'

And what to say now? The truth?

'But I think we must allow them a little more time, sir. The DNA process, as I understand it, is fairly lengthy. And they have quite a large quantity of material to investigate.'

'I suppose so. I suppose so. Well, keep on their tail, keep on their tail. We want a result here as soon as possible.'

'Yes, sir.'

And the call concluded.

Harriet sat there, slumped.

God knows what trouble I've stored up for myself now. Even if I'm lucky, there'll be a great deal of dodging and weaving to keep from Newbroom's prying eyes the fact that the report was delivered today. Must square Pip Steadman, for one thing, and probably the Headquarters post room too. Oh, God.

With a sigh that was more like a groan she reached for the ignition key and turned it.

Nothing happened.

Chapter Sixteen

As if I haven't got enough misery, Harriet had said repeatedly to herself while she tried everything she could think of to get the car started. At last she had to admit defeat and ring for assistance. And then she had to wait. For one hour. For another. And eventually for ten minutes more. The final blow was discovering, when she looked in her briefcase for something to read, that all she had was the copy of *Who Killed the Preacher?* which she had meant to hand back to Pansy Balfour. In the end she was reduced to reading it once more, from cover to cover, seeing it as a way of expiating whatever sin it was that fate was punishing her for.

'Right you are, then,' the cheerful uniformed mechanic said at last. 'And, word of advice, don't give your engine such a caning on your way back.'

Final rebuke, Harriet registered.

It was only when she reached the motorway where she had taken too much out of the engine, tearing down to tell some trainee technician how wrong they had been, that she felt able to give the situation any serious consideration. But, maddeningly, she found she could not stop her thoughts repeating endlessly and ridiculously the lushest passages she had just re-read from *Who Killed the Preacher?*

. . . that group of Sunday-night young men . . . over-eager disciples of the god Bacchus . . .

. . . may have driven a twisted mind to commit the act that can never be taken back . . .

. . . emerged from that deluxe ballroom having carried out their vindictive purpose . . .

. . . where in deep meditation sat alone the young preacher so soon to be brutally done to death . . .

Only, she thought jerking out of her trance with an abrupt laugh, the Boy had not been sitting. He had been – DCI Kenworthy's notes were clear – lying there flat on the dais in that fantastically ornate ballroom. I even saw the photograph of the carpet where the marks left by the body were clear. Left by the body as the Boy had lain there in meditation, or, as dear old down-to-earth Kenworthy had put it somewhere, 'sound asleep, since he seems to have been a great one for nodding off'.

Then another echo, a quite different one, came into her head. A phrase, not from the purple pages of *Who Killed the Preacher?*, but from what John had remarked about his much-enjoyed *Edward Lear*. He had admitted he had never realized Lear was subject to epileptic fits and, talking about such attacks, he had said the short coma that ended each episode was followed by 'a brief sleep'.

So we have the Boy, 'a great one for nodding off', and Lear falling into post-attack periods of sleep. Is there . . .? And, yes, old Mrs Nair told me that on the evening of the murder Harish had had to go with the Boy on the bus in case *another of his funny turns was coming*. And didn't she say, too, something about him smelling sweet smells in the air when there was *nothing whatsoever there for him to smell?* Yes, I can hear her now. And I have a faint memory – must check with John – that such a symptom is not, as I thought at the time, an indication of the Boy's wafty mystic nature, but one that occurs in epilepsy.

In epilepsy. Epilepsy.

Krishna Kumaramangalam had been an epileptic. He was subject to epileptic fits. And in such fits wouldn't he spew out saliva? Spew out saliva all over anyone attending to him?

And, yes, Mrs Nair said something more about those funny turns. She told me that, when the meeting was postponed to the Monday, her husband had worn again the shirt he had put on *for Sunday*. So, yes, yes, yes, this is almost certainly what must have happened, could have happened. The Boy had had an epileptic fit, had, as they say, foamed at the mouth on the Sunday before the meeting, and Harish, in attending to him, had got his green daisy-decorated shirt spattered with the Boy's saliva.

So there was a flaw in Dr Passmore's report.

But it had not occurred during his tests on the clothing. It had arisen even before DCI Kenworthy had arranged for the garments to be taken from those seven people in the ballroom foyer.

And that means – she found she had unconsciously put her foot down and the car was once again going dangerously fast – I can now safely allow Mr Newbroom to see the report.

*

She arrived back at home – she had decided it was hardly worth going into Headquarters – in a state of elation, and at once told John what she had discovered.

'Calm down, calm down. You're right, actually, about the Boy's symptoms, especially smelling those non-existent sweet odours. They do all add up to pretty clear evidence he was an epileptic. I'm surprised, in fact, that nobody knew all along. But, I suppose, thirty years ago, and in a traditional Indian community, such a thing might well be kept secret. As poor old Lear's epilepsy was.'

'So why your rather preachy instructions to calm down? I should have thought I'd every right to be a little excited.'

'A little, yes. But I rather suspect you're on such a high because you think you've won your fight with your Chief Constable.'

'But I have, haven't I? I'll be able to go to him tomorrow and—'

The phone, at her elbow, shrilled out.

With a frown she picked it up and gave her number.

'Ah, Miss Martens. So you're there. And not in your office.'

She put a hand over the mouthpiece.

'Bloody Newbroom,' she whispered. 'Bad penny.'

'Yes, sir, I am at home. I had to go over to Cherry Fettleham because their report, when I saw it, had an apparent flaw in it. I wanted to clear the matter up immediately.'

'The report? It's come? Why wasn't I told? What did it say? Who— Who was it, after all these years, who murdered that boy, the Preacher?'

'I didn't consider there was any point in showing you a report that appeared to have a plain flaw in it, sir. But, now that I've dealt with that, I can tell you at once that its conclusion was that there were identifiable traces of Krishna Kumaramangalam's saliva on just one shirt, the one that had belonged to his older cousin, now dead, Harish Nair.'

'Got him. I told you, when I tasked you with the inquiry, that DNA, as it is today, would give us the answer. A wonderful advance. Did you see the paper this morning? There's a very interesting piece saying that bones, discovered somewhere in Scotland – Stirling, Stirling – are about to be identified as those of King Richard the Second by just these new DNA techniques. After more than six hundred years. Six hundred years. I've been trying to show you the account all day.'

'I'm sorry, sir. I haven't actually seen a paper. I went to my office too early, and then, when I saw the report, I realized I needed to speak to the people at Cherry Fettleham about it before I could take any action.'

'Very well. But now you can take action, Superintendent. I know that fellow Mair, Nair, is dead. But that doesn't mean it isn't up to us to inform the public that we have resolved the case. Even after thirty years.'

'Of course, sir, we should do that. But there is a complication. What I discovered after I had fully informed myself at Cherry Fettleham was that, though their work on the DNA was beyond reproach, the shirt on which they had identified Kumaramangalam's saliva had also been worn by Harish Nair the day before when Kumaramangalam, who was an epileptic, had had a fit. In the course of that fit he may very well have spat out saliva on to Nair's shirt. So there is no sound evidence for stating Harish Nair murdered the Boy.'

'But— But—'

Then Harriet made her mistake.

Exasperated at hearing Mr Newbroom groping for some reason to doubt her freeing of Harish from suspicion, she interrupted him.

'So I'm afraid, sir, this means we really shall have to abandon the re-opened inquiry. There's no proper DNA evidence now against any of those seven suspects.'

She was conscious as she spoke that she was not exactly telling the whole truth. Hadn't Dr Passmore mentioned that there were possible traces of saliva on one, no, two, of the other garments, although not enough, he had said, to produce as evidence? But the chance of calling it quits in her battle with her jealous boss was too good to fumble.

'Abandon the inquiry, Superintendent? Certainly not. Let me say that such a suggestion is yet one more instance of the slackness I see pervading the whole of Greater Birchester Police. A slackness that I intend to root out to the last— To the last— To root out completely. A good police force should periodically re-examine any case that has not been closed. I gather that the dust, the dust, has been allowed to settle on the Boy Preacher inquiry for years. Years. That is why I have tasked you with it now. And I see no reason why you should come to me claiming the matter should be abandoned. No, Superintendent, it has not been properly re-investigated. I want you to complete the task you have been assigned. I want to be told who killed that Boy, and I want to be told within one month. Maximum.'

The sound of a handset being thumped back into place.

Chapter Seventeen

Next morning Harriet found Pip Steadman waiting in her office and decided it was time he should be told how her phone conversation with Mr Newbroom had changed the situation. She sat herself behind her wretched table and launched into an explanation.

'That's it,' she concluded eventually. 'Mr Newcomen is determined that Greater Birchester Police should resolve the murder of the Boy Preacher. He thought DNA would do it. If it could find where King Richard's body was buried six hundred years ago, he believed, it could do anything. But, now it's come to it, DNA hasn't produced his answer for him. It turns out that the evidence he hoped would be found, deeply impregnated in some cotton or woollen fibres, could quite possibly have got there twenty-four hours before Krishna Kumaramangalam was killed.'

Pip, heartened it seemed by hearing he was not the only person in the world to have come a cropper, looked much less nervy than he habitually did.

'So, ma'am,' he asked. 'What are you going to do?'

'Only one thing I can do. I'm going to interview all the people still alive who were in that foyer outside the Imperial Hotel ballroom on the evening of May the twenty-second, 1969.'

'Yes . . . Yes, I suppose that's all there is to do. So . . . Well, who are you going to see first?'

Harriet thought for a moment.

'Barney Trapnell,' she said. 'After all, it was on his shirt that Dr Passmore down at Cherry Fettleham found what might have been the hint of a trace of some alien DNA. Not much to go on, but better than a complete blank. So Barney Trapnell it is.'

A quarter of an hour later she was standing once again beneath the swinging sign that read, if barely visibly, *Clocks and Watches Mended*. If hard questions could produce even the smallest hint that the crippled watch mender had a black secret in his head, then she would ask those questions with all the force she could.

All right, I've been given an impossible task, and one given me deliberately to fail in. But I'm not going to fail. Somehow I am going to beat Newbroom at his own game. And if Barney Trapnell stands in my way, he's going to find himself down in an interrogation room, sweating and sweating till I've sweated every last drop of the truth out of him.

She pushed open the little shop's door. Its old-fashioned bell clanged out.

'Good morning, Mr Trapnell,' she said loudly, leaning forward on the dark shop's narrow counter. 'Detective Superintendent Martens.'

Barney Trapnell, already at his bench, turned lumberingly round.

'You,' he said. 'What you want now?'

'What do I want? I told you when we talked before

that I would come to you again if I found even the smallest piece of evidence that indicated you had not been telling me the whole truth. And here I am.'

'And I told you I've forgotten all about that night, and all about that preaching boy who somebody strangled.'

'Yes, Mr Trapnell, somebody strangled that boy, that preaching boy as you called him. And I am beginning to wonder if he was strangled because he was a preacher. Because somebody violently resented being told by him what they ought to do, how they ought to behave.'

'Dunno what you mean.'

'Oh, but I think you do. I think, though you've tried to hide it even from yourself, that thirty years ago the Boy had words for you that you did not want to hear. Did he tell you that you were wrong to resent the surgery that had resulted in your wearing the first of your callipers. Did you not tell me you couldn't remember what you had felt about it when they said to you as a child that you would have to wear it all your life long? I think you have remembered that moment many, many times since then.'

'Think what you like. And get out.'

'No, Mr Trapnell, I will not get out. I told you before, I don't take that sort of retort for an answer. And I said that I would come back for better answers if I had any reason to believe I was owed them.'

'Well, you ain't got any reason. The police back then didn't have no reason to think I'd killed that Boy, and you can't have thirty years on.'

'But I can, Mr Trapnell.'

Any glint of fear there, of secret knowledge? In the darkness of this shabby hole it was impossible to make out.

She waited. At her elbow on the counter now she became aware of the slow soft ticking coming from an old slate-encased clock, hitherto hardly to be seen in the gloom beyond the bench light.

Then Barney Trapnell broke the silence.

'Don't you try to trick me. Bloody police, all the same.'

'No, I'm not trying to trick you. I mentioned to you before, there have been extraordinary advances made in DNA analysis in the last few years. And I was down at the Forensic Science laboratory in Lincolnshire yesterday when I learnt that, on a certain collarless shirt, there were traces of spittle that might have come from Krishna Kumaramangalam's mouth as someone throttled him to death.'

Curse this gloom. Stuck behind the counter here, I can't really see his face. Should I have got him into the nearest police station? Under the cold scrutiny of neon tubes?

'I don't know nothing about your collarless shirts.'

'No? What kind of a shirt did you used to wear thirty years ago?'

'What sort of a question's that? I don't know what I used to wear ten years ago, five. How should I know what I wore thirty years ago?'

'Then I'll tell you, Mr Trapnell. Thirty years ago the shirt you were wearing on the evening you marched up and down in the foyer of the Imperial's ballroom, waiting while the Boy Preacher meditated inside, was a thick cotton one with a thin red stripe in the material and no attached collar. And how do I know that? Because Detective Chief Inspector Kenworthy had that shirt taken off you and placed in an evidence bag in case there were any signs on it that you had been inside the ballroom. At the time there was little chance of finding anything. Methods of analysis were still fairly crude. But now the tiniest drop of spit from that boy's mouth, if it got anywhere on to your shirt, could tell us with all the certainty of science that you were there leaning down over the Boy. And that shirt, in its sealed evidence bag, has been kept all this time by Greater Birchester Police.'

And still no sign that the shot had gone home.

'Well? Well? What have you got to say now?'

Almost crouching there in front of his bench in the darkened shop, with the light of the lamp all but obscuring his hulking shape, Barney Trapnell simply let out a sound between taut-grinning teeth that was as much an animal growl as anything.

'I asked you, Mr Trapnell, what do you have to say about that shirt you were wearing that evening in 1969? That shirt which has been subjected to analysis at the Forensic Science laboratory?'

'Nothing. I got nothing to say about that, and I got nothing to say about that preacher boy or about who killed him. Nothing, nothing, nothing.'

Harriet stood peering at him in the gloom. The clock at her side seemed to tick more loudly.

Hammer at him again? Or take him at this moment under arrest to the nearest police station?

But I don't have enough grounds really for charging

him with murder, any more than I might have for any of the others still living, thirty years after the Boy Preacher was strangled. And all that my hammering has done so far is to reinforce that steel cuirass he has wrapped round and round himself over all these years.

So . . . So what?

So, one last threat of further questioning, hopefully deeply unsettling, and leave him to stew.

Back at the office Pip sighed at her news. 'And Barney Trapnell is simply claiming he's forgotten all about that evening?' he asked.

'Yes, that's just what he's doing. And, since I've been mulling over it, I'm not so sure that what he said may not be the simple truth, cussed though he was in coming out with it. After all, when last Monday I rather cautiously asked Lucas Calverte for his views on the people with him at the Imperial, his reaction was much the same. He said he could hardly remember a thing about that evening.'

'You believed him then, didn't you, ma'am?'

'I suppose I did. Even though I had a feeling there was something – I don't know – odd about him. If I were a romantic, like that splendid author Michael Meadowcraft, I'd have said he had a dark secret to hide.'

Pip did now produce one of his I'm-taking-a-risk blushes. Harriet thought she could see it extending right down beneath the curly white hairs of that triangular beard.

'Well, you know, ma'am,' he said, 'experiencing

some tremendous emotional shock, such as I imagine being in the ballroom foyer that night must have been, can drive the whole surrounding circumstances right out of one's mind.'

Harriet was about to jump on that as a piece of pop psychology. But then she realized, just in time, that the little detective must be thinking of his own state of mind when he had heard that the wife-murderer in whose favour he had given biassed evidence had gone on to kill his own two children.

'Yes, you could be right,' she said, and then thought of Barney Trapnell as he had been an hour or so earlier. 'You could be right, if the person who truly forgets a terrible experience is basically a sensitive individual. But I doubt if Trapnell comes into that category, not from what I've seen of him. And, come to that, I don't think my Mr Calverte is all that sensitive. You should have heard him sermonizing away about the youth of Birchester today.'

'So you think, ma'am, Calverte might be worth tackling, as it were, with the gloves off?'

Harriet weighed this up for a moment.

'I don't see why not,' she said. 'After all, there's nothing left for me to do but interview each of the people outside the ballroom that evening, little hope though there is of getting anything out of any of them. But I think I'll go now and see, why not, that dubious lady Bubsy Willson.'

'Well, ma'am, you're right, of course, about interviewing them all. But I— Well, I think perhaps you should leave Mrs Brownlow, that's Bubsy Willson's name now, to the last. I gathered from my inquiries that she's not at all well at the moment. I don't know whether she's just got that so-called summer flu, or whether it's something worse. And she must be pretty elderly now, too.'

For a moment Harriet wondered if she should show that much consideration for any of the four remaining suspects. But there seemed to be no good reason to see any one of them before any other.

'Right,' she said, 'I'll go and visit Mr Calverte again.'

'Do you want me to come with you?' Pip asked, almost shivering with excitement.

'No. No, I don't think so.'

She saw the jaw-dropping look of disappointment on the little man's face.

Hell with him, she thought. If I take him with me to Calverte's his nerviness is more than likely to irritate the man. All that stopping and starting, blushing and wriggling, will only serve to annoy an ex-Indian Army stiff-upper-lip type. And I need to have him concentrate on what I'm saying.

But then she thought it worthwhile to do what she could to bolster Pip's fragile self-confidence.

'If I can't physically transport myself back to the time the Boy was murdered,' she said by way of a sop, 'the next best thing is to talk to a man who was there on the case at the time. So what I want you to do, still, is to find DCI Kenworthy's Sergeant Shaddock, if he's yet in the land of the living. We're going to need every scrap of information we can possibly dig up. And Shaddock may turn out to be – you never know – our way to the answer.'

*

This time Harriet, when she drove up to Lucas Cal-verte's cottage, Travellers, did not find the former Undersheriff in his garden, tearing out intrusive clumps of grass. When she knocked at the sturdy oak door, the old gasbag, as she thought of him, opened it himself and ushered her inside.

'Well now, Miss Martens, what can I do for you?'

'I'm afraid I have to tell you that our investigation has met with something of a setback,' she said. 'I think I told you, when we met, that we were hoping the newest methods of DNA analysis would provide us with evidence with which we could proceed, even after thirty years.'

No sign of any reaction. No hint of relief.

Does that mean he never had anything to fear from what new DNA techniques might reveal? Or is he simply a man who by long training, even from childhood days, has learnt to stay tight-lipped in all circumstances?

We'll see.

'But, no, sir, unfortunately the Forensic Science people were unable to find significant traces of Krishna Kumaramangalam's saliva on any of the garments that, you will remember, were taken from you all under Detective Chief Inspector Kenworthy's instructions.'

The old gasbag gave a faintly puzzled frown.

'Yes,' he said. 'Yes, I do seem to remember that happening. Or I think I do. I told you before that I find I really have almost no recollection of that evening. Do you mean to tell me that the police have retained some garment, or garments, of mine all this time?'

A feeble little laugh.

'I suppose I should claim them back now whatever they were.'

'There was a waistcoat, sir, a dark grey waistcoat, a white shirt and a tie, a club tie of some sort.'

'Indeed? Well, I don't suppose that the suit the waistcoat went with is still in existence, and I wouldn't have much use for the shirt now, or for the tie. Whatever club it came from I'm bound to have resigned from it now I so seldom go anywhere. So, no, Miss Martens, Greater Birchester Police may do what they like with them all.'

A chuckle.

Rather a put-on chuckle, Harriet thought. Can he still be uneasy?

'But I mustn't keep you standing here. Come in, come in. Come to my study. I could offer you a cup of coffee. But, to tell the truth, my daily lady isn't here, and my own attempts to make coffee are by no means invariably successful.'

Again some chuckling.

And again Harriet asked herself, is the old boy uneasy? Why should he be this uncomfortable in the presence of a police officer, especially one investigating a case he claims he can no longer remember?

She followed him into the room. It was, she saw, all one might expect of the study of a former Undersheriff living in an ancient cottage that, from its name, had probably once been a travellers' inn. Oak beams, gnarled with age, ran across the low ceiling. Diamond-paned windows looked out at the well-kept garden. In the fireplace the ashes of the last fire that had burnt there were still heaped. There was a settee and an armchair, covered in cretonne in a pattern of cottagey flowers, both sagging with age. A sturdy oak table served as a desk, the leather-cornered blotter with its white paper unsmirched.

'What a nice room,' she said, dutifully.

'Well, yes. Yes, it is. My late wife, you know ...'

'And you've lived here a long time? All your life even?'

A little gentle probing may be worthwhile. I still feel there's something not quite right about him.

He gave her a hesitant smile.

'Well, no. Not my whole life. Not quite. But we'd been here a good time before my wife left me.'

And it was plain in every syllable that she had left not for the milkman but for a better place.

Probing checked, whether consciously or unconsciously.

'So, sir,' Harriet was constrained to say, 'I would like, if I may, to try and bring back to you the circumstances of that terrible evening of May the twenty-second, 1969. I know you have put it all out of your head, very understandably. But, you see, the only chance now of clearing up the whole business is for me to reconstruct as exactly as possible what happened during those two hours while the seven of you were waiting outside the ballroom at the Imperial. Someone must have quietly entered, strangled the Boy – two minutes would very possibly have been long enough – and then quietly come out again. Or perhaps, and this may be more likely, have come out shouting that they had discovered the Boy's body.'

'Well, if that's what happened, I've no doubt you've got on to it, Superintendent. But, no. No, I cannot confirm, or indeed correct, any of it. I have simply no idea who told us the Boy had been killed.'

'You can't remember if someone said later, or implied even, that they had found the body?'

A pause for thought, brow creased.

'No. No, Superintendent. I have absolutely no recollection of that.'

'Right. So may I go back further and ask you this? Perhaps it will start up a train of thought that will lead us on. Do you remember arriving at the hotel? It was, of course, in the evening or late afternoon of the day after the meeting was originally going to take place. Do you at all remember that?'

Lucas Calverte stood there looking down at the soft grey ashes in the fireplace, once again in obvious cogitation.

Too obvious? The old gasbag could be someone acting in a play, rather badly. He really could. But then a good part of his life, certainly in his Undersheriff days, must have been spent play-acting. After all, what else does an Undersheriff do but play a part in an outdated charade?

Then, still with that touch of theatricality, the ex-Undersheriff rose up from his reverie.

'Superintendent,' he said, 'I must tell you that I have no remembrance whatsoever of arriving at the Imperial that night. I have, of course, vague recollections of what arriving there was like. You know they're knocking the old place down now? I saw the hoarding all round it just yesterday. Of course, I had occasion to go there time and again in the old days. Various occasions, you know, various occasions. But that particular evening, terrible as it became, I cannot remember at all.'

Harriet had left him then realizing that, whether of set purpose or not, Lucas Calverte was not going to tell her any more about what had happened there in the Imperial Hotel on that May evening thirty years before.

Back at Headquarters she found, to her surprise, a transformed DC Steadman.

'I've found him, ma'am. I've found him.'

His excitement positively bubbled up.

For a moment Harriet was tempted to say chillingly *Found who?* But she told herself that Pip's fragility ought not to be played with.

'So,' she said, 'ex-DS Shaddock, within our sights at last.'

'Yes, ma'am, yes. It was all so simple in the end. I got on to the police pensions people, and they told me they were still sending cheques for him to an address in Gloucester. A hotel there.'

'And you didn't ask the pensions people before? You should have done, you know.'

Slack work could not be allowed to go uncriticized, even if the one responsible was in a precariously nervous state.

'Yes. Yes. Well, I'm sorry, ma'am. I— Of course I

should have thought of that first of all. But— But I didn't. Sorry.'

Ah, we're improving. A little criticism accepted.

'Right. We'll go and see DS Shaddock. And let's hope he remembers rather more about the case than Undersheriff Lucas Calverte.'

Chapter Eighteen

'You— You didn't get any more out of Lucas Calverte than before, then, ma'am?' Pip asked once they had settled themselves in the car on their way to Gloucester.

'Even less, if that was possible. And yet, you know, I still got the impression that there's something not right about that man. He was play-acting a lot of the time, I'm sure of it. Going into a big deep-thinking act when I asked if he remembered this or that. It was plain enough to me.'

'So . . . So, you've got him in your sights for it?'

'Hardly that. But I'll enter my thoughts in my Policy File, definitely.'

'And— And, well, ma'am, will you also be noting that it's possible that Mr Calverte is simply in denial of an event that made a terrible impression on him at the time? After all, the Boy Preacher seems to have been a sort of pet of his.'

Harriet sighed.

'Yes, DC. I will include that notion in my Policy File, and give you credit for suggesting it to me. But what I won't do is use that piece of half-baked psychiatric jargon *in denial*.'

Oh God, she thought at once, will that criticism send him into another stream of babbled apologies?

It did not, though for nearly all the rest of the trip he was suspiciously silent.

By stopping at the main Gloucester police station, under the shadow of the city's ancient prison in the street called Bearland, they were able to find without difficulty the Laurels, a private hotel on the far outskirts of the city looking across to the tall tower of the cathedral glowing golden in the late sunshine.

The hotel, by contrast, was by no means a pleasing sight. A gaunt weather-worn building with two gables in patently mock 'oak' beams, its broken-tiled path led up to cement-repaired stone steps and a dulled red-painted front door. The only thing that validated the name *The Laurels Hotel* on the faded board running across its front – *hotel* seemed a grave misnomer – were the bushes that crowded the small front garden. Dusty and drooping, despite this being the full flush of spring, they were at least laurels.

'Right,' Harriet said, pushing open the iron gate, once also painted red, now rust-pocked. 'Let's see if former Detective Sergeant Shaddock can transport us back to the days when he was DCI Kenworthy's bagman.'

Pip, carrying with care the tissue-wrapped bottle of whisky they had stopped off to buy in the city's Eastgate shopping centre, offered no comment.

Harriet pushed hard at the grudging button of the doorbell.

No response.

But on the door itself there was an iron knocker, again with signs of once having been painted red. She seized it, hauled it back and then thumped. Once, twice, half a dozen times.

At last the door was pulled open. A big blowsy woman in apron and slippers stood there.

'Yes?'

'We've come to see ex-Detective Sergeant Shaddock.'

'Oh, you have, have you? Well, you can see him, I suppose, though whether you get a word out of him's another matter. But he's there in his room. Hardly out of it. First floor, on the right. Number three.'

Harriet pushed past and tramped up the thinly-carpeted stairs, wrinkling her nose at the odour of stale food seeping up from some basement kitchen. At the top she turned and waited for Pip.

'Jesus,' she said, 'I hope when our time comes to be thrown on the dust-heap neither of us lands up in a place like this.'

Pip now produced his quick little smile.

'I hardly think that'll happen to you, ma'am, though I wouldn't like to be as optimistic about myself.'

'Oh, no. I see a good career ahead for you, Pip. And there'll be a nice soft job in Security at the end of it.'

Pip's head dipped until Harriet could not see whether another smile had divided white moustache from white beard.

'All right. Room three. And there it is.'

She stepped across and gave the door a brisk tapping.

'All ri', come in, damn you.'

She gave Pip a glance, mouth down-turned. And thrust the door open.

The man who must be ex-Detective Sergeant Shaddock was lying sprawled on the unmade bed, one flabby hand above his head grasping a bar of the black-painted headrail. He wore only a shirt, open almost to the navel to show a slobby mound of belly, and a pair of baggy blue serge trousers wide open at the waistband. His large slack-cheeked face was covered with enough white stubble to make it a toss-up whether he had been growing a beard or not shaving.

And the whole room smelt so strongly of whisky, and of something else which Harriet could not immediately identify, that the odour of stale food outside was utterly banished.

Harriet thought she could at least try to get something out of the fellow.

'Mr Shaddock,' she said sharply. 'I'm Detective Superintendent Martens from your old force.'

She had seen herself, after reciting some such words as these, introducing Pip and getting him to offer the gift of whisky. But now, instead, with a quick jerk of her head, she sent Pip and the tissue-wrapped bottle back out on to the landing. There had been altogether too much whisky – she glimpsed an empty bottle that had rolled halfway under the bed – in the room already.

'Mr Shaddock, I have been tasked by the Chief Constable with re-opening the investigation which you conducted under DCI Kenworthy into the murder of Krishna Kumaramangalam, known as the Boy Preacher.'

She waited to see whether the news that the inquiry was alive again would cause the flaccid body on the bed to stir.

It did not.

'Mr Shaddock, let me ask, do you at all remember that case from thirty years ago?'

'Preacher.'

It was an acknowledgment of a sort.

She ploughed on.

'Mr Kenworthy, as I dare say you know, has been dead for some years, and, though I have his excellent record of the investigation, with I may say some very useful suggestions from yourself . . .'

She paused to see if that blatant flattery might produce the response she had so far not succeded in arousing.

It failed to.

'Mr Shaddock, you can see, as the sole officer remaining from those days, that you may have memories which would be extremely useful to us. I may tell you, frankly, that the latest DNA tests, on which the Chief placed his hopes, have produced no evidence we can rely on. So—'

'DNA.'

That and no more.

'Yes, Mr Shaddock, the extensive DNA tests made at the Forensic Science laboratory eventually all came to nothing. So it's back to old-fashioned policing.'

Again she waited, this new piece of flattery dangling thinly from her line.

'No good, DNA, lotter nonsense.'

'Yes, a good many people share your view. And that really does make it all the more important for me to hear what you can recall of the investigation back in the old days.'

And now the bulk on the bed did stir.

Is this . . .? Have I managed . . .?

But all that happened was that the hand that was not grasping the rail above his head moved fretfully to and fro among the tangled yellowish sheets.

'Can I help you?' Harriet asked. 'Is there something you're looking for?'

Could it be a diary? A diary dating back thirty years? No, not in the bed here.

'Sugar alm—'

What's he saying?

Wait. Yes, the other smell I noticed when I came in here besides that reek of whisky. It was the sweet perfumed smell of sugared almonds. I'm sure of it. It must have been. Sugared almonds. I haven't set eyes on them, surely, almost since the days of the Boy Preacher.

Now suddenly the flabby hand groping over the surface of the bed rose up. In it there was grasped a little crumpled white paper bag. Two fat fingers plunged inside, moved about. And a groan. What might have been a heart-rending groan.

'Bloody gone, bloody empty. Could of sworn . . .'

A tear slid out of the rheumy left eye in the big bloated face.

*

Harriet had left him then. She had had an idea.

'Pip,' she said when she found him standing at the top of the stairs. 'Where would you go to buy sugared almonds?'

'Gosh, I haven't seen a sugared almond for years.'

'Neither have I. But I need one, I need a whole bagful. Now.'

Pip stood thinking.

'Well, I suppose an old-fashioned sweet shop. If there are any like that any more.'

'Right. There must be. Whisky-sodden old Shaddock in there had a bag of them. He must have got it from somewhere.'

'But does he even go out?'

'I suppose he must sometimes. But, I tell you what, we'll ask that awful woman who opened the door for us.'

'I heard that.' The voice came floating up from the foot of the stairs. Floating, or roaring. 'And whatever you want to ask, you can forget about it. I'm not going to tell you nothing.'

So they were reduced to patrolling the nearby streets in the car. It took them nearly an hour, and all that they found was a small general store. Closed.

'Down in the town,' Harriet said. 'I think there's a little souvenirish street somewhere. Forget what it's called. But I was there once, when my twins were seven or eight. Looking for the supposed shop of the Tailor of Gloucester. It might . . .'

'Oh, yes, I used to love that little book when I was a kid. Beatrix Potter. Takes me back.'

'No, you take me back, fast as you like to the town centre.'

They found the little alley. They spotted the Tailor of Gloucester place. And then Pip pointed out a sweet shop.

A man in a brown shop-coat was just putting the shutters across its window. But he happily left them where they were, went inside and emerged, less than a couple of minutes later, with a large bag – 'As many as you've got,' Harriet had shouted – of pink and white, sweet-smelling, sugar-coated almonds.

When they got back to the Laurels Hotel and hammered once more with the knocker on its faded red-painted door, they turned out to be in luck. The door was opened, not by the blowsy creature Harriet had unwittingly insulted, but by a morose-looking man wearing a napless green baize apron.

'Thank you,' Harriet said. 'We've come to see Mr Shaddock. We know where his room is.'

They were watched, with suspicion, as they climbed the stairs once again. The smell of greasy cooking was as strong as ever. Though more fishy than oniony, Harriet thought.

Once again she tapped on the door of room three. And it seemed that Shaddock's short spell with neither whisky nor sugared almonds had benefited him. His voice now was noticeably less fuzzy.

'Who's that? If it's the rent money, you can sing for it. You'll get it when I've got it.'

Harriet interpreted this as *Come in*.

She saw the former detective sergeant was slumped now in the room's single battered-about armchair. He was looking much as he had a couple of hours earlier, though he had managed to hook together the two sides of his trousers and to get most of the buttons of his shirt through the buttonholes, if not always the right ones.

'Good evening, Mr Shaddock,' she said. 'It's Superintendent Martens back again. And this is DC Steadman. We've brought you a little present.'

Shaddock had been blinking at her throughout the introduction, and she had begun to wonder if he had any recollection of seeing her earlier. But when Pip stepped forward holding open the big bag of sugared almonds he sat forward at once, eyes glowing with greed.

Harriet decided she would let him have just one of the softly glossy sweets before she began asking about the Boy Preacher. But his podgy, trembling fingers had succeeded in getting the bag out of Pip's grasp altogether. Dipping in it, he had extracted three of them and in instant he had shoved them all into his mouth.

So she waited, checking her impatience, until she heard from inside that slack cavity the crunching of one of the thin sugar shells.

'Mr Shaddock,' she said then, firmly as a schoolmistress, 'you will remember that I wanted to talk to you about the Boy Preacher murder, which you investigated thirty years ago under DCI Kenworthy. I told you earlier that, owing to the failure of DNA testing, we are having to go back to Mr Kenworthy's inquiry itself if we are to have any hope of getting a result.'

Shaddock, his mouth full and teeth still crunching, was unable to answer in words. But she saw in his eyes an acknowledgment that he had taken in what she had said.

'Very well. So, first, tell me if you have any recollections of working on the case.'

'Yer.'

And a small cascade of pink and white sugar chips.

'Good. Then it's worth asking you, first of all, whether Mr Kenworthy confided in you anything he couldn't put on to paper due to lack of evidence. Did he tell you perhaps that he had an idea which one of the seven possible suspects was the killer?'

'Nah.'

'Very well, if he did not, he did not. But you yourself, at the time did you have some idea who the murderer was?'

'Idea? You don't want to go on ideas. That what they do nowadays? Wrong way. Stupid way to go about it.'

Still chewing hard and noisily, he managed to add, 'Old Kenners could of told you what you ought to do.'

'Kenners? DCI Kenworthy? What could he have told me?'

'One who found the body. Old rule.'

Harriet suppressed her fury. How dare this worn-out idiot preach to her about the way a murder investigation should be conducted.

'Yes, DS,' she answered. 'I'm well aware that the person who reports the finding of a body does automatically become the first suspect in any investigation.

My trouble is that, after all the time that's elapsed, no one I've questioned has been at all clear about who did find the body.'

A glint of malice in the bloodshot eyes looking up at her. And fat red fingers fumbling at the bag on his lap.

Harriet sighed.

But I mustn't call it all off. I can't have come all this way for nothing.

She began again.

'Mr Shaddock, do you remember Barbara Willson?'

She got a better response, just.

'Bubsy. Bubsy, that's what she was called. The whore. Bloody lucky not to have had a swarm of little bastards at her tail, ask me.'

'Yes, Bubsy Willson. One account of what happened in that ballroom foyer indicated that Bubsy, whether or not she was the one who found the Boy's body, had at least yelled out that he was dead.'

Two more sugared almonds, one white, one pink, transferred one after the other into the gaping, black-toothed mouth.

Harriet wondered for an instant if she should jump in, snatch the bag away and make its return dependent on getting better answers. But, as quickly, she decided that the risk of making the unco-operative old man even less helpful was not worth taking.

'Yes,' she went on, 'Bubsy may or may not have been the person who found the Boy's body. But if she didn't, I've no idea who did, any more than Mr Kenworthy said he had thirty years ago. His report concluded that the events in the foyer were so confused there was no hope of getting firm evidence that any one of the possible suspects had entered the ballroom. But did you have an idea, Mr Shaddock? An idea you either failed to put forward to Mr Kenworthy, or that, if you did, he decided was not worth recording?'

Shaddock, lolling back in his grotty old chair, barely grunted.

'Mr Shaddock, I asked you a question.'

He sat up a little more straightly.

'No,' he said. 'No, I suppose I didn't never have an idea about that. You should have heard those people there, each of 'em as bad as the other. There was that little schoolteacher, snooty nose. Wasn't going to give me the time of day, and not much better with old Kenners. Then, if you're on the snooty line, what about that Undersheriff. Undersheriff? Believed everyone was under him, far under. And that bloody reporter. From *The Times*, wasn't he? Gave you answers all right, but he took bloody good care they meant fuck all. And that cripple they had there. Couldn't give you an answer if you shook him. Little Indian was no better either. He'd answer you all right. On and on he'd go, and at the end you didn't know nothing more than when he'd begun. And as for the whore, well, no use listening to anything a whore tells you, right? And the same goes for that market trader, what's-his-name. Bigod? Well, by God, there's another who'll never come to no good.'

For a moment Harriet thought of telling the unpleasant old man in front of her that Sydney Aslough was now a prosperous car-showroom owner in Norwich. But, no, game not worth the candle.

And, damn it, she said to herself, I don't think the game of coming lickety-split down to Gloucester has been worth its candle either. Yes, nasty old ex-DS Shaddock does remember the case. But it's pretty evident, from what he's just been saying about those seven, that he never gave it much attention at the time. A typical just-get-by detective. On the point of reaching his *thirty*, that looked-forward-to day when enough years of service have been accumulated to attract the full pension.

So – what's it my father used to say? – it's *Home, James, and don't spare the horses.*

Chapter Nineteen

It was not until the next day that Harriet, after her fruitless trip to see former Detective Sergeant Shaddock, was able to advance her inquiries. Only two of the seven people who had been in the foyer of the Imperial Hotel ballroom remained to be seen: Bubsy Willson and Priscilla Knott. Pip Steadman had said that Bubsy, now Mrs Brownlow, was possibly too ill to be interviewed. So she told him they would visit head teacher Priscilla Knott, waiting until the lunch break at St Peter's Primary School.

They arrived shortly after midday, to be confronted by chaos in the sunshine. The playground on the far side of the tall black-painted gate was a mass of screaming, running, leaping, cavorting small children.

Pip, at the sight, plunged his hand into a pocket, drew out a squashed pack of cigarettes, stuck one in his mouth and lit up.

'Come on,' Harriet snapped. 'What's there to be afraid of? Even though you're not married and not a father, you must have had dealings with noisy kids when you were on the beat.'

'But— But— But, well, ma'am, in those days I could

handle them. I managed very well, actually. But—
Well, now . . .'

'Now you're accompanying me to see Priscilla
Knott, head teacher, Mrs Joseph Johnson until she
reverted to her maiden name. And, let me remind you,
she was the only one of those seven people asked
to surrender their top garments thirty years ago who
demanded to have hers back, that mimsy pale-pink
blouse.'

Perhaps being reminded that the woman they had
come to see had once possessed a mimsy blouse made
Pip pluck up his courage. He stepped forward now and
rang at the bell in the pillar beside the locked security
gates.

They did not have long to wait for a response.

A large, markedly upright woman broke off from
talking to another teacher and looked with suspicion
over to the gate. Sternly grey-haired, dressed in a
severe grey skirt and, billowing forth, a pink-striped
shirt that could not by any stretch be called mimsy,
she advanced towards them.

'Our woman, I'll bet a shilling,' Harriet said, finding
herself reverting to the language of the pre-decimal
days in which her investigation was rooted.

Miss Knott, if it was her, pressed a little silver-
coloured device she had taken from where it had been
clipped to her narrow leather belt. The gates swung
open.

Harriet stepped inside with Pip at her heels.

'Put out that cigarette.'

It was more than a command. It was a one-phrase
sermon on the evils of tobacco.

Pip dropped the cigarette as if it had been a fork-tongued snake and trod it firmly to extinction.

'And kindly pick that thing up. I will not have my playground contaminated in that way. There are children here. You have set them an appalling example.'

Blushing like a child beneath his neat white beard, Pip obeyed.

Harriet stepped forward to screen him from further wrath.

'Miss Knott?' she inquired, holding up her warrant card. 'Miss Priscilla Knott? I am Detective Superintendent Martens and this is Detective Constable Steadman. May we—'

'A detective superintendent?'

Miss Knott gave them both a glare.

'Let me say at once then that I expect a better standard of behaviour from members of the police.'

She gave poor Pip another look of cold disapproval.

'Miss Knott,' Harriet said, with some force. 'I am here making inquiries in connection with the murder, some thirty years ago, of one Krishna Kumaramangalam, known as the Boy Preacher. May we see you somewhere in private?'

'Some thirty years ago? I think, as a detective police officer, you should achieve a somewhat higher standard of accuracy. That event occurred in 1969, on May the twenty-second.'

Ah ha, Harriet thought, brushing aside the reproof she had received. Someone who's going to remember what happened that night. At last.

'Yes, you are perfectly right,' she said. 'May the

twenty-second. I am glad to find your memory is as fresh.'

'And why should it not be? But I cannot allow this discussion to take place out here. Little pitchers, you know, have sharp ears. Something I have more than once had to remind my staff about. Some of them make little effort to control their language.'

Following this dragon into the school building, Harriet reflected that, for once, Michael Meadowcraft had got it more or less right. As he had written in 1969, Miss Knott certainly appeared to be someone who was prepared to do whatever she felt necessary to keep what she saw as the evils around her 'under proper control'. She had been such at the time of the murder. She was such today.

'Zoe,' came the stern voice, 'we do not pull up our skirt like that, even if we have grazed our knee.'

The poor little seven-year-old with the blood-red patch on her knee abruptly ceased her snivelling.

Miss Knott moved on, a cruise liner among rowing boats.

'Nathan. I will not have fighting. Come and see me after school.'

Pip, Harriet saw as they entered the head teacher's study, looked as apprehensive as the boy called Nathan had moments before. And even into her own mind there had come a long-buried memory of the matron at her first school who had had an obsession about not allowing the cuticles at the base of the girls' fingernails to be apparent. She felt a twinge now as she recalled having her own rigorously pushed back out of sight.

Other days, other creeds.

In the study they were instructed, rather than asked, to sit. Harriet took one of the two chairs facing the immaculately tidy desk, noting with approval that Pip had slid on to a child-size chair in the corner, almost behind Miss Knott. There he had discreetly perched his notebook on one knee.

Opposite Harriet, Miss Knott spread her hands flat on the desk.

For an instant Harriet recalled Mr Newbroom sitting at his desk in his Headquarters suite when he had tasked her with the inquiry. The fingers of his hands, too, had pointed at her like so many attacking aircraft.

Seizing the initiative, however, she spoke out.

'Miss Knott, can you tell me why it was that, unlike the rest of the people who were requested to surrender their upper garments after the murder, you asked to have back the blouse you had been wearing?'

For a long moment Priscilla Knott was silent.

'Superintendent,' she said at last, 'all that was a very long time ago.'

'Yes, as you reminded me, it was on May the twenty-second, 1969.'

Again, a silence.

But now Harriet ended it.

'Miss Knott, I am sure that, however long ago that murder took place, you can remember all the circumstances connected with something that must have deeply affected you. So could you, please, tell me why you requested to have your blouse returned? Let me remind you, it was a pale-pink cotton blouse with scallopped edging.'

'I remember it perfectly well, thank you.'

'So, why then?'

Opposite, Priscilla Knott drew in a breath deep enough to swell yet more her full bosom.

'The blouse was mine. It was a favourite. I saw no reason not to have it back.'

'Very well. It wasn't then because you feared some traces from Krishna Kumaramangalam might still be on it, despite any forensic examination it may have undergone?'

'Superintendent, that is an outrageous suggestion. I deny it absolutely. And, let me say, I have a good mind to report it to your superior officer.'

'Miss Knott, however offensive that suggestion may seem to you, it was one it was my duty to ask. I am conducting a murder investigation.'

'Then, let me tell you, you are hardly conducting it in the way I would have thought it should be carried out. You told me you were glad to find my memory of that dreadful night was still fresh. Yet you have failed altogether to ask what I do recall.'

Harriet suppressed an urge to shoot back some sharp comments on how a school should be run. With some sympathy for the children.

'Very well,' she replied, conscious that she had been reduced to taking the one piece of advice that slobbery DS Shaddock had given her. 'Perhaps you could tell me who it was who emerged from the ballroom at the Imperial Hotel and announced that the Boy Preacher had been strangled.'

No answer came back at once.

'Well? You were there, Miss Knott, who did you see?'

'I— I am afraid I cannot give you an answer that would be absolutely correct. Any more than I succeeded in answering that question when that man Inspector Kenworthy put it to me.'

Harriet refrained from restoring to DCI Kenworthy his proper rank.

'And why was that?' she said sharply.

Miss Knott gave a little exasperated snort.

'For the very simple reason, Superintendent, that I happened not to be near any of the doors leading from the ballroom at the moment someone shouted out that the Boy was dead. However, from the way that word was, I might say, yelled, I assumed it was the woman, Barbara Willson. But I would not be prepared, as I was constrained to say in answer to Kenworthy, to give evidence to that effect in a court of law.'

'I must accept that,' Harriet said, irritated once again by this disrespect for solid DCI Kenworthy. 'But, you did tell me in the playground that your memories of the evening are still fresh, so can you explain exactly where you were when you heard that – what did you call it? – that yell?'

Miss Knott's hands, still pointing towards Harriet on the far side of the desk, contracted into loosely held fists.

'You are asking a good deal, Superintendent. You expect me to say exactly where I happened to be at one particular moment during a stay of a full two hours in that large foyer?'

'Yes, but I am not asking about a moment that

was indistinguishable from all the others during those hours. I am asking about the moment you heard someone shout out that the Boy Preacher was dead. You have just told me you were not near any of the three sets of doors into the ballroom. So where were you?'

'I— I was— As a matter of fact, I was just leaving the Ladies.'

'I see. And from near the door there – I saw it for myself just the other day – could you, or could you not, see the exits from the ballroom?'

Miss Knott straightened her already straight back.

'Very well, Superintendent. I could see the set of doors which were nearest the entrance to the foyer. I suppose, had I turned my head far enough, I could have seen the set at the other end. But what I could not see, because there was a large clump of pampas grass in the middle of the round bench at the centre of the foyer, was the middle set of doors.'

'Good. What you have said does establish for me that it was from the central doors that the person who found the Boy's body emerged. My congratulations. No one else that I have questioned was able to do that.'

Miss Knott's loosely held fists slowly lost the last of their aggression.

'As I said, Superintendent, my memory of that appalling night is crystal clear, as everyone else's should be.'

'Should be, but, perhaps naturally, is not. Time blurs the edges, and indeed with some of those I have spoken to it had the effect of blotting out all recollection of those hours.'

Miss Knott gave a snort of derision.

And Harriet, though she had not meant to put her next question as bluntly, leant sharply forward.

'And did you, Miss Knott, enter the ballroom yourself at any time that evening?'

'Certainly not.'

Pistol shot for pistol shot.

'And did you see anyone else enter?'

Miss Knott glared back again with defiance.

'Had I done so, Superintendent, I would have told that man, Kenworthy, thirty years ago. And then he might not have let this matter remain a mystery for so long.'

A picture of walls, stubborn wall after stubborn wall, came into Harriet's head. But had there, she asked herself, been a tiny chink somewhere in one of them? If there was, she thought, I'm damned if I can see it now. Perhaps Pip, sitting quietly with his notebook on that ridiculous little chair there, will have done better. But for now I think I've got as far as I can get.

Right, one last question. See if I can get a hint of whatever motive this terror of a woman might have had.

But how to get to it? Ah, yes. Yes, this may be it.

'So can you tell me, Miss Knott, what was your exact standing thirty years ago in the circle that surrounded the Boy?'

Miss Knott's lips tightened into a hard line.

'My standing, as you choose to put it, was, I am happy to say, entirely of my own making. It so happened that the Boy Preacher had been invited to enter the pulpit at the church I normally attended. I cannot say I approved of allowing such a privilege to one who was not a member of the Anglican communion, but I nevertheless felt it my duty to go and hear him. And, I will admit, I found his message not unworthy.'

Harriet could not help intervening.

'But you must have been very young at the time. Surely scarcely into your twenties?'

'I do not see that my age should be an issue. I had my view of what was fitting then, as I have my view of what is fitting now.'

As that poor bloody-kneed child Zoe has just found out, Harriet registered.

'However,' Miss Knott steamed on, 'I also found, at that time, that the majority of the people in the Boy's circle were by no means fit to be there. The only one of them with something to be said for him was Mr Calverte. But, though he was a man of some distinction, he lacked the determination to put things right where they had gone wrong. Look at the way he allowed that disgraceful drunken man from *The Times* to infiltrate the Boy's circle. As for the rest of them in it, what was there? A street trader with the most vulgar manners. A wretched cripple watch mender with no other qualities than some muscular strength in his arms. Then the Boy's cousin, with some good intentions but none of the will to put them into effect. And finally that girl Barbara Willson, a creature of the very lowest sort.'

'So you decided you ought to take the Boy under your wing?' Harriet said, keeping back with some effort the words *despite being almost as young as the Boy himself*.

'He was worth it.'

A simple declaration.

Harriet was unexpectedly struck by it, coming, as it had, from someone who had regarded every member of the Boy's circle with all the uncompromising disparagement of a hellfire preacher. She found herself filled with a new determination to name the person who had deprived the world of a preacher the very opposite of hellfire.

'Well?' Harriet had demanded, almost before Pip had closed the car door and pulled the seat belt round himself.

'No. No, sorry, ma'am, I didn't hear any sort of giveaway, not once. Perhaps— Perhaps I shouldn't have been taking notes. I should have been just listening instead. But— But— I didn't hear anything at all that made me— Well, sit up and think.'

'If you didn't, you didn't. When I come to read your transcript I may find something you were too busy scribbling to respond to. Or I may not. In the meantime, have you got an address for the ex-husband – Johnson? Joseph Johnson?'

'Yes. Yes, ma'am. I have. I have. It's—'

'Just take me there, DC.'

Joe Johnson, who, Pip had told Harriet, now worked as a jobbing gardener, was eating lunch between visits to two of his regular customers. He was sitting in the dining room of the boarding house where he had settled after the break-up of his marriage. He was the only one of the lodgers, it appeared, who ate a midday meal there. So the bare room, lino under-foot, a skimpy cloth on the table, was at Harriet's disposal.

'I've just been talking to your former wife about the murder thirty years ago of the young man they called the Boy Preacher,' she said as soon as she had taken a chair on the other side of the table, with Pip beside her. 'I dare say you're aware of the case.'

'Aware of it,' Joe Johnson responded cheerfully. 'I heard about that business in some way or another on every single day of my marriage to that woman.'

'Did you? So you must have got a pretty clear idea of what happened during that long evening outside the ballroom at the Imperial Hotel?'

Joe Johnson laughed, waving his earth-smeared hands wide.

'Not at all, not at all. Do you think if time after time you'd been told about all that, and each time told exactly what everybody else involved ought to have done, you'd have remembered a single detail of it?'

Harriet experienced a slight descent of disappoint-ment, though it was nothing, she guessed, to the abrupt loss of hope Pip's face was expressing.

'You mean nothing?' she asked. 'Really nothing?'

'Honestly, yes. And, even if there was anything, in the past couple of years I've succeeded in putting out of my mind almost every single thing that woman ever said to me.'

'*That woman?* That's twice you've used those words. Surely that's a little harsh, if your divorce was as long as two years ago?'

'Two years, one month and twenty-eight days.'

'Right. And how long were you married?'

'One year, seven months, seventeen days.'

'So, if I ask you for an assessment of your former wife's character, I'm not going to get anything like a true picture?'

Joe Johnson, across on the other side of the table with an almost emptied plate of eggs and chips in front of him, pondered for a moment or two.

'No,' he said eventually. 'No, I think, if I restrain myself, I can give you a pretty fair assessment of Priscilla.'

'Then do.'

'All right.'

He stopped and thought for a moment.

'Well, how shall I put it? She means well. She always means well. That's the first thing. I really do believe she's a good woman.'

'A good woman?'

'Yes, absolutely. That was why I married her, in spite of my doubts.'

'Your doubts? Doubts that she really was, as you put it, a good woman? Did you ever feel she might have been capable of actions that were less than good?'

'Ah, I know what you're getting at. You're wondering if she could actually have been the one who strangled the Boy Preacher.'

'Right. I was.'

'Well, yes, after we were married I did sometimes think she would stop at nothing if she'd really taken it into her head that someone had done something unforgivably wrong. But—'

'No, wait. Answer me. Did you ever think that, for

some reason, she could have decided the Boy had done something unforgivable?'

Again Joe Johnson sat in front of the neglected last few thick, glistening chips and thought.

'No. No, I never did. As far as I can remember she always spoke of the Boy in glowing terms. In fact, towards the end of our marriage I had worked up quite a hatred of him, simply because she would keep praising him, glorifying him.'

'Understandable. But, tell me, now that it seems you're beginning to think about her a little more impartially, was there any one particular person outside the ballroom there whom she spoke of in such a way as to make you think she believed they had killed the Boy?'

A longer period of thought. A hand even, unthinkingly, stretching out towards the plate and fingering the longest of the congealing chips.

'No. No, there never was.'

'You're sure?'

'Sure? How can I be? I told you I've tried to put all that right out of my mind. I'm not too pleased, in fact, that you've come here and tried to push that woman back in, though I suppose that's your job. But why you can't let it be forgotten after all this time, I can't see.'

'Justice, Mr Johnson. Justice ought to be done.'

'Now you sound like that bloody preaching woman. I think you had better go.'

Harriet sat where she was. Was there more to learn? But, before she could tell Joe Johnson that, preaching or no preaching, she would come back if she needed to, her mobile twittered out.

'Excuse me.'

She put it to her ear.

'Martens. Yes?'

She listened intently, snapped the little machine off, stood up.

'I must go. Come along, DC.'

There was enough suppressed urgency in her words to make Pip leap to his feet and hurry out of the house after her.

Standing beside the car, she explained.

'That was a message from a detective from C Division. He's at the shop owned by Barney Trapnell. The shop that was owned by Barney Trapnell. He's dead. Left a note mentioning my name and hanged himself. Pip, get in the driving seat and take me there, just as fast as you can.'

Chapter Twenty

Barney Trapnell had hanged himself over the narrow stairs at the back of his dark little shop. In the cruel light of the high-intensity lamps rigged up by the Scene-of-crime team his body could be seen in full unlovely detail. His neck was drawn out by its weight in such a way that Harriet could not thrust from her mind the thought of a plucked chicken in the window of a butcher's shop. His head, the face engorged, the swollen tongue protruding, lolled above the rope biting into the neck like that of a discarded puppet. And, curiously more affecting than anything else, his feet were bare, just perceptibly swinging only a few inches from the highest stair tread.

He must have unburdened himself at last, Harriet thought, of the confining callipers he had had to wear all his life. She felt a stab of pity.

But did I do this?

She stood where she was in the shop doorway, still holding the warrant card she had flicked at the constable on guard outside. In her ears were the reverberations from the clanging doorbell which, when she had first heard it, had reminded her of jaunty bustling Mack, whose sausages were 'the best'. And she could not help but ask herself that question with new insistence.

Had Barney Trapnell hanged himself because, thirty years after the Boy Preacher had been murdered, he had felt persecuted by—

By the Hard Detective?

And – a new thought came rushing into her head – was this the end of the trail? Had whatever persecution the Hard Detective employed driven the murderer of the Boy Preacher to take his own life?

'Who's there?' she called up into the darkness beyond the dangling body.

'Is that you, Superintendent Martens?'

A man's shape appeared in the dazzling light behind the hanging body.

'DC Jones, ma'am. When I found his note with your name in it I thought I'd better let you know.'

'Quite right, DC. Have you got the note still?'

'Left it where it was, ma'am. Evidence. It's on the counter just next to the clock there. Hang on, I'll give you some more light.'

From behind the body, DC Jones manoeuvred one of the Scene-of-crime lamps until it shone more directly on to the shop's narrow dusty counter.

Harriet looked down.

Next to the old slate-cased clock, which she remembered had softly ticked away the last time she had been here and still ticked now, there was a torn scrap of bright green card. She guessed it was the back of some advertisement – takeaway pizzas? Cure-all medicines? – that had been hopefully thrust through the letter box.

On it there were just a few words written in blue

ballpoint. *That Martins super.* And then on the next line, the sole next line, *Cant stand it no longer.*

Somehow what struck Harriet as the most pathetic aspect of it was the contrast between the crudity of the words, with the mis-spellings and the missing apostrophe in *can't*, and the extreme neatness of the writing. But of course, she thought, this was written by a skilled and practised watch-mender's hand.

And then she asked herself again: did I drive this simple cripple to take his own life?

The bell just above her head clattered out.

Pip, who had been having a word with the constable securing the site, entered.

'Christ,' he gasped as he saw Trapnell's oscillating, stretched-neck body.

'Yes,' Harriet said, yielding to the internal pressure before she could stop herself. 'And what I've got to ask myself is, did the way I questioned him make him do that?'

'But— But—'

'Oh, don't bother fudging your way round it. Think what happened. I saw him on Wednesday. A not particularly rewarding interview. So I threatened to come back, if I found any new evidence to link him with the Boy's death. And this morning I did come back and I threatened him again. Then, just an hour later, perhaps not as long, perhaps a little longer, the poor bloody cripple unstraps his callipers and contrives to hang himself from some hook or other up there.'

Little Pip drew himself up, triangular beard jutting out.

'No, ma'am,' he said, more forcefully than Harriet

had ever heard him. 'No. You may have put pressure on him, but I'm very sure it was no more than it was your duty to do. Nor can it have been more than the sorts of pressures he was subjected to every day of his life. From my ex-colleagues in the advertising industry, from the media, from life in general. You tell me if I'm not right.'

Almost reluctantly, Harriet brought herself to say to him that, no, the pressure she had applied to Barney Trapnell, as a suspect, was no more than was proper. And perhaps, too, Pip was right in saying it had been no worse than the daily, hourly pressures Barney was used to.

'But what if he was the one who strangled the Boy all those years ago?' she asked. 'And my coming here tipped him into— Into doing what he's just done?'

She made herself look up again at the slowly twisting and turning body in the unrelenting glare of the Scene-of-crime lights.

'You didn't have any definite evidence pointing to him, rather than any of the others?'

'Well, no.'

Harriet could hear the indecisiveness in her voice. Angrily she shook herself free of it.

'Right. There's one thing to be done straight away. I want a thorough search of the whole premises. There may be something he left behind that he's been hiding all this time. Some indication that he did commit murder back in 1969, a diary, an unsent letter, even some sort of sick souvenir.

'Can we have more light down here?' she called up to the invisible officers at the top of the stairs.

In a moment the lamp that DC Jones had adjusted so that she could read Barney Trapnell's wretched last words was swung further round and the whole little shop was revealed in all its long-accumulated grime.

And then Harriet saw, just jutting out from the base of the tick-ticking slate-cased clock, a tiny rim of green. The same colour as the note Barney Trapnell had left, pathetically, behind before he had mounted those narrow stairs, taken off his constricting callipers, put his neck through the noose and, barefooted, shoved himself into the air.

'Just tilt this clock up a little for me,' she said to Pip. 'Mind you touch it as little as possible. There may be prints. But I want to see if anything more is written on this scrap jutting out here. The writing on the note comes right up to where the top's torn. There may be something more above it.'

Pip quickly pulled one sleeve of his ancient linen jacket down as far as he could tug it. Then he was able safely to lift the clock up, and Harriet, with a ballpoint pen, edged the thin strip of card fully into the light.

And, yes, there was more writing on it. In Barney Trapnell's neat hand. Three words. *It wasnt me.*

Harriet at once called off the search. There could be no reason, bar some freak of psychology, not to believe those three words. *It wasnt me.* Barney Trapnell's last testament must mean that he had not, thirty years ago, strangled to death the Boy Preacher.

'So,' she said to Pip as they got back into the car, miraculously untouched by the juvenile riffraff of the neighbourhood, 'we can be pretty certain now that, of our friend Meadowcraft's Seven Suspects, only five remain, whether dead or alive. Plainly Marcus Fairchild, the Trufflehound, was never a real possibility, once we knew who he really was. And now poor Barney is off the list too, whatever reason or half-reason he may have had for—' She came to a full halt. 'For doing what he did.'

She took a breath.

'Right then, now we've got, among the living, the censorious Miss Knott, the somehow slightly wrong ex-Undersheriff Lucas Calverte, that dodgy car salesman over in Norwich, Sydney Aslough or Bigod, the lady you told me is ill, Bubsy Willson, now Mrs Brownlow, and, I must add to them, the other dead suspect besides Fairchild, Harish Nair.'

And will he, she asked herself, despite his widow's fierce denial, prove after all to be the one? She quickly and sternly told herself that the little Indian was as likely a suspect as any of the others.

'So which of them do you think it was?' Pip asked, newly emboldened.

'It could be any one of them, couldn't it, for God's sake?' Harriet snapped, still weighed down by the thought that Trapnell's suicide might have been triggered by her unyielding tactics. 'How can we get evidence of any sort now the lab at Cherry Fettleham has produced its dusty answer?'

Harriet had felt too depressed and exhausted to want to go home. So it was somewhat later than her usual time – unless an ongoing investigation had detained her – that eventually she arrived there. The large whisky and ginger John poured for her, appropriating the bottle of Black and White she had not needed to give to sugared-almond-gobbling ex-DS Shaddock, did something to revive her. Soon she was able to tell him about Barney Trapnell.

He listened in silence, pondered for a little, and then delivered much the same verdict that Pip Steadman had.

'From what you've told me, and I can't see the Hard Detective sliding in any neatly extenuating circumstances, I wouldn't say you've really anything at all to reproach yourself with.'

She felt a wave of genuine relief. And decided to forgive him for that *Hard Detective*.

So she was able to go on to tell the story of her dash down to Gloucester and visit to the Laurels Hotel, and even made it decently amusing.

'All the same,' John said, 'whizzing off down there at a moment's notice? I still think you're over-reacting to your Mr Newbroom's demands.'

For a moment or two she forced herself to consider this.

'No,' she said at last. 'To tell you the truth, I think I've hardly given the man a thought all day, though now that you've put him into my head . . . No, but honestly, I'm quite clear about this. What's motivating me now is simply a determination to find out who it was who, thirty years ago, strangled that really remarkable young man, the Boy Preacher.'

'All right. But you can't tell me that haring off to Gloucester the way you did has helped get you any nearer to finding that person.'

'Well, no. No, it didn't. Or not unless I'm going to take to heart that old drunk's advice to pin it on whoever it was who found the body. Nice little Pip Steadman, before I packed him off to the place where he has lodgings, did try to persuade me, too, that we hadn't quite had a wasted day. He said he'd remembered something one of our suspects, Miss Knott, the ferocious head teacher, had said when we were interviewing her. He thought it might be significant.'

'Oh ho.'

'Well, I don't know how *Oh ho* it really is. I can't logically give much credence to it. But what Pip claims is that she was altogether too vehement in talking about Bubsy Willson and the way she had yelled out that the Boy was dead. And I suppose he may be right. I am actually quite inclined to trust his judgment. Certainly ferocious Knott spoke of Bubsy as a creature of the very lowest sort. And though, from all I've heard, Bubsy used to look pretty much like a street-walker thirty years ago, I don't think she actually was one. All right, DCI Kenworthy's notes said she had been up in court for soliciting. But in fact she'd never actually been convicted. And, damn it, I know there are prostitutes who are far from being obvious sex objects. But, from what everybody who's described Bubsy told me, she really was so ugly to look at that, well, no male was likely to give her a second glance.'

John raised an eyebrow.

'No. No, I'm right about her appearance. Too many people have commented on it. So Miss Knott's moral condemnation was hardly justified, especially coming from a so-called good woman who ought to have been more charitable. Her ex, whom I also saw today, actually called her that, *a good woman*. And that was despite his having left her because he couldn't take being preached at day and night.'

'But that's all your DC Steadman was able to produce?'

'No, he said a little more. He pointed out that, the moment I appeared to have left the subject of Bubsy, Miss Knott's hands on her desk visibly relaxed. Did I tell you that her hands had pointed at me in just the same aggressive way Newbroom's had when he first saw me?'

'You told me about them,' John put in. 'But it's my belief the chap probably just likes to rest them on his desk that way.'

'If you say so. But you weren't there to see them. I was.'

'All right. Go on, though. What was it your once disparaged DC Steadman told you about Miss Knott's hands?'

'Oh, just that he wondered if it was possible that Miss Knott wanted to say she actually did see Bubsy come out of the ballroom, but that she couldn't quite bring herself to accuse her of killing the Boy. I don't know. As I said, I can't altogether believe in it. Not even taking into account something she told me about when DCI Kenworthy interviewed her. She claimed that she said to him she would not be prepared to state in court who it was she had seen coming out of the ballroom, or whether she had seen anybody.'

'Well, then . . .'

'Oh, yes, I know, it sort of adds up. But what she

said back then, as a twenty-year old girl, damn it, may well have just been her telling DCI Kenworthy how he should do his job. She was capable of that, you know, even at that age.'

'So it seems. I've definitely got the impression from you that the lady still preacheth too much. But—'

'She certainly doesn't preach with any of the sweetness everybody says the Boy did. Not one bit, I'll tell you that.'

'But apparently she had her limits, if it's right that she refused to point the finger at Bubsy Willson, despite what she believed about her immoral life.'

'Ah, but you see, that's where it doesn't quite gel for me. On the one hand there's her readiness to condemn everybody everywhere. You should have heard the tongue-lashing poor Pip got over the fearful crime of smoking a cigarette within the sacred limits of the school playground. On the other hand, there she is apparently refusing to name a woman she may well believe killed the Boy. It doesn't altogether add up.'

'But do I gather, all the same, that you're beginning to have your sights on possibly immoral, ugly Bubsy?'

'Yes. And no. For one thing, I'm not at all sure about her alleged immorality. She got married, you know, soon after the murder. And, so Pip says, is reported as being still happily married today.'

'But are you going to go and talk to her tomorrow? To see if you can discover something that will get it to add up?'

'Yes. Yes, I am.'

Chapter Twenty-One

'She's ill, you know,' Pip Steadman said the next morning as they drove up to a terraced row of narrow houses. This was the edge of the police area covered by B Division, where once Harriet had run the 'Stop the Rot' campaign that earned her the now much-disliked title, the Hard Detective.

It was perhaps because of this reminder that she abruptly felt at odds with the world. So now she turned sharply on the little white-bearded detective.

'Yes, I do know that she's ill, DC. You've told me often enough. And it's thanks to your soft outlook that I haven't, up to now, so much as seen the woman who, according to you, may well have been the one who strangled the Boy.'

Pip positively shrank away.

But Harriet refused to let this renewed onset of timidity affect her.

'Right,' she said. 'There's the house. In we go.'

She briskly manoeuvred Pip into preceding her up the short strip of path and then stood watching him as he pressed the button in the centre of the door. From inside she heard the loud buzz it produced. But no one came to answer. The minutes passed. One. Two.

'Buzz again, buzz again. If she's as ill as you say, there must be someone in.'

Pip pressed the little white plastic button once more, keeping his finger on it as he gave her an anxious look over his shoulder.

'All right, that's—'

But the door had been pulled open.

The man who stood holding it was jovial. It was, Harriet thought as her bad temper slipped away at the sight of him, the only word to use. His large round face, skin glowing red from the top of the forehead to the depths of the neck, radiated goodwill. The eyes behind a pair of cheap tortoiseshell-rimmed spectacles beamed with irrepressible cheerfulness.

'Mr Brownlow?' she asked, finding it hard to believe this could be the husband of a seriously ill woman.

'Yes, yes. Ted Brownlow. What can I do for you?'

Harriet showed her warrant card.

She might have expected an abrupt shutdown to the welcoming grin. In this part of Birchester it was almost the universal reaction to a visit from the police. But, if anything, the grin broadened.

'So, who do you want to see? We've got the whole boiling here just now. Me, the wife, two daughters-in-law. Let alone all the kids, every one of 'em our grandchildren. Bless 'em.'

'We—'

Harriet felt a certain hesitation.

'We'd like to see Mrs Brownlow,' she said. 'That is, if she's well enough. I understand she's been ill.'

'Oh, aye. Well, she is ill, poor Bubsy. But just now she's better. Been on her feet yesterday and again today. Bright as a button, and you should see her with the grandkiddies.'

'Then, yes, we'd like a word with her. But in private, if we may.'

'Oh, right. Don't want to frighten the little terrors, do we? Not that they wouldn't frighten you, the tricks they get up to. Tell you what though, come through and I'll settle you up in my little greenhouse tacked on over the kitchen. Then I'll fetch Bubsy in. She'll be able to see the kiddies from up there, and that'll keep her happy.'

They followed Mr Brownlow – even his back in a big blue cardigan seemed to pulse out goodwill – through the house, up a flight of stairs and into a tiny glassed-in extension looking down on to a small garden.

'All my own work,' he said, ushering them in. 'E. Brownlow, building repairs promptly executed.'

'It's very nice,' Harriet answered, swept up in his undisguised pleasure. 'A very clever piece of work.'

'Right you are, right you are. I'll just fetch the old girl, and then you can have your little chinwag in peace.'

He went bouncing down the stairs.

'Did you know he was like this?' she asked Pip in some amazement.

'No. No, ma'am. I never called at the house, just made inquiries at the neighbours. You said we had to be discreet.'

'Quite right. It would never have done to reveal Mr Newcomen's secret plan.'

She felt, at once, that she should not perhaps have

allowed herself such lese-majesty. But Ted Brownlow's exuberant outlook was catching.

'In any case it looks as if the neighbours were exaggerating the seriousness of Bubsy's illness,' she said. 'Certainly from what her husband's been saying.'

'Well, ma'am, I did—'

She cut him short. Enough apologizing.

'No, Pip, it's understandable. There are people who love to turn even an early summer cold into a matter of imminent death.'

She turned to look down at the little garden below. It was, she realized, almost alive from one end to the other with small children. There must have been at least a dozen of them, all Brownlow grandchildren if what cheerful Ted had said was correct. Three or four were babies at the crawling stage. Others were walking, though apt to fall over and need picking up. Another three – or was it four? – were apparently of school age. And there in the middle of them, sitting in a cane-work armchair that must have been taken out of the house for her, was the woman they had come to question.

It was difficult to see her properly from above, just a head of grey hair and a substantial body dressed in a bright pink summer coat. But, though she was sitting well back in her chair and resting her arms on its sides, she did not otherwise seem to be very ill.

Harriet looked on as Bubsy's husband emerged from the back door and went over to her, leaning forward to speak.

Will she react to the mention of police officers, Harriet asked herself. But there was no sign that she seemed in any way disturbed. Slowly, pushing with her hands on the arms of the chair, she heaved herself up.

Harriet had expected her to come straight in. But instead she stood where she was, holding out her arms to one of the toddling grandchildren. And when he – if it was a he – staggered into them she attempted to pick him up and hug him. Then, it seemed, she had trusted too much to her returned health, because she had to drop to her knees before she could clasp her arms round the little red-faced laughing object.

Nor was that the only delay. As, solicitously helped up again by her husband, she made her way slowly indoors there were more halts to pat a head or, bending low, coo an endearment.

'Well,' Pip said, looking down from beside her, 'I must say after what we've heard about the lady I didn't expect to find someone like that. All those kids, well, smothered in love. That's what I'd have said if I was concocting an ad back in the old days. Smothered in love.'

'Yes, a good slogan. And it makes the interview ahead one layer more complicated than I'd allowed for.'

The comfortable grandmotherly figure below was shepherded into the house at last by her cheerful spouse. Then there came the sound of slow, heavy steps on the stairs.

Now I'm about to find myself face to face with Bubsy Willson, Harriet said to herself. Bubsy, described by that indefatigable assigner of blame, Michael Meadowcraft, as he elbow-nudged her into second

place as the Boy Preacher's murderer on the grounds of
her being an unsavoury young woman. Bubsy, whose
black-and-white photo falling out of DCI Kenworthy's
file had revealed, faded though it was, the unmistak-
ably suet-faced young woman. The woman whose
gaudy blouse had failed to provide Dr Passmore with
enough DNA to pin it down as harbouring the dying
Boy's spittle. Bubsy, cheerily referred to by Sydney
Aslough as 'that tart', even though Marcus Fairchild,
Trufflehound, had declared firmly that she was 'not a
prostitute'. And, finally, the Bubsy whom old DS Shaddock had called a whore 'lucky not to have collected a
string of little bastards', and Miss Knott had contemptu-
ously dismissed as a creature of the very lowest sort.

A last few heavy steps on the stairs, and she was there
in the doorway, puffing hard from the effort of
climbing up to this first-floor eyrie. And at once Harriet
saw that, in spite of the passage of more than thirty
years, Bubsy Brownlow was every bit as unattractive
to look at as she had been when she was Bubsy Willson.
Her face was still an almost featureless, flat, suetty
surface, with, yes, two or three stubs of wiry hair protruding from it, thickly black even now, despite the
scanty grey on her head.

Harriet's first thought, one which she wished at
once she had not had, was to wonder how cheerful
Ted Brownlow had come to marry her so soon after
the time of the murder.

'You're the police,' she puffed out now. 'What—
What d'you want?'

'Come in, Mrs Brownlow, come in,' Harriet said. 'Do sit down. You sound exhausted.'

She led the elderly woman – realizing as she did so that, in fact, she could not be much over fifty – to the sole chair in the little greenhouse, a cane-work twin of the one in the garden below.

Waiting till Bubsy had settled herself, still breathing heavily, she answered her question, *What d'you want?* by using the unalarming formula she had produced so often before.

'Mrs Brownlow, Greater Birchester Police are looking into a number of unsolved crimes where recent advances in the techniques of DNA analysis might make it worthwhile to go into them further.'

Bubsy Brownlow looked baffled.

And was there something more? Harriet asked herself. Had there been even a tiny flick of fear in those dulled brown eyes? Nothing I could see. Nothing at all.

'I don't really understand,' Bubsy said at last. 'I think I must of read about that stuff, DNA, somewhere, 'fore I got ill. But I can't remember.'

'It's the substance in our genes, all our genes, that makes us what we are,' Harriet explained carefully. 'Back in 1985 scientists discovered that by using it they could identify who had left any small quantity of bodily fluid, hair or flakes of skin on any particular surface. And recently they have managed to improve their techniques to the point where very, very small amounts of, say, spittle left on some garment could, even after many years, identify the person it came from.'

Not until she had come almost to the end of the

explanation had she made up her mind to drop into it the detail that might set alarm bells ringing in the head of the heavily breathing woman sitting in front of her. Then she had used that single word *spittle* and watched, hard as a laser beam, to detect the least reaction.

She saw nothing. The big, lard-coloured moon of a face showed not a twitch. The big inexpressive brown eyes stayed as dull as they had been all along.

'Have I made it clear to you?' Harriet asked at last. 'I'm afraid it's rather complicated. Do you understand now?'

'S'pose so.'

Again there was nothing in the two reluctant words to indicate whether the explanation had sent Bubsy's mind back to that night when the Boy, as he was being throttled to death, had spat out what might yet prove to be a clue to his murderer.

And Bubsy had been pointed to, more than once, as that murderer. Her garish nylon blouse of thirty years ago had held a minute unidentifiable trace, lost among the tea stains on it, of what might have been the victim's saliva. The probing had to go deeper.

'Very well. Among those unsolved crimes from the past there is the one that you were involved in yourself, if only because you were there when it happened. I'm referring, of course, to the murder of Krishna Kumaramangalam, known as the Boy Preacher.'

And, yes, now at least, a reaction.

The slumped form in the battered cane-work chair heaved forward. The moon face looked up.

'Shouldn't never . . .'

Harriet waited to see if that sentence was going to

be completed. *Shouldn't never* ... Shouldn't ever have ... what? Put my hands round that slender brown throat?

Or, perhaps, kept silent about ... About who?

But the eyes in the suetty face, which had gleamed momentarily with light, had dulled again now. It was as if in Bubsy's brain, slowed by illness, events of long ago were being slowly dragged to the surface and turned over and over.

Harriet waited yet longer.

Then she guessed that, if she left it for even half a minute more, all that had happened that night might sink back into oblivion.

'Mrs Brownlow, what is it you feel that you should never have done?'

The question put gently as a blanket being laid on a cot.

Bubsy looked up again.

'I shouldn't,' she said with thumped emphasis on each word, 'not never have listened to that boy preaching that day, that Boy Preacher.'

Harriet stayed standing above her for two seconds of silence. Then swooped.

'Why shouldn't you have listened to him, Mrs Browlow? Thousands and thousands of people did. And they went away the better for his preaching.'

'No.'

'No? You don't think people gained from hearing the Boy preach? People have told me that they truly did.'

'Not me.'

An ambiguous answer. Harriet quickly considered

it. And decided it might be best to move on by taking its less obvious meaning.

'No, Mrs Brownlow, you have not told me that, like those others, you gained from the Boy's words. But did you in fact gain from what he preached?'

The heavy body leant fiercely forward. The old chair creaked sharply.

'No, no, no. I told you I shouldn't never have listened. Not that day when he was there standing up on the steps of that church in Chapeltown, there in the sun. That lovely summer day. That black, black day for me.'

The voice, harsh with undirected anger, came to a sudden halt.

'A black day for you? But why was it so black?'

''Cos I listened. That's why. I listened to him and . . . And he had me caught. I had to find him again, to hear him. But I shouldn't of. I shouldn't. That's why that day was black.'

Harriet stooped down nearer to her.

'And you did find him again, didn't you?' she said as softly as a priest in a confessional. 'You found him. You did listen to his preaching. You went to hear him again and again. And then you joined that little circle of people close to him. You joined the cousin he lived with, Harish Nair, and someone very different from you, the Undersheriff of Birrshire, Mr Calverte, and little Miss Knott, the teacher, and poor crippled Barney Trapnell and that street trader, Sydney Bigod. You joined all of them. They helped the Boy, each in their different way. But what did you do for him, Mrs Brownlow?'

Bubsy Brownlow considered. Harriet could almost see her ranging back to those distant days.

And perhaps back to one evening on one of those days in particular. To the two hours and more during which she had been with those five, and one other, the journalist Marcus Fairchild, restlessly waiting in the foyer outside the Imperial Hotel's fantastically decorated ballroom for the Boy Preacher to emerge from his state of meditation.

But, no, it seemed, it had not been back to that fateful Monday evening that Bubsy's thoughts had sent her. It had been to the time when she had been most enthralled by the curious power that emanated from the youthful Krishna Kumaramangalam.

'I did what I could,' she said. 'I know they all thought it wasn't much. But what could the likes of me do for him? I wasn't even strong like that Barney. I wasn't a gentleman like Mr Lucas, I wasn't sharp like Syd. But I did what I could, and I listened. When he preached I listened and listened.'

In the shabby cane-work chair she suddenly went into a fit of shuddering.

Damn it, have I gone too far? Harriet asked herself in momentary panic. She's meant to be over that illness, whatever it was, but what if she isn't? What if I've sent her back into it?

'Are— Are you all right, Mrs Brownlow?'

'All right? All right? I thought I was. I thought when the time came that I could tell my Ted I was having his baby, I thought I was all right for ever then. And when we got married I thought I was even more all right, and with every single one of the little darlings

247

that came along I thought I was more and more all right. And with the grandchilder, it was the same. I was all right. All right.'

From the eyes that were no longer dull there came a glare of pure hatred directed up at Harriet as she stood leaning over.

'And now it's not all right.'

Is she going to tell me why? Harriet asked herself, hardly daring to breathe.

'It's not all right? Mrs Brownlow, will you tell me what happened when you went into the ballroom that night? Tell me.'

A very faint flush appeared on the moon surface of the big face just below.

'I didn't never go in. I didn't. Not never, that night.'

Chapter Twenty-Two

A blank denial. It was the last thing Harriet had expected. She had been by no means sure that, when she asked Bubsy what happened when she went into the ballroom, she would get a confession to having strangled the meditating Boy Preacher. But a total denial of ever having entered that fantastically elaborate room, uttered with a vigour that seemed to spring from the simple truth, was as far as could be from what she thought she would hear.

'You did not go into the ballroom that night after the Boy had begun his meditation?'

'No. No, I never.'

Harriet looked at her.

'But, Bubsy,' she said reproachfully, 'more than one of the people there have told me it was you who shouted out that the Boy was dead. How could you have known that unless you had been in the ballroom?'

Bubsy looked from side to side as if seeking a way of escape from the little greenhouse made for her by her cheerful Ted, E. Brownlow, building repairs promptly executed.

'How could you know?' Harriet repeated, still as quietly as before.

'I— I was told.'

'Told? Told by somebody who had come out of the ballroom while you were near one of the doors?'

It was possible. Just possible that, concealed by chance from the other five in the foyer, perhaps by the flourishing pot of pampas grass in the middle of the round bench there, Bubsy had done no more than see someone emerge. If they had told her that the Boy was dead, Bubsy, his worshipper, might have yelled out in horror.

But who was it, if that was so, who had come out of the ballroom? Who, almost beyond doubt, had just a few minutes earlier strangled the Boy Preacher?

'Bubsy, who was it who told you? Who, Bubsy?'

'It was— It was that Harritch.'

'Harritch? Harritch? Do you— Do you mean Harish Nair, the Boy's cousin?'

'Yeh. Harritch.'

Harriet felt herself caught in a dizzying down-spinning whirlpool of dismay.

Harish. The only one of Michael Meadowcraft's Seven Suspects for whom from the start she had felt whole-hearted sympathy. Harish Nair, on whose shirt Dr Passmore had detected ample traces of the Boy's saliva. It was, after all, possible that his daisy-dotted pale green shirt could have been impregnated twice with the Boy's spittle. It could have happened once when he had had an epileptic fit on the Sunday, and again when he had been throttled to death that Monday night.

And now Bubsy, whether she realized it or not, was

saying in effect that it had been Harish Nair who had killed the Boy Preacher.

Harriet took a deep breath.

Then, forcing herself, she began digging for any confirmation from the heavy-set woman slumped in the cane-work chair in front of her.

'Bubsy, if it was Harish Nair who told you that night that the Boy was dead, do you remember, afterwards, when you were questioned by Detective Chief Inspector Kenworthy? Do you remember him questioning you?'

'Yeh. Yeh, that Mr Kenworthy.'

'Right, when he was questioning you do you remember why you didn't tell him that you had seen Harish Nair come out of the ballroom, and that it had been him who told you the Boy was dead? You didn't say a word about it, you know. If you had, Detective Chief Inspector Kenworthy would have written it down.'

Bubsy thought.

'I didn't tell him anything because,' she said slowly, 'if that Harritch had gone in there and strangled the Boy what he was like a father to, he would of done it for a good reason. He wasn't the sort to go about everywhere strangling and killing, old Harritch. No, he'd have had his good reason to do it. Every murder ain't a wicked act, you know. Not every one.'

So, yes, Bubsy was saying that Harish Nair had committed the murder.

Harriet experienced a flood-wave of sheer disbelief. Harish Nair was not a murderer. He was not. And, immediately, she told herself that, with a woman like

Bubsy, whose powers of reasoning seemed almost non-existent, such an unlikely thought process could well have taken place in her confused head. It was possible, even quite likely, that she was simply not telling the truth when she had virtually accused Harish. She was producing pure and purposeless fiction.

Bubsy, she saw now, had slumped back in her chair, and her face, which had earlier taken on that momentary faint flush, was now yet paler, glistening yet more lard-whitely.

Harriet glanced back at silent Pip Steadman, standing by the door. He, too, was looking at Bubsy with marked concern.

'Bubsy, Mrs Brownlow, are you all right?' she asked urgently.

'Funny. Feel funny.'

The words were hardly distinguishable.

'Pip, go and fetch the husband, quick.'

Harriet knelt in front of her, reached for a plump wrist and after a moment found the pulse beneath. There was a beat there. But it was faint, and worryingly intermittent.

There she stayed kneeling, her face within inches of the bright black and red cotton skirt Bubsy was wearing beneath her long pink summer coat. A mingled odour of cloying talcum powder, sharp body sweat and a tinge of urine came to her nostrils.

Then at last she heard the rapid pounding of footsteps on the stairs outside, and an instant later Ted Brownlow burst in.

'Bubsy, Bubsy. You all right?'

'Now you've come I'm all right again, my old Teddy. Just tired, ever so tired.'

When Harriet got back to her office, the first thing she saw, right in the centre of the old table that occupied most of the little cubbyhole, was a memo form, kept in place by a box of paperclips. On it, clear to be seen: *From the Chief Constable, Greater Birchester Police*. She was unsurprised to see that the message below was yet another request to be kept informed of *any progress*.

She snatched up the telephone and got through to Mr Newcomen's dithery secretary, Pansy Balfour.

'Could you tell Mr Newbr— Could you tell Mr Newcomen that I have nothing to report at the present time? As soon as there is anything I shall be careful to let him know.'

Then, sitting either side of the little table, she and Pip, with much of the morning still before them, settled down to review the situation.

'Tell me truthfully,' Harriet said, 'do you think I'm right to feel that all Bubsy said about Harish Nair was somehow distorted? That she's more muddled than seems possible?'

Pip, bright blue eyes intent, sat in silent thought.

'I know what you mean, ma'am,' he said eventually. 'I met people like her when I was in the mental ward after— After, you know . . .'

'After your experience that seems increasingly now to be of service.'

'Well, yes. Yes, ma'am. I suppose so, though I hadn't thought of it like that before. Well, except when I suggested that any of the people there outside the ballroom thirty years ago could have, well, expunged that whole time from their memories.'

'Yes. An insight, I'll grant you that. But you haven't really answered my question. Do you think I'm right in distrusting Bubsy Brownlow?'

Again Pip considered.

Or perhaps felt obliged to appear to be doing so, because in almost no time at all he came up with his answer.

'Yes, ma'am. I don't think you're wrong to discount, at least to some extent, what she told us up there in that sort of greenhouse.'

'Right. And happily, we've got another account of those few minutes, that minute or two even, before everyone in the foyer knew the Boy had been strangled and Lucas Calverte called out to have the police telephoned.'

'Ma'am?'

'Sydney Aslough. He told me, very vaguely I admit, that he saw that tart Bubsy – his words – come out of the ballroom screaming that the Boy was dead. And, right, he'll be there now at his showroom in Norwich, he'll be at the end of the telephone.'

She pulled out her notebook, riffled through the pages, found the number she had seen displayed underneath that bright red lettering proclaiming *Bargains! Bargains! Bargains!* and stabbed it out.

The phone was answered with promptness. Harriet thought she recognized the voice of the girl in the red outfit whom she had cunningly told she was Mrs Piddock.

'Mr Aslough, please,' she said briskly.

'I'm afraid Mr Aslough isn't available. Can I assist you?'

'No. No, I wanted Mr Aslough himself. When will he be – available?'

'I'm sure I couldn't say. He's on the Continent, purchasing.'

'Over in Europe? But when will he be back?'

'I couldn't say. He left in a big hurry, and he never says how long he'll be over there. It's just a day or two sometimes, and a week or more at others. Are you sure I can't help you?'

'Yes, quite. Thank you. But let me give you my number. It's Detective Superintendent Martens, Greater Birchester Police. As soon as Mr Aslough gets back, will you let me know?'

She dictated the number, put down the handset, and looked across at Pip.

'Foiled again.'

He grinned. 'But not for long, Holmes, I trust.'

Harriet had a reply on her lips, putting Pip into the shoes of Dr Watson, when a sudden flood of doubts swept into her mind.

Aslough. Could something I said to him there in his office have eventually put a fear in his mind? A fear that, after thirty years of safety, the trail he had believed successfully smudged over was being step by step re-opened? Had that sent a murderer, however cheerfully innocent-seeming, scuttling off to Europe? The praise that he, very surprisingly, poured out for the Boy there in Norwich, was it no more than a thrusting-away of possible suspicion? Is Sydney Aslough, after all, the killer?

She had hardly pulled herself up enough to dismiss the idea, and to prevent herself passing this wild notion on to Pip, of whose judgment she was a little in awe, when the phone rang.

She grabbed it, gratefully.

'Detective Superintendent Martens.'

And found herself battered by an entirely unexpected torrent of rage issuing from the instrument.

'Mr Newcomen here. I want an explanation from you, Superintendent. I have just had my post put before me, and what have I found? A letter in which the writer says, in plain terms, that Greater Birchester Police have re-opened the inquiry into the murder of the so-called Boy Preacher. Now I thought I had made it plain to you, Miss Martens, that nothing, nothing at all, was to be said about the inquiry having been re-opened. I did not want, I do not want, at any cost, the media getting hold of the information and then holding us up to ridicule if we do not produce an immediate result. And you, it seems, have flagrantly ignored my instructions. I want your explanation.'

Harriet, while the tea-cup tempest raged, rapidly reviewed everything she had said and done that might have let anybody likely to pass it on know for certain that she was actively investigating the Boy Preacher murder. And she exonerated herself.

She looked across now at Pip. Had he at the early stages, despite her warnings, gone too far with somebody somewhere? It was possible. But she was not going to tell Mr Newbroom that.

'Sir,' she said, now that there seemed to be a lull in the storm, 'let me make it quite plain. I did not at any time say anything to anybody that would indicate the Boy Preacher inquiry has been re-opened. May I ask who it is who has told you that it has been?'

'It— I— The letter was an anonymous communication.'

Harriet fought down a spurt of anger.

A bloody anonymous letter and the man chooses to believe I am responsible for the leak, without so much as considering whether it's possible news of his wretched publicity-seeking move has got about in some other way. Christ.

'Perhaps, sir, I could see this— this *communication*. If we could get some sort of clue as to the writer, we could better assess the strength of his allegation.'

A long silence at the other end.

'Very well, Superintendent. I will have it sent down to you.'

Harriet thought she had better forbear asking how much the letter had been handled. Even if it had got Newbroom prints all over it, it was unlikely that any overlaid ones would be those of someone on file.

Five minutes later Pansy Balfour came teetering in, holding a plain white envelope between thumb and forefinger. Harriet noted at once that it was the kind that could be bought at any W. H. Smith or supermarket.

She got Pansy to slide the envelope flat on to the table, and with her own silver ballpoint slid out the letter.

It read: *Now Greater Birchester Police are looking once more for who killed that Boy Preacher back in 1969 why don't you take a good look at Undersherrif Lucas Calverte. He's not and never has been the gentleman he likes to make people think he is.*

That and no more.

'Right,' she said. 'Handwriting not up to much, and Undersheriff spelt incorrectly. All the signs of a pure and simple mischief-maker. But Mr Newcomen's right about one thing. Whoever put this together is plainly quite sure we are re-investigating the case.'

She sat up and looked straight across at Pip.

'Was it you?'

Under the tidy triangular cat's-cradle of white hair on his face she saw a deep redness come swelling up. A blush of shame? Or a reaction to a baseless accusation?

It was a moment or two before he replied.

'No, ma'am. No, I never said anything to anybody that could have given them any clue that the inquiry was being re-opened. I never said any more than the sort of guarded words I've heard you use, about looking into the possibility of re-opening various unresolved investigations.'

'Very well, DC. I believe you. Unreservedly. So take this to Fingerprints. It's a thousand-to-one chance there'll be any marks on it that are on record. But I'm not laying myself open to any more criticism from above.'

'Thank— Thank you, ma'am,' Pip stuttered.

He eased the envelope – it was addressed simply

to *The Chief Constable, Greater Birchester Police* – into an evidence folder and added the letter.

'You know, Pip,' she said, 'I've always had a niggling doubt about Lucas Calverte. It's quite possible that whoever wrote saying he isn't the gentleman he likes to make people think he is does know something about his early life. And another thing. I noticed when I first read *Who Killed the Preacher?*, though it didn't seem significant at the time, that, although Michael Meadowcraft produced his neat little potted biographies of all of his Seven Suspects, the one on Calverte failed to say where and when he was born.'

'Yes, that does seem odd.'

'It does indeed. So, I'm putting aside finding out who wrote the letter, something all too likely to take a hell of a lot of time and effort and wind up nowhere. No, what I'd like to do now is find out the strength of the claim in it. It may, after all, be a final pointer to Lucas Calverte.'

'Do you really think so, ma'am?'

'I said *may be*. And that's what I meant. But take the damn letter to Fingerprints now.'

When Pip had scuttled away Harriet gave herself to thought.

Yes, I need to know whether there's anything iffy about Calverte. It's my duty. But— But the truth is I still believe Harish Nair did not murder his cousin, despite what Bubsy said before she collapsed. Why should he have done, after all? There's never been the least indication that he had any motive. All right, I haven't found any reason why Calverte should have strangled him either. But I can see a man like him, a man who thinks he knows best and does not hesitate to say what it is, coming close to the point of murder.

She jumped up from her chair.

Right, I'm going out again to Travellers. It's where I saw Lucas Calverte with sudden viciousness twist and twist a clump of long grass he had pulled up and toss it away to destruction. Yes, aged he may be, but there's still strength in those hands of his. And thirty years ago there would have been even more.

Chapter Twenty-Three

By the time Pip had returned from his errand with the anonymous letter, Harriet had decided that, before she went to visit Calverte, she would find out what she could about his origins. And she had thought of a simple way to do that.

'Listen, Pip,' she said, 'this may not work, but even if it doesn't we're no worse off. What I want you to do, straight away, is simply ring up Lucas Calverte saying you're a journalist writing about the history of the office of Undersheriff for the county magazine—'

'I've seen it,' Pip broke in. 'Glossy. Called— Called something. Yes. Of course. Just called *Birrshire*.'

'Right. Then all you've got to do is ask the old gasbag where he was born. Was it, you could ask, within the county boundary.'

Pip's knobby cheeks above the neat beard shone with sudden glee. He seized the telephone. Harriet flipped through her notebook and read the number out. Pip punched it up.

Almost at once the phone was answered. Pip went into his spiel.

Listening, Harriet admired the way he was bringing

conviction to his role. Early years in advertising paying off, she thought.

Impossible to make out what the gasbag was saying at the far end. But whatever it was, after one short interruption, it seemed to be enough.

'Thank you, sir. That's very helpful,' Pip the journalist said, with a nice touch of obsequiousness.

He put the handset back in place.

'That's curious,' he commented.

'Curious? Why?'

'It turns out Calverte was born, not in any of the posh places in Birrshire, but in the next county. In Gralethorpe. He was a bit reluctant to say so, but, as you heard, it needed only one tiny prompt before he realized his birthplace wasn't the sort of fact he could hide from a persistent journalist – like me.'

'Gralethorpe,' Harriet said. 'I see what you mean, *curious*. I know Gralethorpe, I made an inquiry there quite recently. No, a small mining town like that, friendly enough but covered in coal dust from one end to the other, is not at all the sort of place where one would have expected Undersheriff Lucas Calverte to have entered the world. You know, I think that before I go and see him, I'm going to visit Gralethorpe again. This very afternoon in fact.'

'With me, ma'am?'

'No. No, I don't think so. I don't think I'll need to go to Gralethorpe as the second half of a pair of investigative journalists. No, I'll leave you with the dangerous task of fending off Mr Newcomen when he wants to know why we're not making enough progress.'

*

Before setting out, Harriet got Pip to check the Gralethorpe register of electors for anyone 'with that
distinctly upper-crust name of Calverte'. He had no
luck, but he did find a Miss Abigail Calvert, without
the *e*. That comparative lack of success did not make
Harriet abandon her decision. So she set out to see
what she might learn from this Miss Abigail.

The address Pip had found for her was in one of
Gralethorpe's many grimed-over working men's terraced houses. When its door was opened to her careful
tap on the knocker, she saw a woman in her seventies
or eighties who seemed to cry out to have applied to
her the epithet 'apple-cheeked'. She was as upright as
a signpost, too, and her brightly alert eyes were giving
this newcomer a sharply inquiring look.

'Good afternoon,' Harriet said, rapidly abandoning
the persona of a council official which she had decided
was likely to be her best way of finding out what she
wanted to know. 'I am a police officer, Detective Superintendent Martens, and I'm hoping you can assist me
with an inquiry we have about a namesake of yours,
or almost a name—'

'That'll be Luke,' Miss Calvert chipped in, quick as
a darting squirrel.

'Yes. Or Lucas.'

'Well, you can't be here because Lucas Calverte's
done something wicked. He was always too concerned
with what folk might think to do anything amiss.'

'Miss Calvert,' Harriet said, the scent now breast-
high, 'may I come in and ask you some questions?'

'I don't reckon I could keep you out. But come in,

and welcome. I was just going to get myself a cup of tea.'

Harriet was too old a hand at playing a useful witness to decline the offered tea. She sat waiting with happy patience in the little spick and span front room while from the kitchen in the back there came the clink of cups, the whistle of the kettle.

'So you want to know something about my cousin Luke,' Miss Calvert said as she came in with a flower-painted tin tray complete with teapot, sugar basin, two large cups, also flower-patterned, and a plate of shortbread biscuits.

'You call him Luke,' Harriet said, feeling her way. 'But I know him as Lucas, Mr Lucas Calverte, former Undersheriff for the County of Birrshire.'

'Oh, yes, that's my cousin Luke. On away and up, up, up, from the moment he was old enough to fly. To fly away from me in the end, to tell you the whole truth.'

'From you?'

A quick, bright, apple-cheeked smile.

'Oh yes. I don't mind who knows about it now, though I will say I was hurt, hurt in the heart as they say, when one day Luke, who'd shown every sign of liking me, came into this very room – I've lived in this house all my born days, you know – and told me he was off to join the army. Well, worse than that. It was the Indian Army he was going into, and he would be away for years and years.'

Yes, Harriet said to herself, I can see the man who ended up as the scourge of the badly-behaved youth of Birchester telling this nice old lady, who once thought she was going to be his wife, that at a moment's notice he was off out of her life.

'Oh, but he rose up out there, did Luke. Rose up to be an officer, and, when he came back to England, never set foot in Gralethorpe again. That was when he changed his name to Lucas and stuck that extra *e* on the end of Calvert, as if he was ashamed of where he came from. When I saw his photo in the newspaper the time he was made an Undersheriff, whatever that may be, that was the first I knew he was back here and had set up to be a gentleman.'

'And you had once hoped to marry him?'

A bubble of laughter.

'Oh, I'd never have let him be a husband of mine, for all his cajoling ways. And, to tell the truth, I dare say he'd have never tied the knot himself. Not unless I'd let him put me in the family way. And I wasn't going to do that, however much I might have liked it. No, Luke Calvert ran off from Gralethorpe, not to get himself away from me, but because he couldn't stand the narrowness. Chapel twice every Sunday, and being told by everyone just what you had to do and what you'd not. Oh, aye, especially that *not*. Those sermons we got, in chapel and out, and the chapel ones never less than the full hour and hellfire every minute of that. How I hated them.'

She sent Harriet a quickly mischievous glance.

'I may have kept Cousin Luke in his place,' she said. 'But I wasn't one of your goody-goody girls, and Luke wasn't the only one buzzing round. I see you've a wedding band on your finger, so I mustn't say too much about husbands. But from all I've seen in my life, I think I'm a great deal better off with never having let any one of those buzzing bees catch me to cook and clean for him.'

'I dare say you're right, though I must admit my John is about as good as they come, and does his share at the stove too.'

'Then you've been lucky, or you've been deceived. But I never was. I could see what they were made of, in spite of all their sweet talk. And I was proved right. You're from the Birchester Police, aren't you? Well, does the name Ezra Yates ring a bell with you?'

Harriet took herself back to her earlier days in the city and its notorious B Division area. And, yes, the name *Ezra Yates* came up as a flashing light, though she could not at all recall what criminal act had put it there.

'Yes,' she said, 'the name does ring a bell.'

'Ah, well, I can see you don't remember too much about Ezra. But he had a nasty turn to him, even back then when he was courting me, and even though I liked him for it. He left Gralethorpe, too. Loved me and left me. But I've always kept up with him, a card at Christmas if nothing more. And so I read all about his little bit of trouble in the paper. Blackmail, they said it was. Writing letters; wanting to be paid to keep quiet about some old gentleman's naughtiness.'

And now bells were ringing louder and louder.

Ezra Yates, at the time living near enough to his native Gralethorpe to get his name in the local paper for writing anonymous blackmailing letters. Couple that with his knowledge, from half a century ago and more, that Undersheriff Lucas Calverte was no born grandee and it was not difficult to pinpoint who had written anonymously to the new Chief Constable of Greater Birchester Police.

It all fits.

But, no. No, it does not all fit. There's one missing piece. And a very large piece, too. How on earth did Ezra Yates, wherever he is now, get to know that the Boy Preacher murder was under active investigation?

'Ezra Yates?' she asked. 'Did you mention that, even after all these years, you kept in touch with him? That must be true love, even if it's only on a Christmas card.'

Seventy-year-old Abigail Calvert gave a little giggle.

'You've guessed my secret,' she said. 'You're sharp enough. No wonder you've risen up in the police. But, yes, I've always had a soft spot for that bad lad Ezra.'

'So where do you send your cards to now?' Harriet slipped in, casually.

'Oh, to Birchester. Ezra's a shoe mender there, still got his shop in Moorfields, though it's years since I've seen him there.'

Right, Harriet said to herself. I've learnt all I need now. Ezra Yates, anonymous letter writer, a shoe-mender's shop in the Moorfields area.

'Miss Calvert, I've already taken up too much of your time. I'll say goodbye now. And thank you for the tea, and the biscuits.'

Abigail Calvert gave her a sharp look.

'In a hurry to be off, are you?'

*

Right, yes, shrewd old biddy, Harriet thought, speeding out of Gralethorpe on the Birchester road, I am in a hurry. The sooner I find Ezra Yates and put the fear of God into him over his letter-writing activities, the sooner I'll be able to get out of him how he got to learn that the inquiry is active. And the sooner I'll have something to report to Mr Newbroom that ought to keep him quiet for a bit.

She took Pip with her to Moorfields, where they had no difficulty in finding, in a narrow street too rundown even to shelter one of the seedy area's plentiful porn shops, the little cabin where Ezra Yates – his name above the door – offered to mend shoes. An offer, it seemed, in the age of fashion-statement trainers, few people were taking up.

The shop, with darkness setting in, was lit up, if dimly. When Harriet pushed the door open she saw an old man, cigarette dangling from his intent mouth, hammering nails into a shoe on his last.

'Mr Ezra Yates?' she said, infusing her voice with a certain degree of menace. 'Greater Birchester Police.'

At once she saw the back, still bending over the shoe, freeze into rigid apprehension.

'Detective Superintendent Martens and Detective Constable Steadman. We have some questions to ask you.'

Ezra Yates left his last, three or four bright nails still sticking up from the shoe on it.

'I've had all I want of you police,' he grunted.

'I dare say you have, Mr Yates. But, if despite having served a term for one extortion offence you persist in writing anonymous letters, you can expect to have a great deal more to do with us.'

'I never wrote no letters like that.'

'But you did, Mr Yates. You wrote a letter to the Chief Constable of the Greater Birchester Police. It had your fingerprints on it, you know. So you can stop pretending you know nothing about it.'

And thank goodness, she thought, that I did send the letter to be tested. Should he persist in his denials, if by chance Fingerprints come up with something halfway decent, we can charge him. Though not with lese-majesty in daring to address Mr Newbroom.

But there was no need to have any such evidence.

'What if I did write to him?' Ezra Yates growled. 'If Luke Calvert murdered that preacher boy all those years ago, then he ought to have swung for it. And so he ought today. If I've helped him on his way, then you ought to be thanking me, not coming in here and telling me I done wrong.'

'And how do you know the Boy Preacher case is being investigated again now?'

Will he spill out the answer? Or will I have to tussle with him over it? And perhaps lose out?

'I heard, didn't I? Heard somewhere. Everybody must know about it.'

'No, Mr Yates, everybody does not know about it. And your correspondent, my Chief Constable, is very angry because you seem to have got wind of it.'

'But I— I ain't done nothing wrong. If I just heard that murder was being gone into all over again, well, I just did, didn't I? Nothing wrong in that. Nothing for no Chief Constable to be angry about.'

Harriet recognized wryly that Mr Newbroom's anger did not always mean trouble for members of his force. It had its uses.

'No,' she said, 'you're wrong. The Chief Constable's right to be angry, very angry indeed. You committed an offence in sending an anonymous letter at all, and to send one to him puts you in very serious trouble. He's very likely to order me to bring a case against you, and one that will stick.'

Ezra Yates looked more than a little scared now.

'So, why don't you tell me just how you heard about the Boy Preacher investigation? And then we'll see if we can't persuade Mr Newcomen that you didn't mean to commit an offence.'

Barely five seconds of thought, and then Ezra Yates looked up.

'It was at the AA,' he said.

'The AA? Alcoholics Anonymous? You belong to that?'

'Yeh. Years ago I started. Don't need to be prayed at about the drink any more now. Been off it a long time. But I go once a week still. Company, much as anything.'

'And someone at the meeting said they knew the Boy Preacher's murder was being investigated again?'

Harriet failed to keep the doubt out of her voice. It all seemed so unlikely.

'Not at the meeting. Out on the steps afterwards. Nobody wouldn't say something like that when they were all telling how they'd kept off the stuff for however long it was.'

'No, I suppose not. But someone after the meeting told you? Who was it?'

'Who was it? Who was it? I couldn't know, could I? Nobody at the meetings uses their name. Wouldn't ever go otherwise. Should have thought you'd know that. Bloody detective superintendent, aren't you?'

'That's enough of that. And, if you really don't know your informant's name, you'd better tell me all that you do know about them, and pretty quickly.'

The old shoe mender's moment of defiance trickled into nothingness like the last spurt from a defective water tap.

'A lady. It was a lady.'

'All right, that's something. But tell me more.'

'Ain't no more to tell. She's this lady, well-spoken if you like, and somehow she's taken a bit of a shine to me. So we stop after and chat. Couple of minutes. About the weather. Anything comes into her head.'

'I see. And how did it come about that at one moment you were saying it's wonderful weather for May and the next she was telling you—'

She came to a halt.

Ezra Yates, reformed alcoholic, she thought, may not know the name of the lady who has taken 'a bit of a shine' to him. But I do.

'Oh, very well,' she snapped at the miserable shoe mender. 'If you know nothing, you know nothing. And I suppose, as you've done your best to co-operate, we'll say no more about that letter to the Chief Constable. But you take care you never do anything like that again. Understood?'

And she swung out of the little shop.

Outside, Pip almost tugged at her sleeve as if he were an importunate child.

'Ma'am, why? Why leave all of a sudden like that?'

'Because,' Harriet said, 'I know who it was who blabbed to that awful old man about the inquiry. Can't you guess?'

Pip's forehead creased in perplexity.

'No, I can't.'

'Think. Who, among the very few people who actually know the inquiry into the Boy Preacher's death is live again, is likely to be a member of Alcoholics Anonymous.'

'I— I can't think of anybody.'

'That's because, Pip, you're going over in your mind a list, a very short list, of likely women police officers. But it isn't a police officer. It's someone else on the Headquarters staff. So who will it be?'

A slow dawning of recognition.

'I know. I know. Or at least I think I do. It's— Don't people always say that the Chief's secretary, Pansy, seems half-drunk all the time? It's her, isn't it? Her.'

'Yes, of course it is. But keep this strictly under your hat. Pansy may have a drink problem but she doesn't deserve, especially working for who she does, to be the victim of any worse Headquarters gossip than she already is. Okay?'

'Yes, ma'am.'

'Right. Now, there's something rather more urgent to be done than stopping office gossip. There's what I've found out about once-upon-a-time Undersheriff Lucas Calverte, otherwise Luke Calvert, humble son of Gralethorpe.'

'Ma'am?'

'Yes. I've a notion that I'm going to be able to use that to get somewhere with Lucas Calverte. When I cheerfully call him Luke, I've an idea that I may learn at last, in the words of Michael Meadowcraft, who killed the preacher. Or, at the very least I'll bring back to his mind just what did happen that night at the Imperial Hotel.'

Chapter Twenty-Four

Harriet abandoned her customary late Sunday morning visit to the croissant shop in Aslough Parade in favour of waiting, as she had said to Pip the evening before, 'till our former Undersheriff has been to church and heard an improving sermon. Then when he's been, for a change, on the wrong end of a bit of preaching he may be rather more ready to tell the truth.'

But before setting off for Westholme and hopefully sermon-bettered Lucas Calverte she went into Headquarters, where poor Pip had been consigned to wait in case there were any demands from Mr Newcomen to be fended off. There she begged for some expert knowledge.

'Just as I was dropping off to sleep last night,' she said, 'I hit on what we used to call when I was at school a wheeze.'

'A wheeze? I know what that is, however long ago it was that people used to use the word. But what wheeze is it? And why do you need one?'

'Right, Answer One: I think I may need my wheeze if the old gasbag hasn't taken in what the vicar's going to preach to him. The usual stuff about always speaking the truth, that sort of thing.'

'Well, I see that a sermon might not be enough to make an old hypocrite like Lucas Calverte come out with the whole truth and nothing but the truth. But how's your wheeze going to make him cough up? What's your Answer Two?'

'Simple. If dodgy. Let me tell you something. Right at the beginning of this business I thought I ought to go along and see the scene of the crime before the bulldozer and the wrecking ball knocked the Imperial Hotel flat. And it was when I came out of that extraordinary ballroom – I wish you'd seen it, Pip, walls all covered from the floor right up to that great glass roof with mad tile-pictures of luscious nymphs and lusty gods, with twisty pillars in yellow and blue all writhed round with a wild tangling of every sort of flower and foliage – it was when I came out of there, still not convinced that anybody ought to be re-opening such a long-ago case, that I encountered little plump Mr Popham, who used to be the hotel's general manager and is now the caretaker, if he's still there at all. And he was smoking what I imagine was some pretty cheap sort of cigarette. But the smell of that smoke, very much like the Woodbines they used to puff at thirty-odd years ago, took me back in one single instant to those days. And then I felt that, yes, this was my case and I was going to pursue it to the end.'

Pip's little blue eyes were sparkling.

'And you're going to try the same thing on Lucas Calverte?' he said. 'To make him actually confess?'

Then a look of blank dismay overcame him.

'But— But, ma'am. You don't smoke.'

'No, Pip, I don't. I haven't since I had an illicit fag

behind the school pavilion, the pavvy, and was caught there and sent up to the headmistress. The dressing down I got – irresponsibility, unladylike behaviour, setting a bad example – was enough to cure me of smoking for the rest of my life. Well, almost. Because I did take it up for a month or two when I was first in the Met and wanted to act like one of the boys. But that didn't last.'

'Wish I had your strength of will, ma'am.'

'Right. But I can understand why you need something like that, which, thank goodness, I don't. And it's a very good thing now that you are a smoker. Because I want you to lend me the wherewithal. It may or may not get a confession out of that old humbug. But, if we're wrong about him, which we well may be, then at least, if all goes according to plan, he will tell me what he actually saw in the foyer that night.'

Harriet, once Lucas Calverte had settled himself in the sagging cretonne-covered armchair in his study, jumped up from the equally sagging sofa on which he had placed her. She stood looking down at him.

'Mr Calverte,' she said, 'I have visited you twice before now, and on each occasion you have told me you can remember nothing of the events of the evening of May the twenty-second, 1969. Can you do rather better now?'

Calverte looked back at her, eyes filled with sudden anger.

'Superintendent, what is the meaning of this? I told you distinctly before. That whole terrible evening has been mercifully blotted from my mind. Why should you think it should suddenly cease to be so?'

'Frankly, sir, I did not expect any other answer now. But I thought it only fair to give you the opportunity to— To, shall we say, remember what happened again now.'

'Superintendent.' He made an effort to get up out of the deep armchair. 'Superintendent, I think this conversation has gone far enough. I have yet to meet your new Chief Constable, and I would very much dislike having to see him for the first time in order to make a complaint about one of his senior officers. But if necessary I shall do that. I hope you understand.'

'I do understand. All too well. However—'

She left a long pause, all the better to emphasize her next two words.

'Luke Calvert, I am going to ask you once more. What did you see, or do, that evening at the Imperial Hotel?'

Now Lucas Calverte, Luke Calvert, sank slowly back into his flower-patterned chair.

'How— Why— How did you know?' he asked, actually broken-voiced.

'I went out yesterday to Gralethorpe, and saw an old lady who, I understand, is a cousin of yours.'

'Abigail. Damn her.'

'Mr Calverte. What you have chosen to call yourself these many years is no business of mine. But, let me say, I shall not hesitate to tell what I have learnt to whomever I care to. That is, if I think that you are holding back from me events which I am entitled to know about.'

'But— But what if I can't remember? Really can't remember. It was thirty years ago, and— And I did not want to have to think about that evening any more than I had to. So, yes, I deliberately put it out of my mind. And now . . . Now, really, I can remember very little of it, if anything.'

Harriet looked at him. A humbled and confused man.

'You still tell me that?' she said. 'That you cannot remember that evening thirty years ago?'

'I can't. I can't. I blotted it out. You must believe me, you must.'

With a sigh, Harriet took from her pale fawn bag, matching the tussore summer suit she had carefully chosen to wear this Sunday morning, the half-empty pack of Royals Pip had lent her. His lighter followed.

A little awkwardly – she would have been the first to admit it – she pulled out one of the cigarettes, put it between her lips, flicked once, twice, a third time and a fourth at the lighter's wheel, and at last put flame to tip. She sucked in a mouthful of smoke that all but set her choking, and then expelled it. Not quite into Calverte's face, but near enough.

'Miss Martens, I wish you—'

There were smoke-tears in his eyes. He blinked to rid himself of them.

Harriet sucked in, puffed out again.

'Mr Calv—' she began.

And realized speaking was made difficult with a cigarette clamped between her lips. She snatched it away.

'Mr Calverte, I am asking you once again, what happened in the ballroom foyer there at the Imperial?'

'I tell you—'

Now the harsh tobacco smoke, as Harriet hastily managed another puff, sent a splutter of coughing up from Lucas Calverte's unaccustomed lungs.

'I don't know, I don't know,' he said, tears at the edge of his voice. 'I blotted it— No, wait. That evening . . . That terrible, terrible moment. Now I can see it. Yes, see it all.'

A tremendous gulp. Harriet saw the Adam's apple in the old man's stringy throat heave and shift.

And she thought – words beat out in her head – *It's working. It's working, my wheeze. My absurd wheeze that came to me on the edge of sleep last night. That whiff, as near as I could get it, of the old coarse cigarette days of the sixties, the end of the Woodbine days. It's working. Lucas Calverte is going to come out with it all.*

But what he said was not what she had expected to hear.

'It was the end of my life,' he croaked out.

What? What's this?

'I— I was sitting waiting on that round bench with the big pot of pampas grass in the middle, on the far side from the ballroom. Waiting for my dear Boy who had changed my life, for my dear Boy to emerge when he felt himself ready, and— And I heard that loud screech one of those doors made when it was opened too quickly. I turned round. I thought it would be him, coming out. But it wasn't. It was that dreadful Bubsy Willson.'

Bubsy. Harriet pounced now. So it had been Bubsy

after all who went into the ballroom. It was Bubsy who walked along the aisle made by those little red plush chairs, past those fantastic tile-pictures, those foliage-wreathed columns, and—

But Lucas Calverte was going on, seeing it all again.

'I remember, I remember. I had had time to think after I saw her come out. I thought, *She looks uglier than ever*. And then she lifted up her head and shouted. She shouted out, yelled or screamed out, that the Boy was dead. My Krishna.'

Another dreadful gulp, a fighting for mere breath.

'Dead,' the old man said again. 'And I knew then, I knew at once, that I was dead, too. All that I had come to live for, the— The chance to do some real good with my life, through his life, the Boy's life, had gone. I knew then in one instant that the real me, Luke, Luke— Luke was dead. Only the waxwork was still there, the waxwork I had taken so long to make and form, the image of the good man, the Undersheriff, the one who knew always what was for the best, and would tell people what it was. He was back with me. Back with me for ever.'

He came to a halt.

'Thank you, Mr Calverte,' Harriet said.

She could think of nothing more to add.

Pip Steadman was delighted to hear of the success of Harriet's wheeze, such as it was.

'I must admit, ma'am,' he said, 'I never thought it would come off. I mean ... Well, it seemed to be— Well, almost ridiculous.'

'You wouldn't have said anything other than *ridiculous* if you'd seen the way I went about attempting to smoke in the old gasbag's face. Unless you'd said *farcical*.'

'But it came off, ma'am. It came off.'

'It did, Pip. In its way. But just think where it's led us. It looks—'

The ring, ring, ringing of the phone on the table beside her brought her to an enforced halt.

'Oh, for God's sake. It'll be bloody Mr— It'll be the Chief. You'd better answer it, Pip.'

Pip picked up.

But the quacking voice Harriet could hear was clearly not Mr Newbroom's.

'Yes, yes,' Pip said. 'She's here. Detective Superintendent Martens is here.'

He handed the phone to Harriet.

'It's Mr Sydney Aslough, the girl said.'

'Sydney. Then you haven't run off to Europe?'

'Hey, you thought I had,' Aslough's voice came happily back. 'You believed old Syd had done a bunk thinking he'd got the law treading on his tail after all this time. You know, I hoped you'd got a better opinion of me.'

Harriet felt a wave of shame. Which turned in an instant to warmth.

'No, Syd,' she said. 'I don't know what made me have some momentary doubts when I heard from your secretary you'd gone to what she called the Continent. But I certainly should have known better.'

'So you bloody well should. I might sell a dodgy vehicle, get the chance. But I wouldn't never have harmed a hair of that Boy's head. Sydney Aslough knows real goodness when he sees it. Which is almost never.'

'Yes, you're right. From all I've heard and read about the Boy, real goodness is what he had.'

'So you going to find out who it was? Who went in there, to that crazy ballroom, and did in the poor little sod?'

'I am. I think I am.'

'And was it something to do with why you called me when I was away in old Deutschland buying a few motors cheap?'

'It was.'

'Then it's me that's got something to tell you.'

'Right, let's hear.'

'I been thinking. Thinking about when those ballroom doors opened that night. And finally I remembered. I heard that sorta screech the door made. And then I did see, for definite, who came out of there.'

'All right, say the name, though I've a pretty good idea what it'll be.'

'Bubsy Willson.'

'Yes, Bubsy Willson. Thank you, Syd. That may be the final proof I need. Or as much proof as I'm likely ever to get. After thirty long years and with no DNA to help.'

Abruptly into her head there popped the sight of bloated, slummocky ex-Detective Sergeant Shaddock. The man who, she wryly remembered now, had told her to look for the *one who found the body*. *Old rule*. So, it seemed as if he had got it right. The dreadful old soak.

*

'Yet, all the same,' Harriet said to John some time after supper that evening, 'despite having evidence from two witnesses that it was Bubsy who came out of that fantastic empty ballroom thirty-plus years ago and shouted out that the Boy was dead, despite all that's implied by that, more than implied, I'm still not altogether happy that she strangled him.'

'Because it's possible she did no more than find him lying there, strangled?'

Harriet sat frowning, the book she had been trying to read, John's copy of *Edward Lear*, flopped on to her lap.

'Well, no,' she said at last, with wholly uncharacteristic indecision, 'no, it's not that. Or I don't think it is.'

'But it could be that, you know. Logically. And just think what defence counsel would make of the possibility. If, after all this time, it comes to a trial.'

'Right. And I've considered it. Believe me I have. But I honestly think a defence of that sort wouldn't really stand up. Of course, it's possible, logically possible, that one of the others entered the ballroom before Bubsy did. But nothing that I've heard from the surviving witnesses makes me believe anyone did. And, more to the point, nothing old DCI Kenworthy got out of those witnesses at the time led him to believe anyone had been seen entering the ballroom.'

'Not even Bubsy,' John put in. 'Don't forget that.'

'Oh, I haven't forgotten that. I've forgotten nothing, and I know I could go to Mr Newcomen tomorrow, as I really think I shall have to, and tell him in all truth that there's a good case for Barbara Willson, now Mrs Brownlow, to have been the murderer of the Boy

Preacher. And, God, how pleased he'll be with that. A trial, more than thirty years after the murder was committed, and such a murder, too. What a picture he'll be able to paint of the newly directed Greater Birchester Police.'

'But?'

'Yes. How well you know me. Yes, there is a *but*. I think it really comes down to this. I cannot for the life of me understand why that terrible sloppy girl, all those years ago, would have wanted to end the Boy Preacher's life. If I could imagine the slightest, feeblest reason why . . . Oh, I know the prosecution never has to present evidence of motive unless it wishes to, just the facts that will secure a guilty verdict. But only if I knew why Bubsy needed to kill the Boy could I go happily to Mr Newcomen and let him have his triumph.'

'Happily? Really?'

John grinned at her.

'All right, not happily, if you like. But in all sincerity, knowing I was simply putting the truth in front of him. To maul about, as he liked, like a puppy with a rag doll.'

'And you can't think of any reason, however unlikely, however bizarre, for Bubsy to have strangled the Boy?'

'Right, bizarre. If that means totally illogical, gone right round the twist, then, yes, she could have had a bizarre reason, or unreason. But, no. No one has ever suggested that she was behaving, either before the murder or after, in any such fashion. And that, again, includes DCI Kenworthy, whose judgment I'd certainly trust.'

'Well, I can see why you want some sort of a motive, however obscure, before you feel satisfied,' John conceded.

'But you? You know as much as I do about the inquiry now, or nearly as much. What do you think? What motive could Bubsy Willson have had for killing the Boy that night?'

John, now, sat in silence. And at last spoke.

'No, I can't see it any more than you can. Why should that decidedly unattractive, rather simple girl have committed such a savage murder? Because, after all, that's what it was. Savage.'

'Yes, and how Mr Newbroom will love that.'

'No, forget Mr Newbroom. Think of Bubsy. Bubsy, and why should she have done that.'

'But, damn it all, I have thought, thought and thought. If you've no better advice than that, you'd better go back to your book and I'll go back to mine. If I can concentrate at all on it, good though it is.'

John looked at her, head shaking with mock sadness.

'Well, I do have some advice for you actually,' he said, glancing down at his watch. It's this: early though it is, go to bed. *La nuit porte conseil.*'

Harriet glared back at him.

'And I've got some advice for you,' she snapped. 'It's this: just for once don't preach at your wife. And especially not in a foreign language.'

'And don't you play the Hard Detective with me,' John shot back, caught on the raw.

They sat there, books on their laps, tension crackling across the gap between them.

And dissolving.

No calculating which of them laughed first. But it was Harriet who said, 'All right, I will go to bed. Tell you the truth, I'm utterly worn out.'

Chapter Twenty-Five

Harriet woke up. Her first thought was, muzzily, Where am I? A moment later she almost laughed aloud. Where else should I be, but here in bed at home? And John has, in his usual way, quietly slipped out so as not to disturb me. And he's off to engulfing Majestic House to get his undisturbed hour or so to deal with the paperwork. Or some of it.

Only then did she realize that she had been dreaming. Deeply. Hard. And bits of the dream began coming back to her. That cow – how odd, a cow – there in a field somewhere, with, yes, the barred fence it was stretching over. There it was, neck taut, head raised to the unhearing skies. And moo-moo-mooing. In high distress.

And, yes again, in the dream I knew why. The pink udder, I can see it now. Milk-full, stretched, smarting for relief.

Was it me who ought to have milked the wretched beast? No, don't think so. The farmer? Don't remember dreaming there was a farm— No. No, it was a calf. Or even calves. The desperate cow was mooing and shrieking for her calves.

'Oh, God.'

Harriet realized she had spoken the two words, the acknowledgment of a revelation, out aloud into the empty room, dawn-lit through the not quite closed curtains.

She sat up with a jerk, stretching her arms down behind her for support.

Revelation. By God, yes, I have had a revelation.

Then she remembered almost the last words John had said to her when they had had their – what? – their bit of a spat last thing last night. Or last thing for me anyhow. Because I did then do just what John had said I ought to. I went straight up to bed, hardly knew I'd undressed – she glanced at the chair in the corner, and yes, clothes on it, if only just – and I fell straight asleep. And slept and slept and slept. And dreamt. And my dream produced, in dream fashion, this revelation.

La nuit porte conseil, John told me. And counsel, wisdom even, the night did carry to me. It told me what had motivated Bubsy Willson suddenly to strangle the Boy Preacher whose fervent disciple she had been.

It told me that Bubsy, the Bubsy whom street-sharp Syd Aslough had called 'tarty' while almost in the same breath dismissing the notion that she was a prostitute, had answered to both his contradictory views of her. Yes, she had walked the streets of the city's rougher areas looking for sex. But, yes again, she had never been thinking of inducing anyone to pay for it. Because it had not been to gather money that, appallingly ugly as she was, she had sought sex. It had been to gather, yes, a calf, calves.

But then she had been caught up by the Boy's almost hypnotic preaching, no doubt in much the way

Sydney Bigod, as he was in those days, had been. And, in thrall to the Boy, she would have heard time and again his injunction *Do not bring into world one child without Ma-Bap*. Mother plus father. And, yes, surely, surely, it had been the intolerable strain of that . . .

But can this be so?

I wish John . . . Wait. He could still be here.

Head-to-foot naked – only now did she realize her nightie must still be under her pillow – she flung herself out of the bedroom, down the stairs, tumble, tumble, tumble, and into the kitchen.

John was there. Placidly flipping through the pink sheets of the *FT.*

She stood in the doorway and poured it all out to him. Desperate cow, taut udder; parading the streets, *never a prostitute*, the scene in the garden below that perched-up greenhouse, the Boy's commandment *Do not bring into world one child without Ma-Bap:*

'It was— It was because of her overwhelming desire to have a child,' she announced at last. 'To have a child. Maybe no man will understand, can fully understand, but that was it, that was it. I swear it was.'

John, who had listened with complete patience throughout, looked up now.

'The word you're wanting,' he said, 'is *philoprogenitiveness.* I think the dictionary says it means characterized by love of offspring.'

'So if the dictionary okays it, you agree? Bubsy strangled the Boy out of thwarted philo-whatsit?'

'Yes, I agree.'

*

An hour later, no longer stark naked, with a quick breakfast eaten, with Pip Steadman collected from Headquarters and abreast of the situation, Harriet was pressing the white plastic button in the centre of the door of the narrow terraced house where there was to be found Bubsy Brownlow, with her husband Ted – E. Brownlow, building repairs promptly executed – and probably a handful of grandchildren as well.

Once again there was a long delay in answering. But Harriet did not feel the need now for a second imperative buzz.

And, eventually, the door in front of her was opened. But it was not, as it had been the last time, swept wide by cheerfully grinning Ted Brownlow. Instead it was slowly pulled a little back and a pallid face peered round it at about the level of the keyhole.

Harriet was checked for a moment, while she worked out that, despite the too-big, drooping *Up the Rovers* T-shirt and the crumpled orange shorts, this was one of the girl grandchildren. But then she asked, 'Is your granny at home, love? Can we come in and see her?'

'Nah. She's been took to 'ospital.'

'Hospital? She's worse then?' Darts of remorse. 'When did she get worse? Was it after we'd been talking to her?'

'Yeh. Think so.'

'But your grandad, is he in?'

'Nah. Went with 'er to the 'ospital, did'n he? Middle o' the ni'.'

In the middle of the night. Ted going with her, and

still there. She must be . . . Oh yes, Bubsy must be at death's door. Now. This very moment.

'Which hospital? Which hospital did she go to, love? Do you know?'

'Ozzies, o' course.'

Pip Steadman was quick to translate.

'It's St Oswald's, ma'am. It serves the whole of this area.'

'Yes. Yes, of course. Right, let's go.'

But it was Pip who asked the raggedy girl clutching the edge of the door what her name was.

''s Maggie.'

'Maggie,' Harriet put in then. 'I'll give your Gran your love, shall I?'

'Tell 'er get-better-soon.'

In the St Oswald's reception area, they unexpectedly encountered Ted Brownlow.

'Mr Brownlow,' Harriet called out, suppressing her fear that the big genial man might accuse her there and then of having caused his wife's sudden deterioration. 'We've just been at the house,' she said, 'and your little Maggie told us you were here. I hope you've got some better news.'

Ted Brownlow's large face was no longer the glowing, cheerfulness-radiating one that had greeted them on his doorstep on Saturday before leading them up to the greenhouse looking down over the patch of garden. Behind his big, awkward spectacles, he still retained his bright colour, solidly red from hairline to throat. But it might now have been made of some bright plastic, entirely unanimated.

'No,' he said, dully. 'No, no better news. She's dying, that what it is. My Bubsy's dying.'

Harriet fought for something to say.

'Mr Brownlow, I— I'm so sorry. When— When on Saturday she seemed so happy, with her grandchildren all round her, I hoped—'

No, she thought, not the way to put it. If he doesn't seem to have connected this deterioration with our visit, then just keep quiet.

'It had to come,' Ted Brownlow said, voice still flattened to exhaustion point. 'We knew it. We all knew it. But— But somehow we sort of hoped . . .'

'Yes. Yes, I understand. Of course, you would.'

Then a new thought struck her.

Oh God, is he going to ask if we're on our way to see her? And will that mean he guesses what we have in mind? To try, at this last hour, to get a confession? And what shall I say if he does ask?

But she was spared that.

'Excuse me,' Ted said. 'Got to get on. Fetching some things she'd like from home. Photos and that. Mustn't be too long.'

'No, no, of course not.'

And he left them, at a sort of half-shambling run.

When he had barged his way out through the glass doors, Harriet turned to Pip.

'Do you know anything about dying declarations?' she said.

*

Frustrating dealings with hospital bureaucracy over at last, they made their way to the ward to which Bubsy had been admitted. It was, Harriet had gathered, one assigned to the dying, female and male. Before they reached it, Harriet halted and gave Pip his short course in dying declarations, or at least as much as she could remember about those unusual circumstances.

'Right, a dying declaration is admissible as evidence if, a) it is made, as they say, in extremity, and b) the party is at the point of death when, I quote, correctly I think, *every hope of this world has gone, when every motive to falsehood is silenced and the mind is induced by—* By something. Yes, got it, *the most powerful considerations to speak the truth.* That may be a bit outdated, I don't know. Have to look it up. Later. But you can see why those particular words have stuck in my mind.'

'I certainly can, ma'am. But— But— Well, but are they all you need? Now. When we get to see Bubsy?'

'Oh, I think so, yes. The principle is bound to hold still. So I haven't any doubts. It's a genuine dying declaration we're going to hear, if we do. If we do. And you'll need your notebook at the ready.'

They advanced into the ward, with the long lines of curtain-separated beds to either side, a life-washed face in each one of them, the shapes under the sheets lying in perfect stillness or feebly twisting to and fro. Here and there one of the beds had the curtains drawn right round it. *In extremity.*

Outside the last of them at the very far end of the long ward, a nurse was standing. As they approached he gave them a distinctly surly look. People coming to interfere; the police coming to cause complications.

'Detective Superintendent Martens, Detective Constable Steadman,' Harriet said. 'You've been told we have permission to speak to Mrs Brownlow?'

'That's right.'

With bad grace he drew back the curtain enough for them, each in turn, to slip inside.

And there could be no doubt about it: Bubsy Brownlow, too, was in extremity.

Harriet wondered for an instant if they were, in fact, too late. But Bubsy's hollow-sunk eyes plainly registered that someone had come in, and that it was not her Ted returning with the photos she wanted to be able to look at till the end.

Harriet sighed.

'Mrs Brownlow,' she said, bending over the bed, seemingly absurdly wide for the body that, only a few days before, had appeared to be so substantial slumped into that old cane-work garden chair. 'Mrs Brownlow, do you know who we are?'

'That lady. Police. Up in the greenhouse.'

'Yes. I am Detective Superintendent Martens, and here beside me is Detective Constable Steadman.'

'Yes.' A long pause. 'You come to ask, ain't you?'

'Yes, we have come to ask. You know, don't you, that you are— That— That you have not very long to live?'

A tiny spark of spirit.

'Yeh. Know that. Obvious, ain't it?'

Harriet glanced quickly back at Pip to make sure he had registered that *every hope of this world* had gone.

'I am afraid it *is* obvious, Mrs Brownlow,' she said, making the words as clear as she could without banging them out. 'So, I am going to ask you just one question. Are you ready for it?'

'Yeh.'

'Mrs Brownlow, did you on the evening of May the twenty-second, 1969, murder, by strangling, Krishna Kumaramangalam, known as the Boy Preacher?'

A silence.

And then the words.

'Yes. Yes, that's what I did. I strangled him, the poor kid. Had to. He went on and on about not having babies unless you was wed. And who'd wed me? I used to think. Ugly cow that I was. That's what I thought then. Then I didn't know there was anybody in the whole wide world like my Ted. An' I wanted . . . I wanted an' . . . wanted a baby. I had to have one. I had to have lots.'

Chapter Twenty-Six

Mr Newbroom was sitting, Harriet realized, in precisely the same attitude he had adopted when she had last been up in his airy Chief Constable's suite, facing him. Two hands flat on the gleaming surface of the wide desk, fingers pointing towards her in the way that had made her think of two flights of attacking aircraft. But there was one difference in the desk layout. Beside those two forward-pointing hands there lay the garishly covered copy of *Who Killed the Preacher?* which she had duly returned to Pansy Balfour.

'I asked to see you, sir,' she said, 'to report that I now know who it was who killed the Boy Preacher.'

'I hardly expected you to come to me with anything else, Superintendent. After all, finding that out was the task I gave you. And, let me say, I expected I would have been asked for an interview a good deal earlier than this.'

'Yes, sir.'

Harriet bit back all the legitimate reasons she had had for the delay, especially the failure of the Newbroom plan for rapid DNA recognition.

'Then perhaps you'll enlighten me about this discovery of yours?'

'Not discovery, sir. Proof.'

'Proof? Well, I trust it's proof that will stand up in court.'

'A confession, sir. Mrs Barbara Brownlow, Barbara Willson at the time of the Boy's death, has confessed to killing him.'

'Willson? Well, let me show you something, Superintendent. Something I took care that you should see at the very start of your investigation. Something that might have led another officer to bring the inquiry to a rather more rapid conclusion.'

'Sir?'

But Harriet knew very well what she was going to be shown, that masterwork *Who Killed the Preacher?*

She watched now as Mr Newbroom busily riffled through its pages.

'Ah, yes. Here she is. Barbara Willson, *known to one and all by the sobriquet, Bubsy*. And this is what this fellow Meadowcraft says about her, in so many words, *charged with indecent behaviour in a public place*. You can tell at a glance what sort of a criminal type she was. And then a bit later – this is the really significant passage – Meadowcroft describes her *tramping up and down the foyer*. Why do you think she was doing that, Superintendent? I'll tell you. She was looking for her moment to go into the ballroom there and kill the Boy.'

'Yes, sir. I dare say she was, though of course Mr Meadowcraft was rather relying on hearsay for that description. He had no idea he was going to write his book at that time, and wasn't, of course, actually present.'

A chance thought flicked into her mind. Damn it,

yes. Meadowcraft, despite his horrendous way with the facts, had got it right after all. What were those words of his? *There can be no possible doubt that vindictiveness lies at the heart of this atrocious crime.* Something like that. And, true enough, poor wretched Bubsy had developed a vindictive hatred for the Boy Preacher.

'I dare say, I dare say,' Mr Newbroom snapped out. 'But none of that alters the fact that the woman Bubsy Whatever-she-is-now murdered that Boy. You've arrested her, I take it?'

Harriet resisted the temptation to say something like, '*That arrest has been made, sir, by a higher authority than the Greater Birchester Police.*'

'She died in hospital yesterday, sir.'

'Died? Died? So she's escaped justice that way?'

He thought for a brief moment.

'However, Superintendent, this does not mean that her crime should go unnoticed. Greater Birchester Police have secured an extraordinary result, a confession to murder more than thirty years after the commission of the crime. It is right that the public should know of it. It is our duty, at the very least, to show that such a notorious murder, committed within the bounds of our city, has been detected. So you had better get in touch, at once, with our media people. But make sure I am informed of what they propose to say before anything goes out.'

'I don't think so, sir.'

Harriet might have announced the imminent end of the world, so shattering was the effect of her few quiet words.

Mr Newcomen's hands, until that moment flatly

laid on the surface of his desk, as they had been ever since Harriet had taken her seat in front of him, contracted now into two spasms of pure shock. His brilliantly well-shaved shining cheeks turned first white, then a deep dusky red.

'What the hell do you mean by that?'

'I mean, sir, that I do not think that we in the Greater Birchester Police should go out of our way to claim immense credit for what I have learnt about Bubsy Brownlow.'

Mr Newbroom still looked as shocked as any Chief Constable could be.

'Are you deliberately defying my order, Superintendent?'

Then Harriet saw, dawning behind his eyes, the realization that perhaps now there was in front of him the chance of getting rid, once and for all, of a media-loved officer who could not but be a challenge to the image he hoped to project of the force's new dynamic Chief.

That was not going to happen.

'I am afraid, sir,' she said quickly, 'that any emphasized release of this result would lead the media to discover that news of the inquiry had, first, been deliberately withheld under your orders, and then, rather worse, had accidentally leaked out.'

'Nonsense, nonsense. I don't think news of it really did leak out, as you put it.'

'No, sir? But it did. And the leak occurred, I have to tell you, because you yourself let your secretary, Mrs Balfour, learn all about it. And she, put under no obligation to secrecy, mentioned what you had told her to a certain Ezra Yates, the man who wrote anonymously to you, sir.'

'But— But— How did you discover all this?'

'I discovered it, sir. And I must tell you that, if you persist in doing anything more than quietly stating in, say, your first annual report that the investigation into the Boy Preacher's death has now been closed, then I will feel free to let my concerns about what happened be made known in the appropriate quarters.'

It took Mr Newbroom nearly two minutes of silent thought to come to a conclusion.

'Very well, Miss Martens. Perhaps you have seen what may be our best course.'

He gave a long, almost whimpering sigh.

'And as a matter of fact, perhaps this is the best time to make this announcement. I shall probably be away from my desk for the next few weeks. My doctor tells me I am suffering from strain, acute strain. The whole business of taking over a force that has been allowed to— Well, let us say, that needed perhaps a certain amount of rejuvenating has taken a lot out of me. Yes, a lot. So I have been recommended a period of sick leave, some weeks. Perhaps a month. Or more. Yes. So, perhaps it is best, after all, to announce, in some quieter, more dignified fashion, the successful conclusion of the Boy Preacher murder case. Yes?'

'Yes, sir,' Harriet said.

A Detective at Death's Door

Chapter One

Harriet, as she lay there, heard a voice.

'I think you can take it now that we've pulled you through,' it seemed to be saying.

Something stirring at the bottom of her mind told her that she knew the man who had spoken. He was— His name was . . . She had heard it. There was something . . . Something funny . . .

She felt herself sliding back into the semi-oblivion in which she had been lying, and with a jerk forced herself up from it.

Yes, I know. I remember. He's Mr Hume Jones. And, yes. Yes, this is it. I've got it. He called himself 'Hume Jones, no hyphen if you don't mind'. And he's been treating me.

Treating me? What . . ? Why? Why am I being treated?

John. John's here. There, next to . . . To what's-his-name, Mr No-hyphen, if you don't . . .

Wait, I must think. Think why I'm here.

If I'm very careful, keep my eyes shut and take it slowly, I can think. Think it out.

One: I am Harriet Piddock. Two: John is my husband, John Piddock. And, three: I'm Detective Superintendent Harriet Martens as well. Yes. And this must be a hospital. There's the smell. Sharp and sanitized, but lingering. The hospital smell. And up to my neck there's this stiff white sheet. My head on a starchy pillowcase. Yes.

So, four: I'm ill. In hospital. Very ill. But . . . But, yes, we've pulled you through. That was No-hyphen. And I— I sort of remember I heard him say that. Not now. Hours ago. Days ago? Yes, it could be some days ago.

The sod. *We* didn't pull me through. I came through. I pulled myself through. I refused to die. That's it. I was in danger of death, and I decided— somehow I decided I was not going to die. No, more than that. I decided I was not going to be killed. To be murdered. And . . . Yes, I was not going to be poisoned.

Right, it comes back. I was poisoned. What by? Don't know. But it's there in my memory. Somehow I drank poison. Enough to kill me. But I was determined not to be killed. By the poison. Oh, all right, be fair. I have been treated. By Mr Hume Whatsit. Treatment helped. Helped a lot. But if he thinks they've pulled me through, he's wrong. I came through. I've come through. I have.

She allowed herself to slip back into dulled nothingness.

It was morning. Pale dawn light behind the thin curtains in the window of the private room. The door had been briskly opened. The young Asian nurse who, as Harriet was vaguely aware, had been looking after her, went across and pulled the curtains fully back.

Harriet felt the stronger light as a blow in the face.

She shut her eyes, turned away, felt injured and suddenly helpless.

'Mr Hume Jones says you can sit up today,' the nurse pronounced.

Harriet wanted to say, to shout, *Go away*. But she lacked the energy to utter even a word.

She found herself hauled up, and felt the pillows being rearranged behind her. And, yes, something metallic had been noisily pulled forward. She fell back on it.

Back-rest, yes.

But she was not to be allowed any peace. Bedpan pushed underneath her. A bed-table, she realized when she ventured to open her eyes again, had been efficiently slid in front of her and a faintly steaming basin of warm water was being put on it.

'Now you're so much better,' the nurse said, sharply enough, 'you can manage to wash yourself.'

A slimily soaped washcloth was put in her right hand. With firmness.

And, though the nurse had whisked away in a flurry of blue uniform, Harriet did as she had been told and sat dabbing at her face.

But before very long a hard little rebellious thought popped into her head. All right, I'll do it today. But when I'm feeling just a bit stronger, I'll bloody well wash when I want to wash.

She sat there with her hands resting in the basin and began to pull her thoughts together.

Right then. How did I come to be here? Because I'd been poisoned. Where? How? Yes, it was at the pool. The – I can get it – Majestic Insurance Company Sports and Social Club pool. Good. That's come back. I was there at the pool with John, Majestic Insurance high-up. It'd been hot, bloody hot. It was the bank holiday, August bank holiday Monday. I was in my two-piece swimsuit, the near-bikini I hardly ever wear unless it's really boiling hot. I was lying there, body well-covered with sunscreen, just beside the pool. And, yes, I'd drunk a Campari soda, a bright red, bubbles-tingling Campari soda, and poor John, because he'd said he'd be the driver, had had a bitter lemon.

And, yes, it's all coming back. I'd let John get me a second Campari, and I'd had a swallow or two of it, that delicious sharp herbal bite, and then John got up from his chair, put down on it the book he'd been reading – yes, one of those Agatha Christies he relaxes with – and said something . . .

Yes. *I must go for a pee, shan't be long.*

And I let my eyes close, sort of dozed off. And there was something . . . something black and white. Don't know what. And then John was coming back. And I looked up at him and smiled. Pleased just to see him.

I lifted up that tall, cool glass and took another long swallow.

And . . . And something not quite right about the taste. My tongue tingling, pricking, and *God, I'm cold, freezing*, I said. And then . . . Then the next thing I knew was my head being held over a toilet bowl and, yes, John's fingers pushing hard into my throat.

God, I can suddenly feel them again. As if . . .

Am I going to puke? Into this basin of cooling soapy water?

No. Damned if I will.

*

John is here. The real John, not the John of those all too vividly re-experienced probing, vomit-inducing fingers. And flowers, he's brought flowers. Can't remember what they're called. Deep sort of yellow colours. And lovely smell. One of my favourites. But I can't remember the name. Must ask him. Ask what's been happening to me, too.

Did that man, man in the blue woollen shirt open at the neck, beautiful soft blue, and the white coat just hanging from the back of his shoulders, with the long pale face, man-in-the-moon, did he really say he'd pulled me through? All a blur.

No, wait. Yes, Hume Jones, no hyphen.

'John. Hello. It's you, isn't it?'

'Yes, it's me.'

'John, were you standing beside— Man, doctor. No. Yes, consultant? Called, I think, Hume Jones. Said, "We've pulled you through?"'

'Yes, I was. Three days ago, though.'

'God, as much as that? I— I must have been out, unconscious.'

'You were. You recovered, a bit. And then you had a relapse. And you've been unconscious or asleep ever since then. But that's a good thing. You're meant to get as much sleep as possible. You've had a pretty awful time, you know, though Mr Hume Jones is quite happy that, as he said a little too proudly, "We've pulled you through." Shouldn't mock really. He did a fantastic job.'

'I suppose so.'

'Oh, yes, no doubt about it. But you're going to find yourself very weak, and wandering in your mind most probably, for a good long time to come.'

'Yes. Yes, I feel as if I will be. But— but you can tell me things now?'

'Oh, yes. Anything you want to know. Hume Jones says it'll be the best way for you to get yourself together ag—'

'John. I've just thought. The twins. Did the twins come down to see me? All the way from university?'

'Of course they did. It was touch-and-go with you for days, you know.'

'And – this is right? – I was poisoned. Somehow poisoned?'

'You were.'

'And did you . . ? Did you have to make me vomit? I remember that. Or was that a hullu— Hallucin— No, wait. Hallucination?'

'No, it wasn't any hallucination. The moment I realised what might be happening, I rushed you off to make you spew up as much as possible. Turned out to be the best thing I could have done, according to Hume Jones, though if you'd swallowed one of the corrosive poisons it would have been the worst thing.'

A sudden rueful laugh.

'I was in a terrible dilemma at that moment actually. You see, I knew where the loos were; I'd just been spending a penny. And, without thinking much about it, I rushed you towards them. But when I got there I was confronted with two doors side-by-side. One sign had the figure with legs apart, and one the figure with the skirt. And I simply couldn't decide – only for an instant – which one to take you into, male or female. Both inappropriate in their different ways.'

Harriet found she wanted to laugh. Only she didn't know how to. Tears began to form at her eyes.

She saw the quick look of concern on John's face.

'Well,' he said hastily, 'I actually plumped for the Ladies', and there turned out not to be anyone in there. So that was all right. And then I had you whizzed off here. To St Oswald's. And Hume Jones saved your life, over the course of a week or more.'

'But, John, what was it that poisoned me? It was in that Campari soda, wasn't it? But how did you know what was happening?'

John's face lit in a broad smile.

'That was Agatha Christie,' he said. 'You know you're always knocking her for the way she gets her murders solved. Not exactly by Greater Birchester Police methods. Well, you'll have to thank her for ever now for what she wrote in the book I was reading beside you, *Twisted Wolfsbane.*'

'Yes, I can see the book now. You put it on your chair when you went for a pee. *Twisted Wolfsbane* – odd title.'

'Oh, it comes from Keats. The "Ode on Melancholy". You must remember.'

He lifted up his head and quoted.

'No, no, go not to Lethe, neither twist wolfsbane, tight-rooted, for its poisonous wine.'

He looked down at her again.

'But do you know what comes from twisting, more or less, that root?'

'No idea.'

'Aconitine. The almost-always fatal poison that you swallowed with your Campari.'

'The second one, that I'd taken several swallows from earlier on?'

'Yes, I saw you doing that before I went off to the

loo. So it was a wonderful piece of luck that I'd been reading the book immediately beforehand. Agatha Christie actually describes the symptoms – without going too deeply into unpleasant details, as was her way, bless her. But, yes, she wrote, and I'd just read the words, that the victim's tongue tingles violently, that they have a sudden feeling of chill coldness, and then there's a painful burning sensation in the mouth. Just what you said to me.'

'Yes, I remember the tingling and the feeling of terrible coldness. But after that, not a lot. Except I've a very – what's the word? – *physical* recall of your fingers doing their life-saving work down my throat.'

'Well, life-saving only in part. Most of the credit ought to go to Mr Hume Jones. He and his team did heroic work once they had you here.'

'But, John, who was it? Who put aconitine – someone must have done – into my Campari? And why? Why, for heaven's sake?'

She sank back on the bed then, overcome by exhaustion. Through the haze, very faintly, the scent of John's flowers came to her.

Freesias. Yes, freesias.

OTHER BOOKS

AVAILABLE FROM PAN MACMILLAN

H. R. F. KEATING

THE HARD DETECTIVE	0 330 38988 2	£6.99
A DETECTIVE IN LOVE	0 330 48897 X	£6.99
A DETECTIVE AT DEATH'S DOOR	1 4050 4806 9	£16.99

All Pan Macmillan titles can be ordered from our website,
www.panmacmillan.com, or from your local bookshop
and are also available by post from:

Bookpost, PO Box 29, Douglas, Isle of Man IM99 1BQ
Credit cards accepted. For details:
Telephone: 01624 677237
Fax: 01624 670923
E-mail: bookshop@enterprise.net
www.bookpost.co.uk

Free postage and packing in the United Kingdom

Prices shown above were correct at the time of going to press.
Pan Macmillan reserve the right to show new retail prices on covers
which may differ from those previously advertised in the text
or elsewhere.